For the girls

I escape to the hills and my dreams of old,
Of happy times and secrets untold.
And my soul drifts away, away up high,
To that place in the hills where the eagles fly

1

As she drove across the Clackmannanshire Bridge, Kristen barely noticed the soft low cloud gently hovering above the steely grey waters of the River Forth, or the rays of sunlight dancing through the trees as she approached Helensfield. Kristen could see very little through her tear-soaked eyes, nor concentrate on anything more than the note she had just read. 'Sorry for the inconvenience'. The words repeated in her mind over and over again, 'Sorry for the inconvenience', the kind of note someone might leave their boss if they'd missed a deadline. Kristen sighed in disbelief. These words were casual, ordinary, not the last writing of a troubled friend who had just tried to take her own life. But they were the very words she'd read from the note an agitated Gyle Jamieson had thrust into her hand that morning. She had a terrible feeling of dread, and instinctively knew there was something far wrong. It was a feeling she shared with Laura's friend, Mikey Macrae and their earlier conversation now echoed and churned in her mind as she continued her journey. As she drove through the little Hillfoot villages of Alva and Menstrie images of her dear friend lying in hospital fighting for her life occupied every thought. Kristen looked over her shoulder to see little Kenzie fast asleep in her car seat, oblivious to the chaos around her. The two-year-old had been found alone in the house; the precious daughter of her friend Laura. It was crazy. The Laura she knew would never have done that, surely? Eventually Kristen reached her home in Blairlogie. She pulled into the drive and sat staring ahead. She couldn't remember driving home now; her mind was jumpy, her thoughts scrambled and she was unable to make sense of anything. Eventually grief and despair took over and while still sitting in the driver's seat, she let out a loud piercing wail as she sobbed and screamed "No Laura!"

Later that evening, after the shock and horror of the day's events had given way to exhaustion, Kristen sat quietly cuddling Kenzie on the sofa while she watched cartoons. Her partner Scott sat with them, unable to comprehend the horror of the day's events and tried to comfort them both. Kristen tried to search for reasons, but she could find none. Laura's life had certainly dealt her some cruel blows, but Kristen could see no reason why she would want to end her life now. Try as she might, there was nothing she could think of that would be terrible enough for her friend to end it all, especially now she had little Kenzie. Even Mikey had been baffled and worried, yet Laura's husband Gyle seemed to have accepted the situation without question. There had been little emotion except agitation perhaps, but no tears and certainly no outpouring of grief from him. As the scene at Laura's home in Balerno played out in her mind, Kristen was reminded of the special friendship she had with Laura. And in quiet contemplation now, as she sat with Kenzie on her knee, Kristen shared the story of that special friendship with her partner Scott.

No one knew Laura better than Kristen, and Scott was happy to listen to his girlfriend now as she remembered the young Laura

Duncan, as she was back then when Kristen first met her. Laura had been Kristen's best friend since high school; she was the youngest daughter of Marie and Fraser who ran the local newsagent's store near their home in Stirling before their retirement. Although Laura and Kristen were both fairly new to high school, Kristen was very much the 'new girl' having moved home from the Borders after her father John accepted a senior post with a firm in Stirling. When Kristen started school a couple of weeks later than the other students Laura was the first to welcome her, volunteering to be her 'buddy'. It was a happy time for Kristen as Laura helped her settle into school and the area. Over the years, Laura hadn't changed that much; she was still thoughtful and kind; naturally attractive, medium height and build with long fair wavy hair. She had a young-looking fresh face and a huge smile and, like Kristen, was happiest wearing shirts or jumpers and jeans, unlike most of the girls in their year. Apart from that the two were very different. Kristen was very petite with long straight dark hair and full heavy fringe. She loved sport and animals and proved to be an asset to the school's athletics team. Laura's talents were in music. She was a great singer and played guitar, often writing songs of her own and she was always in demand to take part in school productions. It was little surprise that these skills and interests would take Laura and Kristen on different paths through their school years and beyond, and it was even less of a surprise when Kristen announced she had been accepted to study Veterinary Medicine in Glasgow. A few weeks later Laura discovered she would be heading in the opposite direction to an Edinburgh university, to study journalism and media.

Despite the differences in interests, they were always very close and throughout the years they made time at the weekends to spend together, often exploring the hills. Laura loved the Ochil Hills, with its range stretching more than twenty-four miles across Central Scotland. Their beauty through the seasons had been an inspiration to some of her songwriting. The bright yellow gorse and vibrant wild shrubs signalled spring and early summer, giving way only to autumn's majestic trees standing proud with such radiating colours of green, red and gold. They never failed to take Laura's breath away. Further into the hills red deer ran free while sheep calmly grazed and rabbits scattered as birds of prey hovered high above. On rare occasions a couple of eagles made an appearance and this just added to the magic. Then turning round to take in the stunning views she could see as far across the River Forth to Edinburgh and the Pentland Hills. Northwest, views of the higher peaks of Loch Lomond and the Trossachs presented a different aspect and closer to home, on Dumyat, the spectacular views across Stirling, the Hillfoots Villages, Stirling Castle and the Wallace Monument completed the perfect package. These hills were special to Laura, it was her safe place, and a place she was happy only to share with Kristen, for the first time on the last day of their second year of high school. Until then the hills had belonged to Laura, but now she was ready to share them with her special friend and it became a place they would both escape to when they were stressed out or worried, or after having been dumped by some spotty schoolboy, who in hindsight hadn't been worth the easy climb. The hills shared their dreams and ambitions, secrets, worries and hurts. The Ochils heard them all, and kept their secrets safe.

Kristen smiled now as she remembered the weekend before they both started university. They had walked the four and a half miles from the access point starting at Blairlogie Meadow with Kristen's two German Shepherds, Piper and Zeus. Reaching the summit they sat and looked across the incredible views. It was a clear day and they both marvelled at the beauty of the area around them. Looking closer, Kristen pointed down towards the tiny village of Blairlogie and turned to Laura. "This is where I will live one day," she told her. "I'll have my own vet's practice and I'll live down there."

Laura smiled. "I am sure you will", she agreed, "and I'll write an article about you when I'm the editor of the local newspaper!" They both laughed as they rested a while before heading back down the other side of the hill and on towards Bridge of Allan and then Causewayhead.

"Fancy an ice cream from the café?" Kristen asked. "Last one down pays!" Later they sat with their ice cream in the park in silence. Piper and Zeus were having great fun trying to drink from the water tap as the girls watched in amusement.

Finishing her ice cream Laura turned to Kristen. "Did you know that Dumyat," she pointed to the hill behind them, "is an extinct volcano?"

"No way?" Kristen was unconvinced as she looked up towards the hill.

"Honestly, some people claim there's still energy there and that's why it's rarely covered with snow." She looked for Kristen's reaction.

"Now you are really taking the piss." Kristen laughed.

"No, really, of course it's mainly because the other hills seem to catch the worst of it first from the north but there you go, that's something else you didn't know about these hills," Laura teased.

"Thanks, I'm sure that'll come in very handy at vet school!"

Kristen turned to her friend and sighed. "I'll miss days like these, and you."

"Me too," Laura agreed. "And I don't know what I'll do without these hills to escape to?"

"I know what you mean. It's going to be a bit scary without you to buddy me too!"

Laura laughed, "You're a big girl now Kristen," then looking up and down at the petite young woman standing in front of her, "well as big as you're going to get now!"

"I won't miss your cheek, that's for sure," Kristen joked, and then with hugs and greetings to each other for good luck they both lost sight of each other as they made their way along the footpaths home.

Leaving home to start university was a new and challenging experience for the girls, the run up to the day of departure had been hectic and scary. Now it had arrived and the excitement was mirrored in each home. To Kristen and Laura's parents the event was likened more to moving house, than transferring a few essentials to ease their way through the first few months.

"Do you really need all this stuff Laura?" Marie Duncan wailed as she staggered down the drive with a duvet, pillows, towels, sheets and blankets piled high towards an already over-packed car. "Yes, Mum, the woman at Student Halls gave me a list of things I might need and I might even need you to come back with more stuff!"

Marie stood open-mouthed in disbelief. "You can't be serious?" She looked towards Laura's father Fraser, who was struggling to fit a computer, keyboard, mouse and a collection of Laura's teddies on top of everything else already packed. "I don't think the woman meant for you to take everything on the list?" Then looking over to his daughter, "We didn't have all this stuff in our first home together," he sighed, and then looking into one of the boxes, "I'm sure they'll have teaspoons and cups Laura."

"Did your first home come with teaspoons and cups?" Laura teased, trying to keep the mood light.

Fraser Duncan shook his head. "There'll not be enough room for your mother at this rate!"

Laura smiled; she was going to miss her parents, and their funny old-fashioned ways.

Over at the Campbells' house the scene was much the same. "For goodness sake Kristen, what in hell's name are you going to do with that?" Yvonne Campbell cried as her daughter came struggling out to the car with her rowing machine, in several parts.

"It'll be important for me to keep fit," she argued.

"Fit?" her dad yelled. "You'll not have time for fit where you're going, it'll be all books and lectures and assignments." He shook his head. "You'll not have time for fit!" Eventually, heading in different directions, two overloaded cars with a couple of 'soon-to-be-fresher's headed off to begin a new and exciting challenge, destined to change the course of their lives forever.

Arriving at the University Halls of Residence in Glasgow and fifty miles away at university in Edinburgh, the girls signed for the keys to their rooms. After unpacking, both parents left the university accommodation and headed back home knowing life would be quiet without their daughters and knowing they would worry about them while they were gone. For Kristen and

Laura, however, life was promising to be anything but quiet and the first few days were crammed with induction; the process of registering with doctors and dentists, then lectures about the dangers of drugs, partying, sex, smoking and alcohol. Eventually, after a pastoral talk from the university chaplain about dealing with stress, homesickness and illness, someone arrived to issue student cards for shopping and travel. "I'm not sure I've taken it all in," Laura admitted to Kristen in their first phone call to each other. "In fact I think I might have failed the first test!" she joked.

Kristen agreed. "Will it ever seem normal to us?"

Several days later Marie and Fraser Duncan arrived back in Edinburgh to take half the contents of Laura's room back home again. "I said you wouldn't need half this stuff!" her mother scolded.

"Well, I didn't know, Mum, sorry." Laura helped her parents fill the car again and waved them goodbye. An hour later, they arrived home to hear the phone ringing as they stepped out of the car.

"Quick Fraser!" Marie urged her husband, irritated by his lack of urgency.

"It'll be one of them daft calls," he moaned, as he slowly opened the door and Marie pushed past him to answer the phone. "It'll be that PPI or accident compensation mail shot call, or some other daft stuff," he yelled, as Marie lifted the telephone receiver.

"It's Laura." Marie called to him. "Hi honey did we forget something?"

"What have we forgotten now?" Fraser asked wearily, but there was no reply as Marie listened to the call.

"Hi Mum, I'm sorry for catching you on the hop, I just thought you'd have been home by now, and I know Dad doesn't like answering the phone so I let it ring for a while. Anyway, I forgot to ask you something."

"Uhhuh?" Then looking over to her husband, "It's okay Fraser, it's just a question."

Fraser shook his head as he headed to the kitchen and put the kettle on.

"How do you make a steak pie?" Laura asked her mum.

"Well you need steak, for a start, will you get that there?"

"No don't need that Mum."

Marie laughed. "So, it's one of these student veggie steak pies then?"

"No Mum," Laura protested, laughing at the suggestion. "I just need to know how long to cook it for, and at what temperature?"

"It all depends on the size and weight, like how much meat is in it?" Laura looked down towards the kitchen worktop. "I don't know how much is in the pie Mum it says on the packet serves 2-3."

Marie groaned, "You mean you've just bought the pie from a shop?"

"Yes."

Marie shook her head. "Oh Laura, look on the box or the packet, there should be a little bit in small writing about cooking instructions, do you see it?"

A few moments passed then eventually Laura replied. "It says 25 – 30 minutes at 180° Mum".

"That's it then honey, watch you don't burn yourself."

Fraser was now standing at his wife's side intrigued by the conversation, and then shook his head as he returned to the kitchen and muttered, "Unbelievable! God knows how she's going to manage on her own?"

The following week Laura called again, this time it was part of a plan to ward off what she described as a 'frisky young student' who was making the most of being away from home. "Don't tell my dad," she told her mum. "I told him I was going home for the weekend, and without thinking I gave him this number."

"What? Oh Laura!"

"Don't worry Mum, I told him my name was Maisie, so I need you to help me out if he calls."

"Why did you say your name was Maisie? Won't it cause problems?"

"No Mum, he's actually quite a nice guy really. He'll find it hard to track me down here if he's looking for Maisie and he'll get the message eventually."

Marie sighed. "What do I say then?"

"Just say I am at my boyfriend's house, that should do."

Marie laughed, agreeing to fend off the unwelcome admirer.

"Thanks Mum, and remember not to tell Dad, you know what he's like?"

Marie put the phone down and laughed. "Maisie?" she said to herself and laughed again at the idea Laura had just given herself the name of her little West Highland Terrier. Over the next few days there were several calls made to the home of the Duncans. Many were nuisance calls from call centres and some were from Laura's friends who hadn't been able to reach Laura on her mobile, all of which had been a constant source of irritation to Fraser. This time the caller had been persistent, and to the annoyance of Marie, Fraser now refused to answer any of them. And now the phone rang again and again and for the sixth time in as many minutes. "Fraser!" Marie yelled from upstairs. "Will you answer the damn phone, it's driving me mad."

"I'm going, I'm going!" he yelled back angrily, finally giving in to the irritating noise. Marie tried to listen as her husband answered the call, followed by a long silence. "Who?" her husband boomed. "Are you trying to be funny...? Sod off!" he yelled, slamming down the receiver.

"What was all that about?" she called down to him.

"Some bloody idiot wanting to speak to the dog now!" Marie put her hands up to her mouth to stifle her laughter, realising what had happened. She was certain the frisky young student would almost certainly have received that message loud and clear.

Kristen's calls home to her parents were of a more practical nature. First there was the emergency call to say the iron wasn't working and another more frantic cry for help when her hair straighteners blew a fuse. Queries about how to remove stains and how to juggle bills followed, but over the coming weeks the girls eventually learned how to change a fuse, cook and generally manage to look after themselves as well as unwanted admirers. Life was beginning to settle down enough to enable them to study, budget, party and occasionally sleep. Study courses gradually replaced free time, followed by rotas of practical experience. Kristen was now spending more and more weekends helping out at veterinary practices while Laura was helping to cover events for a local newspaper. Their first semester was soon over, exams sat and passed and the girls enjoyed their first Christmas and New Year at home, for a short break. It was a cold winter, and time didn't allow them their usual visit to the Ochils so they had to make do with looking up towards them

11

and wishing they could be there, before heading back to university. Weeks turned into months, the end of the next semester was taken up with study leave assignments and neither girl managed to go home for more than a few days each, and not at the same time. When the end of their first year arrived they were both elated their hard work had paid off with great exam results. They celebrated at a little Italian restaurant in town with their parents, amid good food, wine and laughter as they all shared the experiences and stories of their first year. Over this break they would spend many visits walking in the Ochil Hills. "Even the dogs love coming here now," Kristen told Laura. "When I say 'Ochil s', their ears go up and they run to the door." She laughed.

"Maisie doesn't like it much, it's too far, too much for her."

"You'd expect that from a Westie," Kristen told her with confidence, "they tend to prefer shorter, more frequent walks."

"Oh really, Dr Doolittle," Laura teased, but she was impressed by the changes in Kristen. She was growing up to be more confident and assured in her manner. Her love of animals was evident, as was her growing knowledge of them.

"You'll make a great vet, Kristen," she told her proudly.

"I hope so." The second year at university was really demanding, but the girls always made a point of chatting on the phone to each other, usually complaining about the lack of social time. They were now fed up with not having 'hooked up' with some great-looking undergraduate, as they became more comfortable with their surroundings, despite promising themselves and their parents they wouldn't get romantically involved until after all studies were over. It seemed to be happening all around them, but by students who were either exceptionally bright and didn't need to study, or by those who had been drawn into the lure of partydom away from the control of their parents. Neither was the case for Laura or Kristen and for the time being at least, it was a case of all work and not very much play. November proved to be one of those cold rainy months and it had rained all day. Laura was soaked through twice on the long walk from the Halls of Residence to the Lecture Halls and now she began to feel the chills, sneezing occasionally. The back of her throat was dry and itchy, and she felt chilled to the bone. She threw a warm blanket round her and heated up a bowl of soup, carefully taking a spoonful or two in between writing and expanding on the sketchy notes she'd made during the day's lectures. How she missed her mum at this time, being home and having a hot meal prepared for her. She felt completely sorry for herself without her mum to look after her, and her dad to take care of repairs and bills. All in all it had not been the best of days until the phone rang and it was Kristen. "Hi Laura," she said, brightly. "How's things?"

"Terrible," Laura croaked. "I'm miserable, tired, cold, fed up, I have a sore throat and a banging sore head. What about you?"

"Ahh poor you Laura, I'm good, what's up?"

"Cold, I think?"

"Have you taken anything for it?"

"No chance, Kristen, you know me. I'll just drink lots of warm water with lemon in it and have an early night, it'll pass in a day or two."

Kristen sighed. "Or you could just take a couple of paracetamols and feel better in an hour or two?"

"Naa, it's okay, anyway what's happening?" Laura immediately felt a little brighter knowing Kristen was there to speak to. "Tell me all your news and cheer me up!"

"Well it's all good," she began. "It's all going well and I've met this great guy."

"What?" Laura cut in. "What happened to 'not getting involved until after uni'?"

"Oh I know, I know, but he's really cute and he wants to study just like me. He's really bright and I actually think he could help me because he's in his final year now," Kristen gushed. "And we've agreed to take things slowly."

"Oh well," Laura croaked amid sniffs and the odd cough. "Lucky you, does he have a brother studying here by any chance?"

Kristen laughed. "No sorry."

Laura sighed. "What's his name?"

"It's Scott. Isn't that a lovely name?" Laura raised her eyebrows, and winced as the action hurt her throbbing head. It was clear her friend was truly smitten with this guy.

"What's his other name?" she asked.

"McCallum," Kristen responded, with a sharp cheerful air to her voice. "We've only been going out for a few weeks Laura, so it's really early days yet, but I did promise to tell you if and when someone special came along, and he is." The line went quiet for a second or two, before Kristen whispered. "I really, really like him."

"I take it he knows your name isn't Piper then?" Laura laughed then choked, as they both laughed out loud, recalling the 'Maisie' incident. "When will I get to meet him?"

"After New Year."

Laura paused. "Promise me one thing Kristen?"

"Sure, what is it?"

"Don't get hurt."

"I won't, and I hope you feel better soon Laura." Kristen sighed.

Laura was feeling so much better now; although her throat ached and her head still pounded, she was much cheerier. She made herself some warm water with lemon and headed for bed. The next day Laura felt worse, but she didn't have any lectures or study/work rotas so stayed in her room. Up until now she had been on her own in a two-bed studio. Most of her roommates had been short stayers while they organised accommodation off campus. Today she would be joined by a new roommate, Jodie Lewis, whose attempt at outside accommodation had failed due to lack of funds. When she had been offered the room Jodie grabbed the chance with both hands. Laura felt sorry for someone coming into this room full of bugs, and hoped the girl wouldn't be put off by the sorry sight of a sick roommate. As Laura began to recover over the next few days she came to the conclusion that Jodie Lewis was crazy. She was one of those mad happy-go-lucky types who loved life and didn't worry about anything. At times Laura wondered how she ever managed to earn a place at university, such was her style and lack of studying or settling down to do anything constructive. No, Jodie liked to have a laugh and Laura knew they would get on well as she was already laughing at her antics. During the week of very important exams, Laura was locked away studying as much as she could, while on the other side of the door, Jodie was either chatting on the phone, or on social media sites. Laura could hear her loud infectious laughter filtering through the thin wall, which separated them, and then the door opened. "Are you still alive in there?" Jodie laughed, poking her head round the door. "Do you want a drink or something?"

Laura looked up. "I could murder a cup of tea." She smiled then watched Jodie as she casually wandered around the room examining most of its contents before clutching Laura's guitar, which sat on a chair in the corner. She twanged a few strings, badly. "Do you play this thing?"

Laura nodded. "Yup."

"Are you any good?"

"My mum thinks I am."

Jodie looked thoughtfully. "Crap then?" She laughed.

"No, not crap," Laura protested, taken aback by her forwardness.

"Give it a go then," she said, thrusting the guitar onto Laura's lap.

"What happened to the cuppa?"

"Too much bother." Jodie shrugged. "I'll get you a proper drink later, just play."

"Ok then, do you know this one, it's called 'You've got a Friend'." Laura took the guitar on her knee and began singing. Two lines into the song she paused. "Ring any bells?"

"Go on," Jodie urged. Laura continued the song while for the first time that day Jodie sat quietly. "Wow!" she whispered as Laura laid down her guitar. "That was awesome."

"Thanks."

"Where do you sing?"

"I don't any more since I started here."

"No way man?" Jodie was shocked. "That was brilliant."

"There's no time, at least not until this assignment is finished then after the exams it will be Christmas, and I am going home." Laura continued. "After that I need to find a job, one that pays!"

"Have you got something lined up already?"

"No, I'll just see what's out there at the time."

"What about bar work?"

"Never done it before, but yeh, I'd give it a go. Do you know somewhere?"

Jodie looked excited. "Hell yeh, there's this great little pub on the Royal Mile called 'Tattie Bogles'; you'd love it."

"Tattie Bogles?" Laura laughed and was already unsure whether this would be a place she should be working in. "What kind of place is it?"

"Ahh it's a great wee place, there's a guy, Mikey who plays piano, he's really nice, just qualified as an architect, but he still wants to stay now his studies are over. It's a small pub and they sell food. Doug, the owner/manager is a friend of my dad, so I could put a word in for you."

"What about you?"

"What?" No way.

"Why?"

"I'd rather starve than study and work as well."

Laura laughed. "But you don't."

"What?"

"You don't study."

"Yes, alright, guilty as charged," Jodie agreed, "but I will have to soon, it's catching up with me now, and there's no way I could do both."

Laura could believe it, she couldn't imagine Jodie studying and working. She found it hard to imagine her studying at all. "Okay then Jodie, put a word in for me. I could even do waitressing or something, but not until I get back after Christmas and New Year, and they might have someone else by then to cope with the Christmas and New Year crowds."

"Great!" Jodie said jumping off the end of Laura's bed and ran to the little kitchen area reaching under the sink for the half bottle of vodka she had stacked away. "Now for a celebration!" Laura groaned as she wondered what she was letting herself in for.

Over the next few weeks most of Laura's time was taken up with exams, and when the news finally came through that she had passed with good marks again she was thrilled. She called her parents to tell them she'd be coming home for Christmas and New Year. Marie and Fraser were delighted. "We're so proud of you," they told her as they hugged each other at the other end of the telephone. "Your dad says we'll come and collect you."

"Thanks Mum, that would be great. I'm going to try and catch up with Kristen too, she's got herself a boyfriend now, and I can't wait to meet him."

"She'll need to bring him over." Marie suggested.

"That would be great Mum, see you soon." It had been the end of the first semester of the second year and the girls had a lot to catch up on. Despite the cold start to November, the winter had become unusually mild, with no hint of snow, so when Laura phoned Kristen to suggest they bring in the New Year on top of Dumyat, the answer had been a resounding "Yes!" Scott was spending Christmas and New Year with his family, but had promised to come over straight after to meet Kristen's family and friends.

Back in Stirling the girls met for a coffee and arranged a walk after lunch. Marie had persuaded Laura to take Maisie with them, against Laura's better judgement. "She hates it Mum, it's too far," Laura protested but her protests fell on deaf ears.

"Go on Laura," she cried, thrusting the lead into her hand, "I've never met a dog yet that didn't like going for a walk!"

Kristen looked surprised to see little Maisie when they met later that day.

"Don't say a word," Laura pleaded with her, apologetically. "It's like talking to a wall!"

"Zeus and Piper are pleased to see her," Kristen remarked then, "come on let's give it a go." Two hours later they were on top of Laura's hills. As expected it had been too much for the little terrier and, much to the amusement of Zeus and Piper, Laura and Kristen had taken it in turn to carry her most of the way.

"I told Mum this would happen," Laura apologised.

"Hey, she'll still have a good walk, and maybe she'll be happier coming back down?"

"I doubt it," Laura laughed. "She doesn't like heights either!" At the summit they each took deep breaths as they looked across the vast landscape before them. Zeus and Piper explored the ground all around them, sniffing out burrows and being startled occasionally by birds springing from the wild stark shrubs while Maisie returned to Laura and climbed up on her lap as she sat on the cool rough grass. "It's good to be back eh?"

"Mm yes, yes it is."

"So tell me about Scott McCallum?" Laura asked.

"You know what Laura, I'm not going to say anything more than I have already told you about him, you can meet him yourself at Mum and Dad's the Sunday after New Year."

"That's just a few days before we go back to uni Kristen, my mum and dad would be mad if I didn't spend it at home with them."

"No they won't," Kristen smiled, "because they are coming too!"

"That's great," Laura said excitedly then, "I can't wait to meet this man of yours. I wish I could find a nice man some time."

"I'm sure you will, you've had boyfriends before."

"Yes, best left unmentioned."

"You're thinking of that boy in high school, what's his name?"

"Gordon Crane."

"That's right, Gordon Crane, weren't you quite stuck on him for a while?"

"Yes, it was a forever thing at the time. I got really sucked into his lies, if you remember; before I found out he was cheating on me with Linda Carson. He'd apparently been seeing her for a while!"

"Wasn't everybody?" Kristen laughed. "Sorry, I remember now you were quite upset at the time. It's just as well you didn't take things to the next level, then you really would have felt stupid."

Laura looked up over the view.

"You didn't!" Kristen gasped as Laura nodded. "You idiot, you never said."

"Well I did kind of start to tell you," Laura began, "but I couldn't. I was too ashamed, and hurt and embarrassed and terrified that I'd be caught out. When I found out he was seeing Linda Carson, I felt really stupid and used." She looked up at Kristen. "I still do."

"We all make mistakes Laura, some girls I got talking to at uni have different guys every night, some more than one."

"You're kidding?"

"No honestly, and what's more they seem to be quite proud of themselves. It's just that we weren't brought up that way."

"You're right, and I already feel I've let my mum and dad down. They'd kill me if they knew."

"Mine too."

"Have you ever done anything like that?"

"No, but I'd like to with Scott, and I think it'll happen soon."

"Be careful Kristen."

"Oh I will, we are going to talk about it this weekend and I'll go and see Doctor Buchanan when I head back to Glasgow."

"For the pill?"

"Yes."

Laura thought for a moment. "I don't think I could do that."

"What, go on the pill?"

"Mmm, you know what I'm like about pills."

"Well, in that case, you had better be careful, when the time comes." They both sat quietly for a while before heading back down the hill. Maisie managed to walk most of the way down, but faltered in parts and now and again Zeus and Piper ran up and down alerting the girls to the fact that they'd gone on ahead while Maisie had remained seated to a spot further up the hill. By the time Laura arrived home, carrying the little terrier, Marie had the dinner in the oven. The smell of home cooking and the homely atmosphere reminded Laura she was home, and she loved it. Marie made her a cup of tea and as she sat down to drink it she laughed at little Maisie snoring away in her dog basket.

Christmas was wonderful. A huge tree stood in the corner of the lounge, with its red and gold baubles and little twinkling lights. Presents lay underneath, wrapped in Christmas paper and decorated with glittery ribbons. Laura's older sister Emma had now arrived with husband Neil from London and the laughter and chatter could be heard several houses away from the path outside. Emma and Neil were both practising lawyers, specialising in business law and their jobs were very demanding, meaning visits home were few and far between. Last year they had spent Christmas with Neil's parents so this year was extra special as they all gathered together, even if it would be only for a couple of days. Then Emma and Neil would head back down south and that would signal the end of Christmas as far as Marie and Fraser were concerned. This year, however, they had Laura at home for New Year's Day and they were looking forward to meeting with the Campbells a few days later.

New Year's Eve was the one day in the year Laura knew would not be spent alone on the top of the Ochils' highest and most popular hill, Dumyat. Hogmanay on this hill had become almost a tradition where locals gather together at the summit carrying torches and candlelight to bring in the New Year. After the countdown, signalling the start of a new year, a spectacular display of fireworks from Stirling Castle lights up the sky all around them. It was always a joyous occasion and Laura liked to think of it as Dumyat's birthday party; that way she could accept having to share the experience with others. Of course she knew that many people already climbed these hills but she rarely met anyone, and it suited her that way. This year on the top of Dumyat it felt special, as though the hill had embraced them and welcomed them back. After the countdown the burst of spectacular fireworks from Stirling Castle again lit up the dark skies. "Happy New Year!" everyone cheered as they hugged each other in turn, with wishes of good health and happiness in the coming year. The girls then followed the crowd back down the hill before making their way home again to wish their families the same.

A few days later the Duncans met with the Campbells and Laura eventually met Scott McCallum. Through the crowd of visitors she could see Scott and Kristen talking to one of her aunts and she knew at once why Kristen was so hung up on him. Laura noticed his strong build. His fair hair and striking blue eyes made him stand out from the crowd and he wore the same type of checked shirts and blue jeans they loved to wear. Laura liked him instantly. As she listened to them chatting she could tell he was genuine, polite and funny and it was obvious he was crazy about Kristen. As she made her way through the guests in the room Laura eventually reached Kristen and Scott. "So you're the famous Laura Duncan?" He smiled as he bent down to kiss her cheek.

Laura laughed, "I'm not sure about famous?"

"You are in Kristen's house. I've heard all about you, all good of course." He laughed.

"And I've heard all about you too," Laura added with a knowing nod.

"Oh dear. I hope she left out all the bad stuff?" He teased as they settled down to the dinner table. Scott was very charismatic and Marie Duncan was quite taken with him. "You know, you might find yourself a nice young man like Scott one day Laura, if you stop wearing these jeans all the time." Laura laughed, shaking her head at her mother's predictable comment. The day passed so quickly Laura felt it was over before it had begun, but she left with the feeling that she would be leaving two good friends behind this time, not just one, as the three parted company once again and headed back to university a few days later.

2

It was a new year and the middle of the second year at university. Life as students was hard going, especially financially, and Laura knew she had returned this time to look for work to subsidise her poor finances. Jodie was quick to remind her about Tattie Bogles when she returned to their room at Student Halls. "I've had a word with my dad," she blurted, "and he had a word with Doug, the guy who owns the pub, remember?" Laura nodded as she took off her coat and scarf and laid them on the small sofa. "Well, I've to take you over tonight before they open, if that's okay?"

Laura gasped. "I'm just back!" she cried, looking at Jodie in disbelief. "I've not even unpacked yet!"

Jodie was undeterred. "Look, if we do this tonight, then it's job done isn't it?" She looked up at Laura's startled expression. "You're lucky the job's still open for you, it was very busy over Christmas, but I persuaded Doug to wait till you were back." She paused. "What do you say?"

"Okay, okay, okay." Laura threw her arms in the air. "Tonight it is."

Tattie Bogles was much nicer than Laura had dared to imagine, coming as a recommendation from the lively Jodie, she had half expected a rowdy, clubby sort of place, but this was classy, despite its quirky name, and very un-Jodie like. To the right of the bar a raised half-moon area set the stage for the piano. A young man was sitting there looking through music sheets. He looked up briefly and smiled. Before she could say anything an older man appeared from behind the bar and on seeing Jodie he came forward. "I take it you must be the Laura Duncan I have been hearing so much about?"

Laura laughed. "What has she been saying to you?"

"Now that would be telling," he teased, taking a deep breath as he surveyed the little pub restaurant. "Well you've probably gathered I'm Doug, the owner, manager, boss, whatever, and this is Tattie Bogles. Over there," he pointed towards the piano, "is Mikey Macrae." He looked at Laura now, tilting his head to one side. "First impression?"

"Good," Laura smiled. "Not what I expected... better."

"Great, so what kind of work would you want to be doing here?" he asked.

"Jodie thought I could maybe wait on tables or something? I have no bar experience." Laura glanced up to see Doug looking back with a puzzled smile.

"And that's what you'd like to do is it?"

Laura shrugged. "Anything really, I need the money."

He laughed. "I'm sure you do, but didn't I hear something about you playing guitar and being a bit of a singer? Surely you'd want to be doing something like that instead?"

"I'd love it!" Laura shrieked as she glanced over at Jodie, who was now sitting beside Mikey with a glass of vodka and cola in her hand.

"Now look," Doug started, trying to subdue her excitement. "I'm giving Jodie the benefit of the doubt when she says you are good, and I am looking for another singer." He paused, bringing his hand up to his chin rubbing the slight stubble as he looked at her thoughtfully. "Mind you it has to be the right kind, and you would have to complement Mikey on piano." He looked across towards Mikey as he sat chatting to Jodie. "I don't go in for all this modern stuff, folk hear enough of that on their MP3 players and the likes. I prefer the older, smoother or catchy things that don't blast my customers' eardrums. And I like the quieter ballads folk can listen to but still carry on having a conversation with the person next to them, if you know what I mean?"

Laura nodded. "That's my kind of thing as it happens, but I didn't bring my guitar, if you want me to try out?"

"Ah, that's where our Jodie is one step ahead, she brought your guitar in this morning." He stepped behind the bar and brought out Laura's guitar, handing it to her.

"What? So that's why she was anxious to get me here so quickly?" Then turning to Jodie, she threw up her fist, jokingly. "I'll see you later."

"You didn't notice it missing?" Doug asked, laughing.

"I didn't have time!" Laura shook her head.

"Sing that one you did for me," Jodie shouted from the other side of the room.

Laura and Doug made their way over to the piano, introducing Laura to Mikey. "Do you know what song she's talking about?" he asked.

Mikey nodded. "Jodie's been telling me, yes I know it." He turned to Laura. "You start and I'll come in."

As the soft music filled the room it was clear Doug was as impressed as Jodie had been. The two were just fantastic together, and it was obvious from the start they had a great

26

chemistry going on when they sang. They looked every inch a couple with similar hair colour and Mikey, he noticed, wasn't that much taller than Laura. They looked good together, that much was true and now as they ended the song Doug jumped up. "And you've got a job!" he yelled. "And two more friends!" Despite being slightly annoyed at the cheek of Jodie Lewis, Laura couldn't help feel excited about the prospect of her new job, and she was pleased Jodie had taken her along to Tattie Bogles. Jodie was right, it was a great wee place and Laura realised she would be doing something she loved. *It was not like a job at all*, she told herself, and she'd be getting paid for it into the bargain. Over the next few months she spent more time at Tattie Bogles and with Mikey. "You'll need to come and see me," she told Kristen after telling her the exciting news, but Kristen was apologetic. "I'm working part-time at the veterinary practice not far from the university campus now," she told Laura. "But the first weekend we're free, we'll come over, I promise."

Weeks passed as Laura got to know Doug and Mikey a bit better, and she loved the chatter and the friendly atmosphere of Tattie Bogles. Mikey's girlfriend Jade made an appearance now and again and Laura referred to her as 'a bit of a girl', a remark Mikey found amusingly old fashioned. And although Mikey thought the world of her, Laura wasn't too sure Jade felt the same way. She felt really sorry for the way Jade treated him, cancelling dates at the drop of a hat as soon as something else came along. "Don't you mind?" she asked him one night when yet another date had been cancelled so she could go out with her friends. "She's got a life too, Laura, you know, and I'm here most weekends. If she doesn't want to be with me then what good would it do to insist she does?"

"Does she want to be with you at all?" Laura asked, instantly wishing she hadn't and apologised for the question.

Mikey looked at her and shook his head. "No, it's okay and you know Laura, to be honest, I don't know? And what's more, I'm afraid to ask in case she says no."

"You're too good for her you know?"

"Relationships are complicated sometimes, Laura, you have to give and take and bend a little or they just snap."

"I could snap her sometimes," Laura laughed.

"Sometimes... I think you've got it right being single."

"It's not out of choice!" Laura protested. "Just lack of time."

"Ah one day Laura, one day you'll meet someone and everything in your life will change."

"Is that a prediction?"

"Hell yeh, have you never heard of Psychy Mikey?"

Together, Mikey and Laura were a great hit with the regulars and the tourists who stopped by. The place was always packed when they were there, but Doug accepted Laura was studying and Mikey was trying to maintain a dodgy relationship, so he was happy to settle for the days they could both manage to come and play. They were certainly bringing in the crowds when they did and he reluctantly accepted the quieter days when they couldn't in between. If he was honest with himself, those quieter days gave him some breathing space as Tattie Bogles soon became the place to be and Laura just loved it.

As the end of the second university year approached Kristen was in touch to say she was spending the summer recess with Scott. Laura spent some time at home, climbing the hills on her own and absorbing the beauty and the peace before returning to begin her third year at university. Laura knew that good exam results were achievable but the constant pressure was overwhelming. She loved the escape of playing at Tattie Bogles whenever she could and catching up on all the gossip from Doug and Mikey was a refreshing change from the conversations she had at university. Their music was gaining in popularity and Laura had even worked with Mikey on some of her own songs. Jodie was hardly around, despite her promise to knuckle down to study, so at least Laura had some peace to study when she needed it. Jade eventually left Mikey for another guy and Laura was left to pick up the pieces of his broken heart. Their friendship grew stronger as a consequence and she knew now she could trust him with anything. Outside Tattie Bogles Mikey was gaining experience in a new job and he was, for the first time in a long while, happy to be single. Life for Laura settled into a pattern, as the routine of study and work became the focus of her life. The extra money was welcome and Mikey was happy to give her a lift back to university after work, so she didn't have to pay for the bus or taxis. Tattie Bogles now attracted its own group of regulars who came in at the weekends, when Laura and Mikey were playing, and she became familiar with their faces. Then one Friday night she noticed a stranger among the usual crowd. He was a stylish-looking man in his late twenties, strikingly good looking, with thick dark hair and an olive complexion. He sat watching her all night, while she sang and played guitar, speaking very little to the beautiful young woman beside him. "Who's that guy?" Laura asked Mikey when they stopped for a break.

"Which one?" Mikey asked, as they both looked up, but the couple were gone.

"He was sitting there, over by the window, in the corner."

"Sorry honey, I didn't notice him."

"You must have?" Laura was astounded. "He stood out a mile."

Mikey shook his head. "If he comes in again give me a nudge, and I'll see if I know him." It was a week later before the stranger appeared again. Laura poked Mikey on the shoulder as he bent down to take his seat at the piano. "That's him again, Mikey, that guy I was telling you about." She whispered, "Don't stare, he's sitting by the window again... don't look now, it'll be obvious." Mikey laughed, keeping his eyes well down focusing on the keys of the piano. Then, lifting his head slowly as Laura checked the tuning of her guitar, he looked over towards the window and nodded in recognition of the customer. "Do you know him?" Laura asked.

"Ohhh yes," he answered. "That's Gyle Jamieson."

"How do you know him?"

"He used to come in here all the time with his girlfriend Natalie, but I see he's not with her tonight, unless she's meeting him here later."

"What does Natalie look like?" Laura was curious.

"Very beautiful, tall, long dark hair."

"He was with her last night, I saw her."

Mikey looked up. "He's one to watch, that one," he said.

"What do you mean?"

"He's a bit full of himself, thinks he's the man." He looked at Laura. "And he has a girlfriend... at least one. Come on, you know the type?" But Laura didn't know the type. She had never met anyone who had captured her attention so much as this stranger, this Gyle Jamieson, who had sat, almost staring at her throughout her last performance. Tonight, he was here again, alone, and Laura was intrigued to know why. They were opening the night with a catchy song, 'Can't get by without you', and as they started Laura tried not to look at the handsome stranger she now knew was Gyle Jamieson, but now and again her eyes wandered over to the window seat, where she noticed him take a sip from his glass of whisky before slowly lifting his gaze to hers. She looked away instantly and carried on with the song. The end of the evening's entertainment now ended with a solo, either by Mikey or Laura and tonight it was Mikey's turn. As he started with 'Leave Right Now', Laura noticed her tall dark stranger finish his fourth drink of the night before leaving. This time as he stood, he paused for a moment smiling towards her, and then she watched as he disappeared through the heavy glass doors. He had again watched her all night, this time alone. The atmosphere in Tattie Bogles the following night was unusually lively. They started off with a duet, 'Love lifts us up where we belong'. Laura loved this number and as they sang, she was reminded of home, the Ochil Hills, and the two eagles that made an occasional appearance. This is where she would always feel she belonged, perhaps not on a mountain high, but some beautiful hills. Tonight the lyrics seemed to spell out how she saw life, and the challenges she faced. There was no sign of Gyle Jamieson, and Laura assumed he must be out with his stunning girlfriend. Somewhere romantic, she imagined, enjoying a meal and fine wine. As they moved to another duet, 'Don't go breaking my heart', the crowd were now humming along to the tune, half dancing in their seats and as Laura surveyed the crowd enjoying themselves, her eye moved towards the door just as Gyle Jamieson walked in. His eyes caught Laura's as he moved towards the bar and ordered a whisky, holding her gaze as he smiled. She smiled back, and when the music stopped for a short break, he walked over to the stage. Laura was freeing herself from her guitar strap. "Hi," he said cheerfully, taking her by surprise.

"Hi," she replied, slightly startled, and then turning to Mikey, "Could you get me a ginger beer and lime honey?" Mikey nodded and moved quickly towards the bar, as the customers took the opportunity to do the same during the short break.

"Boyfriend?" asked Gyle.

Laura laughed. "No, friends and partners in music only."

"I'm Gyle," he said, smiling. "I've been watching you play. You are very good."

"Thank you," Laura smiled, "that's very kind. I'm Laura."

"I know," he said, grinning. "I wondered... if you are not with someone that is, whether I could buy you a drink after work?"

"That's really nice of you," Laura said shyly, "but Mikey usually gives me a lift home, unless he decides to stay for a drink himself."

"I could give you a lift."

Laura thought for a moment. "Err no, I don't think so, but thanks for offering. If you are still around at the end of the night, and we are having a drink before heading off, you would be welcome to join us." Mikey was back by this time, ginger beer and lime in one hand and a lemonade in the other. He acknowledged Gyle still standing next to Laura then, turning to her, said, "I thought we'd start off this time with a Beatles number?"

Laura turned to Gyle. "You must excuse me," she said before turning back to Mikey and they both headed back towards the piano.

"What did he want?" Mikey asked.

"To buy me a drink." The surprise in her voice was obvious.

"And you said no?"

"I said maybe after work, maybe, if we were staying on."

"Do you want to stay on?"

Laura shrugged. "Only if you do."

He looked at her thoughtfully. "Why not? Be careful though with that one, I wouldn't trust him as far as I could throw him."

Laura raised her eyebrows, closed her eyes and shook her head. "Okay Mum," she joked, laughing. "He thought you were my boyfriend!"

Mikey laughed, looking over towards Gyle Jamieson who was now sitting at the bar, his eyes fixed on the two of them laughing. He turned away. "He's watching us," he told her, "don't look towards the bar, he'll know we were talking about him."

At the end of the evening, Gyle Jamieson approached the two of them and very charmingly offered to buy them both a drink. "I'm driving thanks," Mikey said, "but I'd love a lemonade if that's okay?"

Gyle nodded then turned towards Laura. "And you?"

"Malibu and pineapple please." They stood at the bar; Doug joined them and chatted about everything and anything. Laura was determined to keep the conversation light and general, and when she and Mikey had finished their drink she spoke to Gyle directly. "Thanks for the drink Gyle, maybe I'll see you tomorrow or maybe next week?"

"You will," he said smiling, and then took a step back to let Laura and Mikey past as they left Tattie Bogles.

When Laura arrived home that night Jodie was waiting for her. She had a vodka and cola in one hand and a bag of chips in the other. "I'm just in," she told Laura, slightly tipsy. "How was Tatties tonight?" Jodie sat and listened, mouth open wide, as Laura told her of the weekend's events. "So, you're telling me that Gyle Jamieson offered to buy you a drink and drive you home – and you said no?"

"Yes," Laura answered, noting the odd expression on Jodie's face. "I don't know him, he could be anybody?"

"He's Gyle Jamieson," Jodie said, almost breathless, dropping a chip onto the table in front of her, before picking it up again and stuffing it into her mouth. "He's only the most gorgeous guy in Edinburgh, and he only drives a Mercedes sport. And you turned him down?"

"You might also know he has a girlfriend, a beautiful girlfriend he was with just a couple of nights ago?" Laura protested.

"He's always got a girlfriend, Laura, which tells you what?"

"He's a gigolo?"

"He's hot! And loaded, and probably the most desirable man..."

"I get it," Laura interrupted, stealing one of Jodie's chips, before finishing what she thought Jodie was about to say, "in Edinburgh."

"If not Scotland?" Jodie added, staring at her. "I'm coming next week."

Laura laughed; she was certain Jodie would be there, watching Gyle's every move. The following weekend, Jodie proved true to her word, and probably, for the first time in her entire life, Laura imagined, Jodie was the first to arrive. "It's been ages since I heard you two play," she told them, trying to justify her presence.

Doug appeared from behind the bar. "Jodie!" he called, giving her a big hug. "You couldn't help out behind the bar tonight could you?" he asked. "Madeleine has called in sick." Jodie stared at him in silence. "Okay, I can detect a bargaining look here." Doug laughed. "How about three free drinks and twenty quid?"

"Twenty quid?" she gasped, "is that legal?"

"Mates' rates?"

"Thirty," Jodie bargained.

"Done!" he said quickly before heading back behind the bar.

"I think I have been," Jodie sighed, following him.

By the end of the night, Gyle Jamieson had not only bought Laura a drink; he had also asked her out on a date. The conversation took place during the break at the bar and Jodie had almost fallen into Gyle Jamieson's drink, listening to the conversation. She was even more shocked when Laura was again hesitant. "I'm not sure?" she told him, explaining. "I hardly know you. Maybe some other time?"

Jodie stood with her mouth open and her eyes as wide as tea plates. She couldn't believe that Laura had again turned down the most eligible bachelor in the city. Caught up in her own excitement she jumped in at the end of the conversation. "I'll come out with you!" To which Gyle Jamieson laughed and told her not to be so nosey.

Laura was mortified. "Go away Jodie," she whispered loudly and irritably, apologising to Gyle afterwards.

"Do you know her?" he asked curiously.

"She's my roommate."

"Roommate?"

"At university," Laura explained.

"Oh, I didn't realise Jodie was at university, sorry."

"I didn't realise you knew each other."

"Maybe Jodie will put in a good word for me." He laughed before Laura was called back to the stage for the second half of the evening's entertainment. That evening, Gyle left before the end of the evening.

Jodie was astounded by the events surrounding Gyle Jamieson and her roommate. She called Mikey over. "Hey Mikey, you won't believe this one!" she said as she told him of the conversation she had witnessed.

Laura defended her corner. "Look, I'm not going out, in a car, or anywhere with someone I don't know, it's crazy!"

Mikey and Jodie looked at each other in amusement. "Well how would anyone ever meet anyone and strike up a relationship?" Jodie asked, curiously.

"Where I come from, everybody knows everybody so going out with someone isn't scary. And if you don't know them, your friends will know them well and give you a very detailed heads up before you go out."

"That's Stirling, a wee town Laura," Jodie protested.

"A city actually," Laura corrected her.

"Yes okay, on paper maybe, but here in the real city, the capital, you go out and you might not meet anybody you know. Anyway, I know him and I tell you he's a catch." It was obvious Laura was very nervous about the prospect of going out with a complete stranger, and as Jodie continued to convince her this was quite normal city living, even Mikey who had sat in silence throughout the conversation had to agree. However, without the bravado of Jodie, Mikey admitted he had serious reservations about the charismatic Mr Jamieson and warned Laura to be careful.

"Oh shut up Mikey," Jodie yelled at him. "You are just jealous." Then, turning to Laura, "I know Gyle, and Mikey knows Gyle, so there you are. He's not a stranger."

Mikey looked up. "Keep me out of that one," he said as he

gave up on the conversation and suggested he take the two girls back to university just as Doug appeared from the kitchen. "Is it home time then?" he called, and then pitching his voice towards Laura, he asked, "Are you going out with Gyle then?"

Laura was shocked. "How did you know about that, you were in the kitchen?"

"I've been at the bar most of the evening and he's been asking questions and talking about you all night!"

"Do you think I should go out with him?"

"Not at the weekends, when you should be in here!"

"Now, there's another reason why I can say no," Laura teased as Jodie gave a huge sigh; then, turning to Doug, she said, "See you!" Eventually, Laura agreed to go out with Gyle, but only as part of a double date with Jodie and Mikey, who had accepted the invitation under protest and with mixed emotions. Jodie's emotion was one of expected elation while Mikey's emotion was one of dread. However, he kept his promise and the evening paved the way for Laura to feel a little more comfortable in Gyle's company. "Don't you have a girlfriend?" she asked over dinner. "I saw you with a lovely-looking girl one night.

"Ah, so you did notice me?" he laughed. "Actually we had just agreed to end it. We were having a very civilised goodbye drink."

"I'm sorry," Laura said softly, "I shouldn't have asked".

"I'm not," he said, smiling, his eyes catching hers as he held her gaze. Jodie had been her usual lively self, while Laura noticed that Mikey, while being the perfect gentleman, had been very quiet all night. Laura took the opportunity to ask him why he didn't like Gyle a few days later as they worked on a new song together at Student Halls. Mikey's awkward reply was difficult for Laura to understand as he threw just about everything into the mix. He didn't like the way he dressed, the number of girlfriends he had, and used the words smug, smarmy and devious. Then he admitted that he not only knew Gyle Jamieson through his visits to Tattie Bogles, but he had also come into contact with him through work. Laura listened as she learned a little more about this new man in her life. "He works as an estate agent," Mikey began. "I came into contact with him when the company he works for, McArdle and Baynes, were agents for a new development at Gullane." Mikey stopped and looked at Laura.

"Go on."

"Well, the company I was working for designed the development and dealt with all the red tape and permissions that go with it through each stage. I was just a trainee then, so I had been given access to the files and dealings around the major points through the process." Laura nodded. "Well things were going really well, the company I was working for had taken a huge risk at the time, sinking all their finances into it. They had major financial problems and it was a make-or-break deal, but we were up for a prestigious design award and the development was promising to be the biggest break the company had ever had."

"And?"

"It all went pear shaped, almost overnight. The company I worked for had spent months as well as committing every penny they had on design and development and suddenly McArdle and Baynes pulled out at the crucial point, and with them the builders and the contractors."

"How could that have been Gyle's fault, he just works for the company does he not?"

"How many estate agents, or should I say, more accurately, people who work for estate agents, do you know who have their own flat in Manor Place and drive a top-of-the-range Mercedes sport?" Laura raised her eyebrows in surprise. "So where did he fit in?"

"His father, Alastair Jamieson, is a top merchant banker. He was financing the deal. It is rumoured that Gyle persuaded him to withdraw the finance and invest in a development in the Cayman Islands."

"What happened?"

"The deal collapsed as quickly as the construction industry fell and the housing market crashed. The company I was working for had turned other major work away to concentrate on the Gullane development and they struggled to find other work. Eventually the business was taken into receivership, people lost their jobs and I lost mine."

"Are you sure?"

"Yes, I definitely lost my job."

"No, Mikey, all the other stuff?"

"That's what I understand to be true, so you'll forgive me for not trusting the man. If it wasn't for my work at Doug's place, I'd have been stuffed."

"Do you not think his father might have pressured him?"

"I doubt his father had too much to do with the finer details to be honest Laura, but I don't doubt he made valuable connections in the process. There's a lot of money in the Cayman Islands and Gyle Jamieson was the link person at the time. The deal secured him a very handsome personal bonus."

"Hence the apartment in Manor Place and the car?"

"Exactly."

"Was it legal?"

"Perfectly, unfortunately some dodgy deals in business are not always illegal. Immoral, perhaps, ruthless even and it's the latter that gives me the most unease."

"Thanks for telling me Mikey, but there could be another explanation, couldn't there?"

"I think it's called business." Mikey sighed. "But there's good practice, and there's this. It wasn't McArdle and Baynes' shout, but it was done through them and they knew we had everything riding on this deal. The whole thing was underhand, to say the least."

"I can see where you're coming from."

"Well, don't go casting it up to him, it won't do me any good, or you. Some things are best known and then kept quiet, so just take care Laura. If you are going to see Gyle bloody Jamieson again, I'd rather you know what he's like now."

"And I gather you would rather I didn't see him again?"

Mikey looked at her, lowered his head and paused, and then, lifting his head up again, "Yes, I would, but I don't have the right to stop you, or even try." Laura hugged Mikey and kissed him on the cheek. "What was that for?"

"Being you."

A month later Laura started dating Gyle Jamieson, despite Mikey's warnings. Over in Glasgow, Scott McCallum, having graduated, was now working in a veterinary practice and Kristen had moved out of her student accommodation and into a flat with him in town. Laura couldn't wait to tell Kristen all about her new boyfriend, but when Kristen suggested they meet up one weekend Laura said she felt it was early days, and should she and Gyle still be dating in a few months, they would definitely arrange something. It was a date Laura hoped would happen. From then on, Gyle pulled out all the stops to gain Laura's trust and approval. She was showered with flowers at her student flat, and treated to meals out in upmarket restaurants. Gyle was happy to join her and Mikey at Tattie Bogles, while they performed, but it was he who took her back to Student Halls instead of Mikey. Jodie Lewis was surprised by the attention Gyle Jamieson was showering on her roommate. "You know, Laura, I have to say, I am gobsmacked really, that you two are still going out," she told Laura one night. Laura could see why Jodie might think that but she teased her by asking for her reasons. Jodie looked awkward as she tried to be honest but not hurtful in her response. "Well, it's not that I don't think you are attractive, Laura, because you are, but." She stopped.

"But what?"

Jodie looked at her thoughtfully, screwing up her nose. "You are just not the type of girl he usually goes for. Every girl I see him with is tall, slim, elegant and stunningly beautiful, you know, like a model?"

"And you don't think I am like that Jodie?" Laura joked, trying to look serious.

Jodie laughed. "Sorry, but you know what I mean?"

Laura agreed, laughing slightly now as she remembered how Natalie looked, and then eventually admitted it was a mystery to her too; but as she pointed out to Jodie, they were dating, and happy, and it seemed to be working somehow. What's more Gyle Jamieson appeared to be absolutely smitten by this fresh-faced, attractive wholesome blonde girl from Stirling. The reasons why were a mystery to them both. "Maybe these other girls are shallow bimbos?" Jodie offered, looking for answers. Laura shrugged. "Whatever the reason, Jodie, I guess I'll find out sometime?" From that point Gyle was a constant visitor to Laura's student rooms, and she loved the impromptu visits, whisking her off for dinner or taking her out for the day, or to the theatre – but never pushing for anything more. She wondered whether he saw her as a friend, like Mikey, which would explain why she was different to his other girlfriends. *That was it*, she told herself. She was merely a new friend, someone to have a laugh with and no ties; then she realised that he had never taken her to his flat in Manor Place. When she mentioned it a few days later he was surprised. "You want to see where I live?"

Laura nodded. "You know where I live," she reasoned.

"One day," he promised without offering to take her there.

Laura was intrigued and mentioned it to Mikey when she had a quiet moment with him at work. "Why do you think he doesn't want me to see his place?" she asked.

Mikey was puzzled. "I have no idea Laura." He sat looking over the piano in deep thought. "Maybe it's because if you split up, he won't need to worry about you hunting him down?"

Laura laughed. "As if I would!"

Mikey looked to her again. "Or maybe it's because he has other girlfriends who might call there?"

"No way!" Laura scolded him at the suggestion, but it had struck a chord and it now bothered her enough to tackle him about it a few days later. It was the conversation which changed the course of their relationship, as he sat her down on a seat in Princes Street Gardens, below Edinburgh Castle. It was a beautiful sunny day and local office workers sat on the grass enjoying lunch in the sun near the outside stage some few feet away. Gyle held Laura's hands as he explained that he had made mistakes in the past and he had many relationships behind him.

He told Laura that being lucky enough to have a fast car and a smart apartment in town had attracted the wrong type of girlfriend. "There are too many women out there Laura who see these things and think they can manipulate a fancy lifestyle out of my bank balance." He laughed, as Laura listened desperate to butt in and tell him she was not like those girls, but there was no time as Gyle quickly continued to explain. "I've had girls stay at my place often, and when the relationship soured, I felt it had also left a sourness about my home. You know, Laura, my home is my haven, I like to feel I can escape when I go there." Laura understood perfectly. "When Natalie and I split it was because she wanted more, but it was the lifestyle she wanted more of, not me, and I'm no millionaire. I realised that, without the flat in Manor Place, without the Mercedes or the money I make now," he paused while Laura sat listening and wondering where she fitted in to this, "without all this, she wouldn't want to know." He looked up towards the castle. "And unfortunately, during an argument, she as much admitted it."

"I'm not Natalie," she whispered.

"That's just it, Laura. You are nothing like Natalie or anyone else I have ever been out with. I knew that from the beginning when you didn't want to go out with me!" He laughed. "It was a shock at the time I'd have to admit. It had never happened before and it made me realise that, if you did go out with me, you would be going out with ME, if that makes any sense?"

"I think so, but it doesn't go very far to explain why you don't want to take me to your place now, assuming you already realise I am not like Natalie?" Gyle looked into her eyes before pulling her close to him. He kissed her, gently but assuredly and differently from any time before. "I had to be sure this time.

43

When Niamh and I spilt I promised myself that no one else would come to Manor Place, or meet my parents unless I was sure they were the one. I don't want my possessions to be the main focus of the relationship; that has to be me, and the relationship has to survive because of me, who I am, not what I have, otherwise it's not real."

"And you're not sure I am the one, or that I'm real?" Laura pulled away. "Thanks Gyle, I understand perfectly." She started to walk away.

"Laura!" Gyle yelled, jumping up, running after her. "You've missed the whole point!"

"I don't think so?" Laura shook her head as she turned her back again and continued to walk away.

"I love you!" he called. She turned round and watched him as he stood looking helpless and lost. It was a look she'd never seen before and she was stunned. He looked vulnerable, and humble and she realised at once there was another side to Gyle. Hidden behind the flash car and the fancy clothes, there was a more sensitive and sincere Gyle, making him even more attractive in her eyes than he'd been before. "I love you," he repeated quietly. "You are the one, but it has to be mutual Laura. I just had to be sure you felt the same way. If you don't love me, walk away now. If you do, please tell me, I'm in knots here?"

"I love you too," she whispered and as the two embraced their lips met. They stood holding each other while office workers and the world passed them by for a few special moments.

"Will you come to my place tonight?" he asked, as they eventually loosened their hold on each other.

Laura smiled. "Yes, I will."

"And you'll stay with me?"

"What, all night?" Laura asked, shocked at the sudden request.

Gyle laughed. "Isn't that how two people in love usually spend their time?"

Laura gulped, and in a split second she felt panicked, then relaxed as she realised her life was about to take another major turn in its journey. "Okay," she whispered and hugged him.

"I've never met anyone like you Laura," he told her. "You're so damn genuine, you're talented and so refreshingly pretty, and you are so nice. I can't believe you are not with someone?"

"I am," she teased. "You!" She looked more serious now. "I've had boyfriends, and dates," she told him. "They were few, and usually didn't end well. They made me feel I had just wasted my time. When I started uni, Kristen and I promised our parents and each other we'd not waste any more time on worthless relationships, but would concentrate on our studies."

"Kristen?"

"My best friend."

"And she is?"

"At a university in Glasgow studying veterinary medicine," Laura said, with a sudden urge of pride.

"Very good, and I take it she's single too then?"

Laura laughed. "Not exactly, she's living with her boyfriend now in a flat in Glasgow. She's really happy."

Gyle smiled. "I'm going to make you happy Laura, I promise. I will take care of you, look after you and love you... and make you happy."

"I hope so," Laura teased as they left Princes Street Gardens and Gyle returned back to work. As Laura spent a few hours shopping, she felt a sudden surge of romance and all it promised. She was elated, this gorgeous man loved her, little Laura Duncan, and she loved him. She couldn't wait to tell Jodie, but by the time she returned to her room at Student Halls, Jodie was typically out. Laura left a note to say she would be staying at Gyle's that night. It was the first time she had written such a note, and it felt strange, very grown up suddenly and she laughed as she propped the note up against the kettle before taking a shower and packing a few things for her night away in Manor Place. Of course there was Tattie Bogles first, and she expected Jodie would pop in to hear all the details, which of course she did. "Oh my God Laura!" she said excitedly, "I told you it was because those girls were shallow, I tell you he was just needing a good woman and to think he could have had me!" Laura laughed as Jodie outlined her small, slightly chubby frame, and unruly purple hair.

"He missed out there, sure enough," Laura teased.

Mikey was in a less jocular mood, as Laura expected, and he delivered his warning for her to be careful again. "I'm here for you Laura, if you need me," he added before giving her a hug.

"I'm not going anywhere Mikey," she laughed, "I'm not bailing out to another planet, I'll still be playing here with you and going to uni."

Mikey smiled. "I hope so."

Laura felt like a speck of dust in a sandstorm over the next few days as events took over her life. Her first night's stay at Manor Place had been amazing. Gyle dropped rose petals across the bedroom floor and on to the huge king-sized bed where Prosecco and strawberries sat precariously on a little silver tray. He had taken Laura in his arms and gently made love to her, telling her constantly how much he loved her. She felt so happy, so much in love, it all seemed surreal. It was not until the following morning before she was able to take in the amazingly chic and stylish Victorian terraced apartment. The period home had a smart contemporary feel, while still retaining some of its original character. Sleek integrated appliances interrupted marble worktops while natural oak floors enhanced the chic and sophisticated design. Gyle looked on as Laura examined every detail. "You like?" he asked.

"It is so beautiful, did you do all of this?"

"No this incredible style choice was my mum's. She is amazing, Italian, you know, they have style, and she has more than her share of it."

Laura was a little surprised. That was something else she had learned about her new boyfriend. "Half Italian then?" she teased.

"Si." He laughed. "You must meet my parents; they live not that far away in Easter Belmont Road."

"Tell me about them?"

Gyle sighed. "Where do I start? My mum is Italian, she comes from Positano, a beautiful place along the Amalfi Coast and her name is Carlotta, but she's always been called Carla. My dad is Alastair, he's very much a hard-boiled Scot from Edinburgh."

Laura smiled, remembering Mikey had told her already Gyle's father was called Alastair. "Go on then," she prompted, "sisters or brothers?"

"I have one brother, Paolo, and no sisters. My dad insisted his first-born son would have a completely Scottish name, which explains why I am Gyle or, rather, Argyle but no one ever calls me Argyle, it's always been Gyle. Mum won the argument when my brother was born and Dad agreed to Paolo, thinking that everyone would just call him Paul."

"And do they?"

"No." Gyle laughed. "He gets Paolo to this day much to my dad's annoyance and my mum's amusement. My dad is in merchant banking, and my mum just shops and meets with her friends and that's about all really. They are rarely around, Dad's job takes him abroad often, and they don't keep in touch much."

Laura found that strange. Her parents were always in touch but she was amused to hear Gyle's description of his mum and she was fairly sure she didn't just spend her days shopping and meeting with friends. "And your mum dabbles in interior design?" Laura added.

"When needs must; and your family?"

"Not as exciting as yours," Laura started. "My mum and dad used to own a newsagent's in Stirling, before they retired. I have an older sister Emma who is married and lives in London. She's a lawyer, and she doesn't keep in touch much; and there's me, and Maisie."

"Maisie?"

"Mum's West Highland Terrier."

Gyle laughed. "And what's your mum and dad's name?"

"Mr and Mrs Duncan, of course!" Laura teased. "Actually they are Fraser and Marie, and you know they live in Stirling."

Gyle put his arms around Laura. " I love you Laura Duncan, you'll need to take me to Stirling to meet your parents and you must meet mine."

3

Returning to Student Halls after spending the weekend at Manor Place brought with it a sharp reminder of reality. Compared to Gyle's flat, Laura's room at Student Halls was cold, dull and basic. Worse than that, a note left by her tutor reminded her she had failed to meet an assignment deadline; and it was clear from the note that it had not gone unnoticed that her sketchy submissions were the result of missed lectures. Catching up on the missed work and revising what she had already covered would be difficult without burning the midnight oil during the week. Then there were study courses to attend during the weekend on top of her much-needed work at Tattie Bogles. Laura now worried where Gyle would fit into this busy schedule and she suddenly felt under enormous pressure, making her panicked and nervous. Later that day, Gyle's acceptance of the situation had been a great relief as he shrugged off the situation. "It's no big deal," he told her, rather excitedly. "You can come over to mine and use my study. I'll busy myself elsewhere, and when you are finished we'll still have the nights together." Laura looked shocked, as Gyle finished, selling the idea to her. "We'll still be together, even if you are busy. It will be a great feeling Laura, it's what couples do all the time."

She looked shocked, and for a few moments said nothing, then looking into his eyes, "Are you sure you don't mind? I have a lot of studying to do."

"Do I mind? Of course I don't mind Laura, in fact, the more I think about it, the more I think you should just move out of student accommodation altogether and stay here with me?"

"I couldn't do that!" Laura gasped.

"Why ever not, it makes perfect sense to me?" He paused, taking her by the hands, his mood changing slightly. "Of course, I am assuming you want to be with me?"

"You know I do."

"Then what's stopping you?"

"What if you tire of me and all the studying? Where do I go then, if I give up my room?"

"That's not going to happen." Gyle laughed. "If it makes you feel any easier, don't give up your room. Don't tell them you are not there, I am sure Jodie will keep things going and you don't need to pay to stay with me!"

Laura reluctantly agreed, noting how excited Gyle was about his proposition she didn't want to disappoint him. She moved some of her things into Gyle's flat the next day, much to the surprise of Jodie and later Mikey.

"It's all gone a bit fast Laura," Mikey remarked with some concern.

"I know," Laura said quietly.

"As long as you are happy Laura," he chirped, trying to lighten the sombre mood. Mikey smiled but he was worried Laura had been railroaded into a decision she wasn't really ready for, and she certainly didn't seem very excited about it. He had a bad feeling about where it would all lead but he was pretty sure it wouldn't be to the road of happiness and fulfilment, if his knowledge of Gyle Jamieson was anything to go by.

Laura found living at Manor Place to be luxurious and for the first few days Gyle was happy to listen to music or watch television in the lounge while she worked in the little study next to it. He was happy to take her to university when she had lectures, and collect her again later. He would occasionally pop in to the study while Laura was working for a chat or to bring her a drink. When she was studying at home during the day he'd call in for coffee, then again for lunch, before returning to work. Gradually the interruptions increased and with it polite requests to take care of laundry and other household chores. Laura reluctantly accepted she had to pull her weight, but the interruptions were intrusive and annoying. Now it was becoming apparent that Gyle was beginning to feel bored during the evenings as she tried to make up for lost time during the day. His interruptions were now more frequent, and the increased attention he demanded meant even less time spent catching up. Tonight he was particularly restless, interrupting her concentration on a number of occasions with casual unimportant questions. Now he sneaked up behind Laura, kissing her neck. His hands then moved down to her breasts and soon his kisses were everywhere, strong and passionate and they continued as he led her into the bedroom where they stayed all night. The following evening Gyle announced he'd invited his parents over for dinner. Laura was aghast. "What, tonight, as in an hour or so?"

"Less than that, I guess. I thought you wanted to meet them?" He sounded surprised.

"I'd have preferred a little more notice, look at me, I'm a mess." She drew attention to her jeans and shirt and hair loosely tied back in a ponytail, as she cleared her books from the study table.

"You're beautiful, they'll love you," Gyle told her reassuringly.

"Dinner?" Laura questioned, knowing what little provisions they had.

"Arriving soon," he laughed, "via Gianni."

Gianni was a friend of the family who owned a little restaurant in Leith. Gyle had called on Gianni many times in the past to cater for impromptu guests and gatherings. Tonight, he had done so with ease, while Laura felt as though her heart would pound right out of her chest with panic. "Relax Laura." Gyle laughed, kissing her forehead, before she pulled away and ran to the dining room to set the table, irritated at missing out on her studies again. When Carla Jamieson glided into the room some twenty minutes later, she made Laura gasp. She was stunning. Her long thick dark hair fell in large curls past her shoulders, and like Gyle, she was tall and slim with a stylish elegance you couldn't ignore. Moving towards Laura, she offered her a cheek, which Laura duly kissed. "Laura," she said without expression, "how lovely to meet you." Then before Laura could reply Carla continued into the kitchen to see Gyle and poured herself a glass of Prosecco, as another tall thin figure entered the room. Alastair Jamieson was slightly breathless, and very different from his wife. "It's bloody murder trying to get a parking space around here." He said loudly but lightheartedly as he stepped towards Laura. "Sorry, you must be Laura? I'm Gyle's father Alastair." He offered his hand, to which Laura shook and smiled. She liked him. "Pleased to meet you, Mr Jamieson."

"Oh Alastair, please." Then, looking round the room, "Where are they?"

"In the kitchen, I think,' Laura answered just as the two walked back into the room.

"Sorry Laura," Gyle apologised, just adding some finishing touches to the parmigiana. "You've met Mum and Dad then?"

Laura nodded.

"You're not cooking Gyle?" Alastair asked, surprised.

He nodded. "Mm, well via Gianni."

His father laughed. "I should have known."

Over dinner Laura noticed that Carla, although very beautiful, was cool and aloof and not at all like her own mum. She was very different from the stereotypical Italian 'mama' Laura had imagined she would be introduced to. Carla still had a fairly strong Italian accent, which made her sound formal, in an almost forced politeness. Laura worried her coolness was because she didn't approve of her living there and she asked Laura pointed questions about university, her parents and home and her future plans. She felt she was being interviewed for a job, rather than having a relaxed conversation over dinner and she was relieved when, after the meal was over, Carla and Alastair thanked them as they made their excuses to leave for the evening. There was no return invitation, Laura noticed, but she remained polite and cheerful and hoped they would not be too critical of her to Gyle as he led them to the door.

"That was great Laura," Gyle sighed, when he returned a few minutes later. "Mum and Dad just love you, I knew they would!"

"They did?" Laura was surprised, even more so than before. "They didn't stay very long."

"Oh they never do, anyway what did you think then?"

Laura thought for a moment, choosing her words carefully. "They are very different from my parents". Then before Gyle had a chance to pursue the conversation further, she moved towards the kitchen to clear up, before calling back, "You'll have to meet them now."

Carla and Alastair were not only very different in looks and manner to Laura's parents; there was the added complication that Laura's parents had no idea she was now living with Gyle. It was a situation she knew they would not approve of and therefore decided she wouldn't tell them. Gyle was amused by this decision and made reference to the fact they were living in the twenty-first century, they were both adults and that he was beginning to think of Stirling as a backwater town, whose residents had failed to move with the times. Laura found the remark insulting. It was true that life in the city was very different to home and attitudes were very different; but she was sure it was Edinburgh that was different to every other Scottish town she'd ever known, and that Gyle had little experience of life outside the city. The opportunity to expand his horizons came two weeks later when Laura and Gyle visited Marie and Fraser in Stirling. The experience was very different this time and Laura felt relaxed in the surroundings of her family home. Marie fussed over Gyle, and Fraser brought out his best whisky for the occasion. It was clear they were both quite taken by Laura's new boyfriend and more so when he spoke about encouraging Laura to study and make the most of her university life, and all it would promise for the future. It made Laura smile; if only they knew how he distracted her, and how her marks had plummeted since he came into her life.

And there was more bad news waiting for Laura. She had

failed the last exam but would be able to re-sit. If she failed again then she would have to leave. Laura was devastated. It had been a long hard slog, but the constant interruptions to her studying had taken their toll. Gyle had been unsympathetic this time, accusing her of slacking off while he was at work, and telling her to make the most of her time, suggesting she should give up working at Tattie Bogles. Laura even considered it, but she was determined to keep the income and the little independence the money gave her. Ultimately it was a decision which didn't go down well with Gyle. Until now he'd been happy to support her as promised but now she felt he was finding the support a little harder to provide. When he didn't show at Tattie Bogles that weekend, she was a little alarmed. She had tried to call him during the break but he didn't answer and now she was worried he might not show to take her home. She knew Mikey would give her a lift, but she sensed something serious might have happened to Gyle and she could hardly concentrate on her performance all night. The evening ended and the place emptied. There was still no sign of Gyle so Laura gratefully accepted Mikey's offer of a lift back to Manor Place. As the car pulled in to an empty parking place across the road from the flat, Laura could see there was no light on and there was no sign of Gyle's car. She tried calling again but there was no answer. "Do you want me to come in with you?" Mikey offered.

Laura thought for a moment. "No, no," she assured him. "He'll be home soon, something will have cropped up and knowing him, his phone battery will have run out." She tried to be carefree about the situation but inside her stomach churned wondering what could have happened. It was the early hours of the morning before Gyle Jamieson fell in the door. Laura was in bed but she could hear him in the kitchen, opening the fridge door, and then lifting the lid of the bread bin. She got out of bed and made her way through to the kitchen. "Gyle!" she shouted, and he jumped, as he turned to face her.

"What?"

"Where have you been? I've tried calling you, are you alright?" His face was serious and suddenly he looked very different. There was no apology, no move to kiss her or ask how her night went. There was no smile. Instead, his stare was hard and cold, making Laura feel uncomfortable. "Out," he said. "I've been out. That's all you need to know."

He glared at her and suddenly Laura felt scared. "Oh thank goodness." She continued trying to lighten the mood. "I was so worried something might have happened to you. I guess your battery ran out eh?"

"No."

"I thought you might have called?"

He shrugged. "What is this Laura, a quiz?"

"I just wondered where you were, that's all, when you didn't come for me?"

"And now it's the third degree is it?" His expression was angry and troubled, and Laura still felt uneasy.

"Look, I'm trying to keep things light here. I'm trying to keep things happy," she said, encouraging a change of mood.

Instead he pushed past her, knocking her off balance. "Try keeping it shut!" he yelled as he made his way to the bedroom. Laura lay awake most of the night worrying where Gyle had been, and why the sudden mood? She had never seen him like this before and it had been unexpected. She should have been the one in a mood, having been left to find her own way home without an explanation, but his dark mood prevented her from challenging him. She knew if she did there would be an almighty showdown. There was nothing she could think of that could have provoked his change in attitude towards her. The following morning he was already gone before she woke. It was Sunday and there was no reason for him to have left the flat. She tried calling him several times, but there was no reply. Eventually she gave up and started studying. She couldn't concentrate on anything more than Gyle and when he didn't appear until after nine that night she was really scared. She wasn't sure what to say or do that wouldn't make him angry like the night before so she tested his mood with a simple "Hi". He nodded but said nothing for a long time then just walked out of the lounge towards the bedroom. "Gyle," she cried out to him. "What's wrong, what have I done?"

"Nothing," he snapped. "It's not all about you Laura, you know."

Laura shook her head and carried on studying until she was sure he was asleep, before creeping into bed without disturbing him.

It was three in the morning when Gyle woke her, touching and kissing her. She could feel him rub up against her and soon he was on top of her and then inside of her despite her protests. It had come out of the blue, and Laura wasn't ready for the sudden passion. He was rough and relentless and when it was finally over, Laura felt used and hurt as he turned over and went to sleep, without a word. Laura lay for a while, her silent tears soaking the pillow, before eventually falling asleep. The following morning she woke to find him gone. Laura jumped with a start, thinking she'd slept in and he'd left her to get to university herself. She had important lectures and was really worried about being late. She was just about to climb out of bed when the door swung open, and Gyle waltzed in with a tray. "Tea with toast and marmalade, just how you like it," he announced cheerfully. "Take your time, there's plenty of time before uni." Then he turned and walked out. Laura sighed. There was no explanation for the night before, or the day before that. Just this gesture of tea and toast, and a sudden change of mood once again. While Gyle's mood continued to be reasonably bright his unexplained absences continued. He constantly ran hot and cold with her emotions and Laura found him hard work. When Laura challenged him, he brushed the matter off making her feel like some neurotic housewife from the sticks. "You're not my mother Laura, we're not joined at the hip," he told her. "We've been together a lot lately, people sometimes just need space. I need space, and you need to study, so what's the problem? It's not that I don't love you, but don't suffocate me!" Laura was slightly shocked. Suffocating would have been the last thing she felt she was guilty of, between long evenings of study and her weekend assignments and work. She had never met anyone like Gyle before, and his attitude at that moment reminded him of Jade. She wondered whether Gyle had a point, maybe this was how people's relationships worked in the city? It was a style alien to her, but then so was her new way of life. When she spoke to Mikey the following weekend, he was a little taken aback by her analogy of the situation. "I don't know what to say Laura," he said. "Jade was a player, she was never in the relationship for the long haul." He saw her worried face. "That's not saying Gyle's a player," he said kindly, "he maybe does need time out now and again, to catch up with his mates."

"Do you think so?" Laura asked quietly.

Mikey nodded. "It's nothing to do with city folk Laura, I'm not like that and I've lived here all my life."

Laura smiled. "I'm sure you're right."

Months passed and with them the ever-changing moods of Gyle Jamieson increased. Christmas and New Year had both been strange and brief encounters, and Laura missed catching up with Kristen and Scott. Gyle returned to being the loving boyfriend again after a particularly moody festive period but now he couldn't do enough to help Laura. He showered her with love and affection and made sure he was home when she expected him. Despite this, Laura's test marks never recovered to the high standard of the previous years and she was now struggling to pass exams again in the middle of the third year. Keeping house, shopping, working, making time for Gyle all took her away from studying and concentrating. She only just scraped through the last re-sit and now it was exam time once more. Laura had woken that morning feeling light-headed and nauseous but arrived in plenty of time for the exam and for the first time in ages she felt prepared. Halfway through the exam she felt faint, and when she asked for some time out for a drink of water, the plea was refused. Laura continued, but now the pages were turning black in front of her eyes and in the next few moments everything darkened as she fell to the floor. When she came round she phoned Gyle to take her home, and in tears she sat in the car wondering if she would ever be given the chance to re-sit again. A few days later Laura was no better and her tutor called to discuss her future studies. It was clear her tutor was surprised by the sudden decline in Laura's efforts and results. Now she questioned the reason for her illness. She suggested stress, or the fact that perhaps she was taking on too much? Laura agreed. She was certain her tutor was right. She had been taking on too much, but she couldn't tell her that she was living with Gyle now in case she was forced to give up her room. The way Gyle's moods were, she wasn't confident he wouldn't ask her to leave and she was so close to qualifying it would be crazy not to give it her all now.

The next few days were no better, and during a particularly long lecture the following week Laura collapsed again. This time it was different. As people gathered to help, no one could bring her round. They stood looking down at her, as she just lay motionless on the lecture room floor. Eventually someone called an ambulance and she was taken to hospital. It had been a startling experience for the students and the lecture was cut short. Several hours later Laura recovered to receive the news from a young student doctor. "We now have the results of all the tests, and there's nothing sinister going on." She smiled. Laura was relieved. "I'm not sure if the news that you are pregnant will come as a surprise or not?"

Laura was shocked and sat in silence for several minutes, no longer hearing what the doctor continued to say, before answering. "Pregnant? I can't be, are you sure?"

"Very sure." The young doctor smiled. "Just over six weeks sure, in fact, congratulations."

Laura was stunned and sat in silence for many more minutes, as she watched the young doctor move quickly along the long corridor and on to her next patient. "Pregnant?" she whispered to herself before lying back down crying into her pillow.

Gyle's reaction to the pregnancy was worse. He was shocked and angry at the news. "For God's sake Laura, how the hell did that happen?" he said loudly, ignoring the other patients sitting close by. "Did you forget your pill, or what?"

Laura looked at him in surprise. "Pill? I'm not on the Pill."

"What the hell did you expect then, what did you think would happen?"

"I thought you were taking care of that side of things?" she protested.

"Where in hell's name did you get that idea from?"

"The time you spend in the bathroom at night," she said quietly, faltering over her words. "I just thought you must be, you know?"

"What?"

"Sorting things?"

Gyle put his head in hands. He wasn't sure if this was a wind up. "Sorting things?" he questioned, staring at her in disbelief. "Oh sure, I was sorting things, like washing, moisturising, hair grooming, teeth whitening. Those sort of things people do at night."

"You take ages."

He looked her up and down and groaned. "Quite!" he said dismissively. "If this is some kind of trap Laura, it won't work. Just get rid of it!"

Laura was shocked. "I can't!"

He stared at her, in the same way he had stared the night he had come home drunk. "I don't want a child, Laura. Understand? Not now, not ever! So sort this damn mess out." With that he turned and walked out of the hospital.

Laura cried herself to sleep and when she woke she phoned Kristen.

"Oh my God Laura." Kristen was shocked. "What are you going to do?"

"I don't know?"

"Oh Laura, your folks will be livid!"

"I know. Gyle is furious, he wants me to get rid of it!"

"No?"

Laura just didn't know what to do, every inch of what she believed in wouldn't allow her to have a termination, yet this pregnancy was sure to spell the end of university, her future, and very likely her relationship with Gyle. "My God what a mess," she cried as she wrestled with the nightmare situation she now found herself in. The following morning, in the cool light of day, she spoke to the young student doctor and told her of the predicament and that Gyle was insisting she have a termination.

"What do you want Laura?" the student asked.

"I don't know?"

"Well would you want to have a termination if your boyfriend was over the moon about it?"

"No," Laura whispered, "but then he would be there to support me, and what about university? I am almost qualified."

"Support can come from lots of places these days," the young doctor told her, "and you can always pick up on university next year, with some negotiation." She looked at Laura. "The bottom line, Laura, is you can't have a termination just because it's inconvenient at the moment. I'm sure you'd want to have children one day and you have to consider you are dealing with human life here. A life that is in your hands, it's not an unwanted gift to be cast aside. Your day has just come a little sooner than you planned." Laura hadn't thought about it like that. Yes, it was unwanted now, but she had always wanted to have children in the future, and it was clear Gyle had no plans for a family now or anytime. She asked herself what would happen if this had happened five or ten years down the line; would he have walked out on her then? Several hours later Laura made a brave decision. She was going to keep her baby no matter what. If Gyle walked out on her now it meant he clearly didn't love her anyway. She was now ready and strong enough to face him if and when he came to visit. Later that evening Gyle faced the truth but he wasn't happy. "I take it that's your final decision?" He stared at her unsmiling. "Yes," Laura said quietly. "I'm sorry."

"So am I Laura," he whispered as he turned and walked out of the ward and the hospital. The following day Laura was discharged from hospital as expected and she called Mikey to ask him to take her back to Student Halls. "The guy is an idiot Laura," Mikey said to her, and without looking at her, "If I had a girlfriend like you, I would have been delighted with that kind of news."

Laura laughed. "I'm not exactly delighted myself Mikey."

"I know, but that's because you've got all this shit going on. Have you told your parents yet?"

"Oh God..." Laura wailed. "Not yet."

Back at Student Halls Jodie was quick to give Laura tea and sympathy. "At least you won't have Gyle to worry about anymore while you're studying," she said encouragingly. "You can devote all your time here now."

"I wish I had done that in the first place now Jodie. What a bloody mess I've made of everything." The next few days were hard. She couldn't bring herself to deliver the news about the baby to her parents, especially now she and Gyle had split and she was skating on very thin ice at university. She decided to wait a few weeks before mentioning it to them and asked Kristen not to tell her parents either. Gyle had gone. There were no text messages or calls from him and no visits, except to drop off her things while she was at a lecture. At the weekend Laura kept an anxious eye on the door at Tattie Bogles, first hoping he might come in, then hoping he wouldn't. Her emotions were all over the place and she was glad when the weekend was over and she could retreat to her room at university, without fear of bumping into Gyle. A week later she was back in hospital again. She had been violently sick and Jodie called for the doctor. Determining she was badly dehydrated, the doctor called for an ambulance and Jodie went with her. Three days later she was still in hospital when Jodie visited, bringing with her a letter from the university. Laura's face was white as she read the note to herself, then tears welled into her eyes spilling down her cheeks. "What is it?" Jodie asked anxiously, as Laura passed the letter to her. She read it quietly.

Dear Miss Duncan,

Your recent examination results have unfortunately been significantly below the required standard expected at this stage of your studies. I understand from your Tutor that you have been under considerable stress, and that you are now suffering from a difficult pregnancy, which she feels will lead to further absences.

It is therefore with regret that the Examination Board has decided to withdraw your registration from this university. You have until the end of the month to clear your things from Student Halls and secure alternative accommodation.

This decision should not affect further applications for acceptance on courses at a later date, and we wish you well for the future.

Yours sincerely
Malcolm Allison
Principal

Jodie hugged Laura as she sobbed. "What on earth now, Laura?"

"I guess I have to tell my parents and go home," she cried. Two days later the hospital discharged her unexpectedly. The young student doctor she'd seen previously arrived, with her notes. "Could you call me a taxi to take me home?"

The young doctor looked puzzled. "You have someone here to collect you." She left the room, opening the door for Laura's surprise visitor.

"Gyle!" she exclaimed as he entered the room. "What are you doing here?"

"Well to be honest Laura, the hospital phoned me. They still had my number from before."

"Oh, I am so sorry," she said. "They didn't give me a chance this time to call someone. I'll get that changed right now".

"No Laura, don't do that. I'm here to take you home."

"Where's home?" Laura asked, half laughing at the irony. "I've just been kicked out of uni, I'm no longer welcome at your house, and my parents haven't a clue about any of this. So where am I going exactly?"

Gyle lowered his head. "I am so sorry Laura. They've kicked you out of uni?"

Laura nodded, now fighting back the tears.

"After all that studying Laura." He shook his head. "It's all my fault. I'm so sorry."

"No, no Gyle, it's not your fault." Laura was adamant. "It was mine. I should have studied. I shouldn't have got pregnant. I shouldn't have trusted you and I shouldn't have made such a bloody mess of my life. I still have time at Student Halls to clear out, so you can take me there, if you want."

He looked at her. "I'm not sure I deserve it, Laura, but you can trust me and I want you to come back with me, to my place.

I've had a long time to think and the bottom line is I love you, and I think we could make a real go of it. If you're willing to try again?"

Laura looked at him carefully, examining his expression. He looked humble and she wondered if he was genuine. "I have a baby on the way, you know?"

He shrugged. "Our baby, shock as it was, it is still our baby."

"And you are sure this is what you want?"

"I know I want you Laura and if you can love me we can make it work."

Laura was slightly relieved. She still loved Gyle, despite being hurt and angry. Moving back to Manor Place would be the best decision she could make right now, under the circumstances. She owed it to her baby to make a go of it with its father and she hoped it might soften the blow when she eventually faced her parents.

While Carla and Alastair Jamieson took the news cautiously, it was clear neither were delighted. Laura assumed it was because they thought little of her; after all she was nothing like them and she felt intimidated by them, especially Carla. It was a view she held fairly strongly until Carla made a surprise visit one morning a few days after she had returned home from hospital. Laura quickly made some coffee and ushered Carla into the lounge. It was obvious she had something on her mind and Laura watched closely as Carla took a sip of coffee. "Good coffee," she remarked, smiling, and then, taking a deep breath, she came straight to the point. "Darling," she started in her Italian-accentuated English. "You are so different from Gyle's other girlfriends." Laura cringed; it was the moment she had dreaded, the moment where Carla Jamieson would tell her she wasn't good enough for her son. The message was clear. "My darling, you must be careful of Gyle, he will break your heart." Laura was taken aback. Was this a backhanded way of saying she wasn't good enough? Laura wasn't sure. She looked at her but said nothing as Carla continued. "He is, what you say, very complex, you know?" Laura nodded; she could agree with that. "Gyle is my son and I love him very much, Laura, but you know he is very unreliable and he has an impulsive and cruel streak to his nature. I hope you know what you are taking on with him. Just because you are expecting his child, it doesn't mean you have to marry him."

Laura gulped. "Marry him?" She hadn't even thought that far ahead herself; the statement came as a complete shock to her, but not to Carla Jamieson. "Why yes," she went on, "Gyle has told us this news, that you are going to be married soon, certainly before the baby is born." Her expression was of surprise at Laura's reaction, as she continued. "This is why I am coming here, Laura, to warn you. You are too good for my son, too naïve, too kind, too honest." The statement came as a complete shock. Here was Gyle's mother telling her she was too good for her son. She pinched herself, wondering whether she had fainted again and this was a dream. It wasn't. Laura sat for some time in silence before she could say anything.

"This has all come as a bit of a shock Mrs Jamieson," she said quietly.

"No, no, no," she interrupted, "Carla, please. Just call me Carla."

The shocks just kept coming for Laura. "Okay, Carla," she started again. "Gyle has never mentioned marriage. In fact I wasn't too sure he wanted to continue our relationship after he heard the news about the baby. To be honest err, Carla, the last few weeks have been like a rollercoaster for me, and I just don't know where to get off? My parents don't even know yet!"

Carla laughed. "This is life with Gyle. This is what I am talking about Laura." She reached out and touched her hand. "Take very good care Laura, and be careful. Gyle is very secretive and controlling, he's very manipulative and good at it. You might not even realise what he is doing." She took a final mouthful of coffee and stood up, smoothing her skirt. "You mustn't tell Gyle of this conversation, only that I visited for coffee. You understand?"

Laura stood up and stepped forward to give Carla a hug, which she unexpectedly returned. "Thank you for coming to see me Carla." They smiled at each other, and a moment or two later Carla was gone. Laura was left stunned. She couldn't mention marriage to Gyle; otherwise he would know she had spoken to Carla about it. Her head was in a spin; she didn't know what to think. When Gyle came home from work that evening, he said nothing about marriage, or the future or the baby. It was as if none of it was happening. He chatted about his day at McArdle and Baynes and the many clients he had visited. He was in an upbeat mood and insisted they go out to Gianni's for dinner. "You can meet Gianni, you will need to be in touch with him when we have dinner parties, unless you are an expert cook of course?"

She shook her head.

"I thought not." Gyle laughed. "This is why we have Gianni!" He picked up the car keys and then, turning to Laura, "Come on then!"

Over the next few days, Laura noticed that he did take control of some situations, but in a good way, she thought. He was just taking the lead, the initiative, and she told herself that

Carla misunderstood her son's intentions. When Gyle suggested they go up to Stirling that weekend, Laura was terrified. She had avoided saying anything to her parents over the phone, and they were so excited about the impending visit. Laura felt sick at the thought of delivering the news she knew would disappoint and shock them. And all too soon Laura's fears met with reality as she watched her parents' happy, cheerful and bright faces sink and turn grey as they gasped, taking in the news. Marie took a seat, almost stumbling into her chair while Fraser said nothing as he turned and walked out of the room and into the kitchen. There he stood, leaning against the sink staring out of the kitchen window. Finally Marie broke the silence, through tears. "Oh Laura, you stupid, stupid girl. You've ruined your life, what the hell were you thinking?" And, turning to Gyle, "I thought better of you too!" she snapped, wiping the tears from her eyes.

"I'm so sorry Mum," Laura whispered through her own tearful state. An hour later, when things had calmed down, they would receive another shock. Fraser asked Gyle what he intended to do about the mess he'd helped to create and he calmly told him they were getting married in Edinburgh two months later, and they would be moving into a new house in Balerno shortly after the wedding. "You've got it all worked out then?" Fraser sighed, disappointedly, still finding the news difficult to take in.

"I thought you always wanted to get married in Logie Kirk?" Marie confronted her daughter. "You know Laura, I just don't think I know you any more?" Laura hung her head.

"You haven't given us much time to find money for a wedding," Fraser protested, irritated by the cool calm young man standing officiously before him, and the speed of the arrangements they had been completely left out of.

"It's all taken care of Mr Duncan. There's no way I could expect you to pay for the wedding, under the circumstances. Of course it will be a small wedding, but I think that's best considering."

Fraser and Marie were disappointed. Fraser had so wanted to pay for his daughter's wedding. He had imagined a wedding at the small Logie Kirk, packed with friends and relatives, followed by a reception at the Highland Hotel. It would be a grand affair, with a ceilidh and a piper. Marie had always imagined she would be the one organising and arranging dresses and flowers and invitations. Instead, the thrill of it all had been taken away from them, and they were going to feel more like guests than Mother and Father of the Bride. The announcement of the impending wedding and the house in Balerno was as much a surprise to Laura as it was to her parents, despite the early warning from Carla, so she could say nothing about it. Instead, she went along with it, not knowing whether it was just talk or whether any of it was real. She had to pretend the new house in Balerno was lovely, although she'd never seen it or even knew about it. Now, she had to convince them they would have to wait to see it after the wedding. Her mum was right; it had always been Laura's dream to be married in Logie Kirk, at the foot of the Ochil Hills, and she was disappointed that this was not to be, but then she had dreamed of many things since then, and none of them had transpired. Eventually, after Marie's tears had dried and the news had sunk in, although bitterly disappointed, Laura's parents wished the happy couple well. Laura was distraught on her way home, and asked Gyle what he was doing telling her parents they were getting married and moving house. "They'll be expecting all of this to happen now Gyle, don't you think they've had enough disappointment?"

Gyle smiled and turned to her. "It's okay Laura, it's more or less all arranged".

"What is?"

"The wedding at the Balmoral Hotel. You know the one near Waverley Station? It will be really handy for guests coming by train."

"And the house in Balerno?" Laura asked, anxiously.

"Ah, yes, that was just confirmed before we set off. It's a lovely little house with a nice garden in Lanark Road West. You'll love it." He looked at her and smiled, but she was not smiling back at him. "What?" he asked, throwing up his hands impatiently.

"When were you going to tell me? Or maybe I should say, ask me?"

"Ah, not until..." He stamped on his brake and pulled up quickly, almost skidding into a layby. Then reaching into the glove compartment he took out a little box, opening it to reveal a beautiful two-stone diamond ring. Laura looked at it in amazement. "One diamond for each of us," he said as she gazed at the ring before trying it on. "As I was saying, I was going to tell you after this. He looked deep into her eyes. Please Laura Duncan, will you take this idiot of a man to be your awful, lawful husband?"

Laura looked at him. "You've been doing all of this, planning a wedding and buying a house?" She was shocked beyond belief.

"Yes Laura, I couldn't ask you to marry me without having anything to offer you now, could I?"

"I don't believe you sometimes Gyle." Laura laughed. "What if I don't like the house in Balerno?"

"You will."

"And the Balmoral Hotel?"

"Oh, believe me, you will," Gyle told her confidently.

"Well," she teased, "only on the basis that I will, the answer is yes!"

Kristen and Scott came over to congratulate the newly engaged couple the following weekend and Kristen took the opportunity to suggest they all go to Tattie Bogles. Gyle made arrangements to have a meal in town and afterwards he gave them a guided tour of the Balmoral Hotel. Laura arranged the night off work but promised to call in to show off her fancy engagement ring and to introduce Kristen and Scott to Mikey and Doug. Mikey was performing by himself and was well into the song 'Jealous Guy' when they arrived. Laura introduced her friends to Mikey during the break, and later to Doug and Jodie. There was a happy atmosphere about the place with everyone having fun and in a celebratory mood until the second half of the evening when Mikey asked Laura to join him in a couple of duets. Kristen was delighted; she had told Scott all about her talented friend and she couldn't wait to see her and Mikey perform. "Do you mind?" Laura politely asked Gyle, as he joked with Scott but Kristen noticed that despite his feigned approval his mood darkened. "She drives herself too far sometimes," he said with obvious annoyance as Mikey and Laura started with 'Up on the Roof', and finished with 'Will you Love me Tomorrow'. The crowd gave them a standing ovation and Kristen was up on her feet along with them.

"That was great Laura," she said excitedly, and Scott agreed.

"You have a real talent there Laura, I'm sure you could make a living from that alone, if you are ever stuck!" he told her then, turning to Gyle, "She's a real star." But Gyle refused to be drawn into the excitement of his wife's obvious popularity and it wasn't long before he insisted they leave Tattie Bogles, making the excuse that Laura was prone to exhaustion, and didn't know when she'd had enough. Kristen and Scott were staying at Manor Place that night and Laura noticed Gyle was now subdued and polite, far from the happy and carefree mood he had enjoyed earlier. Laura suspected his dark side was about to show its ugly face once again. "What's wrong?" she asked quietly when everyone had gone to bed.

He grabbed her by the throat. "Stop making a fool of me," he hissed as he threw her back on the bed.

She tried to catch her breath. "What do you mean?" she cried.

"You. Making an exhibition of yourself with Mikey up there."

"Gyle, for God's sake it's work, it's performance, it's...."

"It's taking the piss, that's what it is." He glared at her. "Just get to sleep Laura, I can't stand to look at you right now!"

Laura was shattered. The night's performance had been no different to any other night and she couldn't understand why now, with a few weeks to go before their wedding, he could suddenly turn on her. The following morning before leaving, Kristen asked if Gyle was alright, sensing something was wrong. Laura showed her the red marks she was hiding behind a high neck top. "My God, Laura, what the hell is he playing at?"

She shrugged. "He wasn't happy about the performance. I guess he didn't like to see me up there performing with Mikey, for some strange reason."

Kristen looked worried. "You look out Laura, he's jealous of you. That's what that's all about. He doesn't like you stealing his thunder!"

Laura laughed at the thought Gyle could actually be jealous of her, with all he had at his feet, and she struggled to find a plausible reason. By evening Gyle had settled down again, and the incident seemed to have been forgotten. But Laura felt troubled that he was out more than he was at home over the next few weeks, giving work as the reason, to pay for the wedding and the baby, and she felt guilty he was shouldering all the responsibility for the arrangements and finance. Then, out of the blue, he organised a visit to their new house in Balerno, days before their wedding. He was excited as he guided Laura through each room of the bright and spacious house at Lanark Road West. It was everything Gyle promised it would be and Laura was excited and happy. As they strolled through the garden she convinced herself she had the measure of him now and she was quietly confident she could manage his changing moods simply by ignoring them.

When the big day arrived Fraser and Marie seemed in a brighter mood as they stepped out of their car with Yvonne and John Campbell, Kristen and Scott. It was the first time Laura had met Paolo, as he arrived as Gyle's best man, and she was surprised how different he was to Gyle. Apart from being tall and thin, like Gyle, Carla and Alastair, Paolo was of pale complexion with sandy fair hair, like his father, and he was funny and sociable. Then Mikey and Jodie arrived together announcing they were a couple and the news amused Gyle as he welcomed them to the function suite. Kristen chatted to them as they waited for the bride to make her entrance. It was a good day. Laura looked stunning in a simple brilliant white sweetheart neck dress which was cleverly cut to minimise her very large bump, and Gyle sported a silver grey suit which he looked well in, contrasting with his dark hair and swarthy skin. Bridesmaid, Kristen wore a long black sleek dress, decorated with diamanté and the look was classy and sophisticated, adding the final wow factor to the wedding party. Then all eyes turned when the radiant Carla entered the room. She wore a long silver gown, decorated with tiny pearls and crystals, which caught the light as she moved. "That's Gyle's Mum?" Marie asked, clearly shocked. "She looks about the same age as him!"

"That's money for you Marie," Fraser answered with a smile, "but she couldn't hold a candle to you, my love."

"Get away with you," she laughed, "I think all this wedding stuff has gone to your head, or else the whisky has!"

The wedding suite was filled with music and laughter following the short ceremony as the guests danced and chatted and shared corny jokes. Rosy-cheeked children ran around the room creating their own kind of party as the band played on, but in room 742 another more intimate party was beginning between Gyle and the girlfriend of one of his old friends. Gyle had always found Celine attractive; now, as she stood before him in a revealing tightly fitting gown, he had found his pulse race. "I felt I should congratulate you in person," she purred, removing her very high-heeled shoes. "You know? The way you like it."

Gyle smiled, pulling her on to the bed and kissing her.

"Where's Ben?" he asked nervously.

"He's gone to move the car to that parking lot at Haymarket. He couldn't find a long-stay one here and the hotel car park was full. He won't be back for a while yet."

"Oh good," he whispered, kissing her neck and slowly

loosening the zip of her dress. "I think you should be showering me with your good wishes."

"Oh I'll be showering you with more than that," she promised. Celine moved to undo his tie, but he stopped her. "Best not, Celine. I might not be able to get the thing fixed again in a hurry."

She pulled back to look at him.

"Just these." He pointed to his trousers and she started to pull them, soon they were pulling each other's clothes off before passion took over and the next few minutes developed into a frenzied act of sex as they explored every intimate part of each other's bodies. They lay breathless in each other's arms some minutes later before Gyle kissed the end of Celine's nose and then jumped up. "You'd better get dressed." He smiled. "I'll just use your bathroom quickly and head back to the party."

"I think I preferred our party," she told him quietly as she stepped into her dress.

Gyle smiled.

Downstairs Laura had been looking for her new husband. "Where did you get to?" she asked.

"Oh one of the guests had too much to drink, I couldn't get away."

"Typical," Laura laughed. "It's almost time to cut the cake; the photographer was looking for you." As they cut the cake together moments later, Gyle looked up to see Celine and Ben, smiling towards them. He winked at Ben and he felt a smug sense of achievement knowing he had just bedded his girlfriend. Hours later the couple said goodbye to their guests as the crowd waved and cheered them off. Laura could see her parents as she looked back through the window of the taxi. They had one arm around each other while waving with the other. They looked happy, and as she waved back Laura hoped that one day it would be Gyle and herself waving off their child like this; and they would still be as happy and in love as much as her own parents were on this special day.

4

Laura felt as though she had stepped into a fairytale when she returned from her brief honeymoon. Her new mother-in-law took her out to look for fabric and furnishings for the new home while decorators called with colour charts and wallpaper samples offering the latest designer patterns. They hadn't yet moved into their new home in Balerno, but remained at Manor Place while the refurbishments were made. Laura was excited but exhausted and when she fainted one afternoon in Jenner's Department Store while out with Carla, it resulted in yet another short stay in hospital. Carla had been only too happy to step in and take control of things, leaving Gyle free to work and vi r hospital in the evenings. Resulting tests revealed the baby was fine but Laura needed to rest more and they insisted she return over the weekend for another short stay to monitor her progress more closely. Gyle took the opportunity to meet up with Celine again after visiting hospital, then out for dinner before taking her back to Manor Place to spend the night. Although he was reasonably happy with Laura, the thrill of the chase and subsequent reward of bedding other women satisfied his ultimate need for adoration. It underlined everything he believed about himself as a sexy, stylish and desirable good-looking man. Laura's brief but frequent hospital stays provided him with the opportunity he couldn't ignore. The fact that the women he chose to chase wouldn't have needed to be asked twice by anyone willing to pay for a meal and a few drinks went unnoticed. After all, in his mind the reason was clear, it was because he was irresistible. Having the personal space and time to sleep with other women frequently left him in a euphoric state. It was only when Laura restricted his movements, or questioned his timekeeping that he felt resentful of her, so when she was eventually discharged from hospital again he was still on top of the world. Collecting her from hospital he whisked her off to their new home and managed to carry her over the threshold, but only just. As Laura surveyed the stylish work her mother-in-law had created, using the fabrics and furnishings they had chosen together, she had only one word to say: "Wow!" Gyle grabbed her by the hand, pulling her through the house, each room as beautiful as the next. Looking around in amazement Laura turned to Gyle, smiling. "I can't wait for Mum and Dad to see it!"

Gyle smiled. "Why not ask them over for lunch once you've settled in? It'll give you some company while I'm at work." Laura then realised that being that bit further away from the city centre would mean Gyle would be less likely to be home, unless he had properties in the area to view. The flat in Manor Place was up for sale now too, which meant Gyle being on call both during the days, and in the evenings to show prospective buyers round. It was an arrangement which would suit him well for a while, giving him a place and perfect excuse to escape for a few hours. Over the next few weeks Gyle was rarely at home and when a major potential sale he was involved in fell through he was in a foul mood. It was now the middle of October and the peak time for selling properties was over. There was a lot of pressure to push through as many sales as possible before the market slowed altogether. Demands at work had not provided him with any personal space and Laura was now calling on his help more and more. It had all culminated in what became a really bad week and when Laura asked if he could be home when her parents came to visit he blew his top once again, leaving her shaken and rejected. It was a feeling she found hard to shift when her parents arrived and although she tried to appear bright and cheerful while she showed them round her lovely new home, Marie could sense all was not well. Later, on the way home, she felt uneasy with so many questions she had wanted to ask but didn't and a few which had remained unanswered. Over the next few weeks Kristen and Scott visited and then Jodie and Mikey. Gyle had not been around for any of these visits and Laura was relieved, given his recent mood. Her guests were also relieved; none of them quite knew how to take Gyle; even Jodie who had known him the longest found him to be either charming or rude and arrogant. Kristen worried about her friend, she felt uneasy about how Laura coped with Gyle's dark moods and she was sure if it weren't for the baby, due at the end of November, they wouldn't still be together. Mikey worried more. He knew all about Gyle's indiscretions but he didn't dare tell Laura. The revelations would destroy her and he couldn't risk being the bearer of news which could potentially cause her to lose the baby. Instead, he worried constantly about her. She was no longer working in Tattie Bogles and he missed her.

On a very cold and misty evening the following month Marie and Fraser Duncan enjoyed a meal out with friends in Kippen, a little village nine miles west of Stirling, and now they were heading home. "It's freezing." Marie shivered. "Is that heater on?"

"Give it time," Fraser protested, "the car engine has to heat up first." He turned to his wife. "That's the ice light on now."

"I'm not surprised," his wife replied still shivering as she rubbed the sleeves of her thin jacket. "It's freezing out there, thank goodness we've not far to go, it'll be good to get home and take these shoes off."

Fraser laughed. "I don't know why you women go out half dressed and suffer wearing silly shoes?" he said, shaking his head. "In fact I do," he laughed, "it's vanity!"

Marie shook her head. "Ah yes, you'd love it if I turned up in a woolly jumper and little fur boots."

Fraser sighed, "You'd look just as stylish in them too, you know."

Marie looked at him and laughed. It had been a difficult time for them worrying about Laura. The shock of her pregnancy and ill health, together with the disappointment of her dropping out of university, and a quickly manufactured wedding had caused them many a sleepless night. They were bitterly disappointed that Laura would, in their eyes, never have the chance again to achieve her full potential, unlike her older sister Emma who had sailed through university and on to a top job. But if Marie was saddened by all of this, she was even unhappier by Laura's spirit she felt had been oppressed by her forceful and strong-minded husband Gyle. "Do you think she's happy?" she asked her husband, as they continued their journey home.

"Who?" he answered, looking towards her, surprised at the sudden question.

"Laura, do you think she's happy?"

"She seems happy enough to me," Fraser said, without too much thought, and turning to his wife. "What's brought this on?"

"I was just thinking about her."

"Worrying, you mean. The trouble with Laura is that she's just joined the real world. Now she's got it all to do herself, she'll maybe appreciate what she had before – and what we've done for her."

Marie sighed. "You think she doesn't appreciate us?" She glanced at her husband as he cast an eye to the rearview mirror.

"She does now, but I don't think she's that bothered about stuffing up university. She thinks because she's got a fancy new husband, and a baby on the way, she doesn't need to do anything anymore."

"You're just talking stupid now Fraser, let's change the subject," Marie snapped irritably as she looked away from her husband and out of the passenger door window. "Fine by me," he sighed, continuing to glance at the rearview mirror.

To the friends they'd just left, the conversation had been very different. Over dinner, Marie and Fraser Duncan were every inch the proud parents of a lovely daughter and her 'upmarket' husband. Keeping up appearances was always important to Marie and the meal enabled them to celebrate the imminent arrival of their first grandchild. Despite their reflections on what could have been, Marie and Fraser were in a happy mood as they drove home. Looking over to King's Knot Gardens and the magnificent Stirling Castle sitting above, high on the peak of Castle Hill, Marie felt a certain pride of the heritage it portrayed. "Doesn't the castle look lovely all lit up at night?" she remarked, looking towards it. "The way they've done it is fabulous, it looks like it's made from silver and gold shining like a beacon over the gateway to the highlands."

Her husband laughed. "You are in the wrong job Marie, you should have been a tour guide." He turned to his wife and smiled before looking in the rearview mirror again.

"Look at it Fraser," she urged, but he declined.

"I'm watching this idiot behind me, three or four cars back in the Peugeot, he's determined to overtake and it's not a good idea in these conditions." Fraser continued along the road, the visibility was poor and the roads were yet to be gritted, although one was heading towards them on the other side of the road. As the huge vehicle approached they could feel the gravel hit the side of their car as it passed. Fraser watched it disappear into the mist behind them, and tentatively continued along a now fairly icy road glistening ahead of them in the car headlights. He looked at the car clock. "Mm nearly eleven. We should be home by twenty past."

"Oh good." Marie smiled. "I think I'll put the electric blanket on for a few minutes when we get in."

"Good idea, I could murder a cup of tea," Fraser said, still checking the road behind him. Then suddenly and without warning, looming out of the mist behind them, a Lexus came speeding up behind overtaking the line of traffic, chased by the equally fast-moving Peugeot who had been trying to pass earlier. "What the Hell!" Fraser yelled. "Bloody idiots! It's too close to the junction ahead now."

Marie looked alarmed. "Oh my God!" she shrieked, pulling her hands up to her face, just as a young lad on a motorbike careered round the corner, skidding wildly on a patch of ice and then across the newly dropped grit on the other side of the road into the path of their oncoming car. "Jesus!" Fraser yelled, and in desperation braked hard pulling the steering wheel fast round to avoid hitting him. It would have been a difficult manoeuvre in any condition but on the icy road the car lost control and was sent spinning into the path of the speeding Lexus. The Lexus then braked hard while the Peugeot behind followed suit, but he lost control, sending his car turning over and over, catching the back of the Lexus and turning it the way it had come, but it was now on its side, sliding across the road. It then smashed into the side of a little Fiat, which swerved, trying to avoid further damage but was travelling too fast and it shot into the air amid the screeching of brakes and the tearing and crunching of metal, and breaking of glass. The young lad on the motorbike was thrown into the melee as the Fiat landed on top of Marie and Fraser's Toyota. It had all happened in a matter of seconds. But in that short time they were all caught up in a crumpled pile of twisted wreckage, grit and dust, followed by an eerie silence, which was broken only by the sound of sirens some twenty minutes later.

A loud banging on the door at Lanark Road West wakened Gyle Jamieson. He looked at the little bedside clock; it was just after two in the morning. "You stay here," he whispered to Laura. "Who the hell can that be at this time?" He grabbed his robe and headed downstairs to the front door as Laura tried to listen. She could hear voices, but they were speaking so quietly she couldn't make out what they were saying. Downstairs, Gyle opened the door to find two police officers standing there. An older man and a much younger woman spoke as he stood at the door.

"Mr Jamieson?" the male police officer asked, while the young woman greeted him then stood a little way back, leaving her colleague to speak.

"Yes," Gyle replied, searching their faces. "Is there something wrong?"

"I'm Sergeant Graham Morrison, Lothian and Borders Police, this is my colleague PC Denise Millar." Gyle smiled and acknowledged the introduction. "Do you know a Mr and Mrs Duncan sir?" Sergeant Morrison asked.

"Yes, they're my wife's parents, has something happened?"

"Do you mind if we come in?" Gyle ushered the officers inside. "Do you happen to know where they were going tonight sir?" Sergeant Morrison asked.

"Yeh, they were meeting friends in Kippen, I think?" He looked at the two officers standing in front of him, searching their faces for clues.

"Would they have been driving a blue Yaris?"

"Yes," Gyle nodded.

"Is Mrs Jamieson here?"

Gyle sighed, running his fingers through his tousled hair, frustrated by the slow outpour of information. "My wife is heavily pregnant and in bed officer. I think you'd better tell me what's happened and I'll speak to her later."

The officers turned to each other and nodded. "Sir, it looks as though Mr and Mrs Duncan have been involved in a multi-car accident on the A811 near Stirling. As far as we know they've been taken to Forth Valley Royal Hospital in Larbert. Do you know where that is?"

Gyle nodded, then, noticing the change of expression on their faces, he spun round to find his wife standing behind him.

"What's wrong?" she asked shakily, sensing something really bad had happened. Gyle put his arm around his wife and led her to the chair before sitting her down, and then, still holding her, broke the terrible news.

"Oh my God!" she screamed. "Oh my God! No, not my mum! Not my dad!" Then a long loud wail: "Noooooo." She jumped up in panic, not knowing which way to turn before she sat down again and sobbed. Her face was soaked with tears and her eyes were filled with fear and desperation as she quietly whimpered. "Will they be alright?"

"I'm sorry, we don't know what your parents' condition is," Sergeant Morrison apologised. "There have been many casualties."

Then the young woman police officer spoke now, for the first time, turning to her colleague. "Sir, shouldn't we call a doctor out for Mrs Jamieson?"

"No," Laura whispered quickly, shaking her head then looking to Gyle. "We need to go."

"Do you have any other children Mrs Jamieson we need to find care for?" PC Millar asked.

"No, this is our first, thank you, but there's Maisie, my mum's dog." She looked at the woman police officer, and noticed she was very young. Her face was full of genuine concern, and it was obvious she was finding the situation very difficult. Laura felt sorry for her having to bring such terrible news to a family through the night.

"Your parents' neighbour is caring for the dog, Mrs Jamieson. She's happy to hang on to her until she hears from you," Sergeant Morrison explained, then a moment of silence passed before he continued. "We have an escort on standby. We can only take you so far, you know, boundary issues, but another escort will be waiting to take you the rest of the way. It's not likely to be busy at this time in the morning but it means you don't need to worry about speed or traffic holdups, you'll be escorted right through." The officer reached for his radio. "Just give me your car registration sir."

Gyle thanked them, while noting down his registration, realising Marie and Fraser must be in a very bad condition if an escort had been provided to take them through. "Does the escort come here?" he asked.

"No sir, you'll go to Newbridge where you'll see the escort vehicle waiting with its lights flashing. Just give them a flash as you approach and they'll come out behind you and move to the front, just follow them, the next escort will take over in the same way."

"When?" Gyle asked.

"Twenty minutes ok?"

Gyle looked at his wife and she nodded. "Sure," he confirmed, as the two officers made their way out of the house.

"Sorry sir, I hope your wife, and your in-laws are okay."

Gyle stopped them. "Err... how did you know to come here?" he asked, amazed the information had reached them that same evening.

"Your in-laws' neighbour." He smiled.

"Of course, the dog." Gyle sighed as both police officers turned and made their way back to the patrol car. "Thanks officer," Gyle called out to them. "Thanks to you both."

The escort to Larbert happened as the officer had described. Laura said nothing throughout the journey, her face was ashen and she was shaking uncontrollably. Gyle was afraid she was in shock and was relieved when they arrived at the hospital. Doctors were waiting for them, and immediately took a desperate and frail-looking Laura aside to assess her condition. Refusing to take any pills they insisted she have an injection to keep her calm. "It's fine Laura, it's safe," the doctor assured her, "it will protect your baby from shock. We can't let you see your parents yet, and you'll need to wait a few more minutes before we know whether that will be possible at all; they are still in theatre."

"Thank God, they are alive," she sighed, barely audible, before flinching slightly as the needle entered her arm. "How bad is it?"

"We won't know until we have had the results of all the tests, but it's nasty. When we know more someone will come to see you."

"I need to see them," Laura cried.

"You can't I'm afraid, they are in theatre, it's a sterile environment and inaccessible to the public for infection control. I'm sorry, you'll need to wait a bit longer. We have a great team in there, they're doing everything they can." The doctor gave his apology and moved back to the theatre.

Minutes turned to hours as they waited, tired, agitated and absolutely desperate. Gyle stayed by Laura's side, very much the loving, caring husband he had promised to be, but had failed to be on so many occasions. Now in this situation he was compassionate, caring, loving, the way he was when Laura first met him, but Laura was too frantic to notice, or even care. Eventually a figure appeared at the end of the corridor and Laura sat holding her breath, praying the figure was the bringer of good news. Introducing himself as Doctor Neville, he began. "We've been able to stop the bleeding, but your parents' condition at the moment remains critical. We have stabilised them both enough to enable them to be transferred to the Western General in Edinburgh, do you know it?"

They nodded. "We don't live too far from there," Gyle told him. "When will they be going?"

"Later tonight," Dr Neville told them, then, looking at this watch, and realising it was almost six in the morning, "Ahh, it's likely to be late morning now, maybe even lunchtime. We can't really be that precise to be honest so I suggest you go home and try to get some rest. The process of transfer can be timely."

"Can I see them?" Laura cried.

"No, I'm sorry, we are in the process of moving them both to ITU now until they are transferred, it's a lengthy process and it's important to keep them stable. There's a lot going on right now. Given the time it's best you go home." He looked at Gyle apologetically. "It's in their best interests. They are unconscious, they won't know." Reaching into his pocket, he pulled out a little card. "Take this and call the number at the bottom of the card around lunchtime, we should know where they are by then and we'll have been able to let the Edinburgh team know you are coming, so they'll be ready for you. They should have a clearer idea of what's going on by then." He looked across at Laura's white and anxious face. "If your parents' situation changes for the better or for the worse we will call you immediately. There's nothing you can do here, so try to get some sleep Laura, you will need to be rested. Tomorrow will probably be another long day."

Laura reluctantly agreed; she was exhausted and feeling really sick and lightheaded.

"What about the others caught up in the accident?" Gyle asked.

The doctor looked at him and nodded slowly. "Four fatalities and three others critical I believe," he said, shaking his head. "It was a nasty one."

Gyle put his arm round his wife's shoulders and led her away from the hospital waiting room. "Come on honey," he said softly, "tomorrow's another day, things might be better, and you need to get some sleep."

She looked at her husband, grateful he was there for her, and she smiled. "Will you stay with me tomorrow and come to the hospital?" she asked, looking up with such sadness in her eyes it was difficult, even for a normally cold and calculating Gyle, not to be moved by her obvious deep pain. Then, holding her towards him tightly, he whispered, "Of course I will." And he kissed the top her head. When they left the hospital, all Laura could think about was her mum and dad, lying in there fighting for their lives, and she retreated to the deepest, darkest space in her mind and hid there from the cruel reality of life, before eventually falling into a deep but agitated sleep, as the effects of the medication began to take effect. The following morning, Laura woke with a start. "Emma!" she yelled. Gyle was already awake and downstairs making breakfast. "Gyle, Emma!" she shouted down to him, and he ran upstairs to comfort his frantic wife.

"It's okay honey," he said softly and reassuringly. "I phoned Neil this morning, they are trying to get a flight up and should be here later today."

"Did you phone the hospital?"

"Not yet" he said softly, "they said not to phone until lunch time, so I guess, if there was anything new we'd have heard." He looked at her and smiled. "Remember they're still with us Laura. You need to hang on to that, and every day is one day more." He turned to go back downstairs. "Oh and Kristen called, your parents' neighbour called Yvonne and John. She was very upset but she's going over to get the dog and she said she would just keep her for the time being."

"Did she say she would come here?"

Gyle nodded. "Yes honey, she said she would come over soon." Moving back towards the bed, he bent over and hugged her. "There's coffee made downstairs if you feel up to it."

"Thanks," she smiled, "I'll come down." A few minutes later Laura walked into the kitchen and poured herself a coffee. She sat down and gazed out of the patio window. The birds were pecking at the bird feeder, which she'd put out for them a week or two before. "Look at that." She turned to Gyle slowly. "Look at them, as though nothing has happened, what right do they have to be happy and healthy while my lovely mum and dad are fighting for their lives?" She turned away from the door and, putting her head on the table, she cried.

Gyle let her cry for a while before giving her a hug and placed some toast beside her. "Maybe you should try to eat something?" He started to watch the birds on the feeder, then turned to Laura who was sipping her coffee. Her face was white and it made her swollen red eyes look huge. "Will you be ok for a while? I need to get some fuel before we head off to the hospital."

Laura nodded and looked at the clock on the kitchen wall. It was a little after ten. Time had seemed to stand still, and she was now questioning whether it had all been a nightmare. That's just how it felt, her mum and dad would be at home in Stirling as usual, winding each other up and making plans for the day, and this had all been a bad dream. She reached for her mobile and called their number. It rang out. It was horrible and as the cruel reality came back to her she sat and cried again. Gyle left to get some fuel for the car and it was nearer noon before he returned. Laura was now showered and dressed and she was trying hard to feel optimistic, realising there had been no call from the hospital either way, which gave her a strand of hope to cling on to. "Everything okay?" she asked, then in a panic. "The hospital haven't called you have they?"

"No, no, I just had some calls to make, you know, to clear the day?"

Laura stared at him. "And is it?"

"Pretty much," he said. "I might have to leave you for an hour at the hospital if we are going to be a while, but I'll come back for you."

Laura sighed and looked at him. "Whatever." It was typical of Gyle; he couldn't just be there all day, like normal people. "You've only been away for two hours already Gyle, how difficult can it be? Surely someone in the office can cover your calls for a few hours?" Laura was angry. Of all the times for Gyle to lapse into his 'Mr Unreliable' mode she was sure as hell it wasn't going to be today. "I need you here, with me Gyle," she told him, trying to curb the torrent of emotions she felt. "I'll only be hanging around, it's not as if I can do anything," he protested.

Laura took a deep breath. "For God's sake Gyle, I'm your wife, and if you haven't noticed," she stroked her very large bump, "you will soon have a child. It's time to grow up Gyle, if you can't put us first in a situation like this, then what's the point? You can be so bloody irresponsible sometimes."

He looked at her, with irritation etched on his face. "I am there for you," he said between clenched teeth. "Was one of your calls to the hospital by any chance?"

"No, I thought I'd do that when I came home, so you would be there to hear what they have to say. In fact, you might want to call them yourself?" The tone in his voice was weary.

"No." Laura shook her head. "I think I'd rather not hear it raw, if you get what I mean?"

Gyle's call to the hospital was very much an exchange of information. "Head to the Intensive Therapy Unit, or ITU of the Western General, as the signposts will say," the young woman told him. "Your name is on the list for entry, but you might not be able to see anyone straight away. It's a very busy unit; you have to be prepared to wait for a time when it's convenient to see someone."

"Okay," Gyle answered, confirming he understood the procedure.

"You will be asked to scrub up and wear a gown. Coats, jackets and handbags are not permitted."

"Okay," Gyle repeated before asking, "Can you tell me how they are?"

"I'm sorry sir, I am not allowed to discuss patients over the telephone. When you arrive at the unit, someone will be able to give you an update on their condition."

Gyle thanked the young woman for her help then, turning to his wife, "Did you get all that?"

"Yeh," she nodded as she returned her handbag and coat to the cupboard. At the hospital, the news was grim. Marie and Fraser had survived the accident but survival had come at a terrible price. Gyle paced up and down, checking his watch every five minutes agitated by the lengthy wait in ITU. Laura was irritated by his manner. "For goodness sake Gyle, can you not settle down, you are driving me mad here." He took a seat and as he did a young nurse ushered them into a small room a short distance away from the waiting lounge. The Consultant, Mr Daniels, delivered the harsh truth while Laura sat taking in every word, like a stab to the heart. "There has been extensive head injuries, the extent of brain damage is not yet known while the swelling remains," Mr Daniels began. "While your parents have survived," he continued, as though he were reading from a manual, "they will never be the people they were before the accident, nor will they be able to live without extensive long-term care."

Laura was shocked. "Will they be able to come home eventually?" she asked.

Mr Daniels shook his head. "In cases such as this it's unlikely, the damage has been extensive and, in my opinion, they will need professional care, such as a nursing home."

"What about care in the home?" she asked as Gyle shook his head and looked away.

"Of course, it's possible, but you would need to have lots of room, and at ground level. The equipment you would need is vast and it's likely your parents will need twenty-four-hour care."

Laura gasped. She couldn't accept the reality of it all. "Are they going to live?" She could barely ask the question and he looked at her, this time with undeniable sadness.

"It's too early to say. If they are still with us this time next week then it's possible they could live another ten years. But realistically, with the extent of their injuries, I would expect it to be much sooner. It's just too difficult to say at this stage."

Choking back the tears, and unable to process the horror of what lay ahead for her beloved parents, Laura was now unable to speak.

"I'll give you a minute," he continued, "... and I'll check to see if you can go in to see them. You do realise they will be wired up to machines that make lots of different funny noises?" Laura nodded, without raising her head as he continued. "You don't need to worry about these, they are all quite normal, and they are just there to do a job."

"What happens next?" Gyle asked.

"Well," Mr Daniels smiled, trying to lighten a very heavy load, "... next is you both going in to see them for a few minutes, and then we'll take it one day at a time after that." And with those words he left the room, leaving behind a distraught, young pregnant woman who was unable to believe the words that had come crushing in, destroying her world. She turned to Gyle as he said hurriedly, "Look, I think it's best if you go in to see them for a while, and I'll deal with what I have to do and come back for you."

"What?" Laura said, stunned. "You're not coming in with me, after all I said?"

He looked at her with a cold stare. "Look Laura, they're your parents, you spend the time with them, I need to make sure we still have an income coming in, it's not as if you contribute anything. Money doesn't magically appear to pay the mortgage and the bills, and provide for the sodding new baby you know!" Laura stared at him in disbelief as he turned and stormed out of the small room tearing off the fine plastic gown he'd been asked to wear, then turning back, "I'll come back for you in an hour." He paused, put his hand in his pocket, pulled out a five-pound note and threw it at her. "Get yourself a coffee or something if I'm not back."

Laura picked up the crumpled note and in that brief moment she hated him. Inside ITU Laura sobbed as she saw the sorry sight of her mum and dad lying next to each other, hardly recognisable. They were both badly injured, with terrible swelling, bruising and cuts to their face and body. As they lay still and lifeless, looking as if they had been put together by needle and thread, machines around them bleeped and buzzed, while little graphs on the monitors displayed changing images. At once Laura understood the meaning of life support and she was now inconsolable as she sobbed and hugged each of her parents in turn not knowing what to do or say or which way to turn. A young male nurse approached the beds and, placing an arm around her, spoke reassuringly. "They are in no pain, they wouldn't have felt any pain, and it was over in seconds," he told her. "We'll take good care of them for you."

Laura looked at him with swollen red eyes, sore from crying and exhausted by the lack of any good sleep. "They must have known at some point something terrible was going to happen," she whispered.

He shook his head. "I don't think they'd have had time?"

"They look so peaceful now," Laura sighed.

"Yes," the young nurse agreed, "there's no sign of fear or trauma on their faces is there?"

Laura agreed, suddenly taking the edge off her horror. "When can I come in again?"

"You can come in any time you want," the young man assured her, but remember that you might have to wait, it might not be because we are working on your parents, it could be someone else, but we don't have visitors in when something is going on, so don't worry if you have to wait."

"How long will they be in here for?" she asked, in a much calmer tone now as the grave acceptance of the situation began to sink in.

"I don't know?" he said, shaking his head. "It's up to them really." Looking towards Marie and Fraser, "At least they are still together."

Laura agreed, it had given her a little comfort, seeing them next to each other, but now she had to give them a kiss goodbye for the time being before making her way out of the unit and into the main hospital building.

In a little café in town, Gyle Jamieson enjoyed a coffee with Louisa, a young woman who'd called into the estate agents looking for a flat several weeks before. Gyle had been instantly attracted to the leggy blonde and on offering to show her around some properties personally, the young woman was happy to accept. Gyle loved the attention and the thrill of early romance, and he was already feeling trapped by a marriage he wasn't sure he wanted, and the prospect of a child he definitely didn't want. Being there now with Louisa was uplifting. Yet in some ways he thought being married was quite good, if only to provide him with the perfect excuse for ending this relationship, and any other future flings or one-night-stands he might have, once the novelty wore off. Louisa wasn't the first woman he had romanced since his brief moment of passion with Celine on his wedding day, nor would she be the last. That was never his intention, but for now she provided him with an escape, not only from the normality of family life, but from the stress he faced since the accident. Today his stress levels had reached a peak with the trauma of the accident, the imminent new arrival and Laura's ever-increasing demands on his time. Today's date was meant to be lunch, coffee and a tour of some empty properties, he and the attractive Louisa would avail themselves of for Prosecco and sex. It was not to be, however, and Gyle was in one hell of a mood at being put on the spot. He wasn't about to tell the lovely Louisa of his married status yet; there was still mileage in this romance. He hoped to persuade her to buy a prime property first; thereafter the romance would likely have run its course and he would return to Laura, and home and be content until the next time. The sudden events of the day had spoiled his date with Louisa and he was fuming. He now had to make excuses for the disruption to the day's plans blaming it on legal complications relating to a property, which should have concluded that day. Softening the blow, they had lunch together and after they had finished coffee Gyle promised to call to make another date.

It was now two hours since Gyle had left Laura at the hospital and as she saw him finally enter the main arena of the hospital, she stood up, disgusted by his calm and seemingly carefree nature. "Ready?" he asked.

Laura nodded, and without speaking started to walk out of the hospital as he followed behind. In the car Gyle asked, "Well?"

"Well what?"

"How are they?"

"As you might expect," she said sharply

"Well don't think you'll be bringing them back home to our place," he snarled. Laura realised now that this could never be an option, but she was angry and hurt at the cold and heartless remark and even more so by his next words. "It'll be bad enough with a screaming baby without two brain-damaged geriatrics?"

"That's my mum and dad you're talking about you heartless moron!" she yelled at him and, without even looking her way, Gyle struck her a blow to the mouth with the back of his left hand, leaving her cut and swollen by his ring, as Laura screamed in pain, then sat sobbing.

"Enough Laura!" he yelled. "It's hard for everyone you know. And we are not having the bloody dog either."

Laura didn't lift her head to look his way; instead she sat in silence, tears flowing down her cheeks as they continued their journey home.

Later that evening, Gyle Jamieson was charming and agreeable as he welcomed Laura's sister Emma. She had taken the last seat on the earliest flight she could without husband Neil, who had only been able to find an available seat on the next day's flight. Emma laughed as Gyle explained Laura's sore mouth. "You know Emma, I've told her I don't know how many times about stacking things carefully in the cupboard, but oh no, Laura knows best, then I hear this almighty crash. There's Laura sitting on the floor in the cupboard with all sorts around her. She's just lucky it was an old recipe book that caught her and not something heavier."

Emma shook her head. "Laura, you need to be more careful, you could have really hurt yourself – and in your condition too."

Laura said nothing, quietly disturbed her sister could laugh at all, and waited for the mood to change, as the realisation of their parents' situation sunk in. Later that evening Gyle escorted Emma and Laura to the hospital and he managed to stay with them this time, fulfilling his role as the considerate and caring husband everyone thought he was. He even provided a shoulder for Emma to cry on, wiping away her tears, as the horrific sight of her parents lying in ITU confirmed her nightmare. Up until then she had believed the description had been exaggerated but now faced with the harsh and cruel reality of the situation the shock in her voice was undeniable. "Someone will pay for this," she cried as Laura shook her head at the typical lawyer talk.

"I don't think so," she told her sister. "It would seem it was what police describe as a multi-fault accident, with all of those possibly responsible killed. I think you could say they've paid the price for their mistakes."

"And Mum and Dad?" she cried, looking towards her sister. "Haven't they paid the price for a mistake that wasn't theirs?"

"Just leave it Emma," Laura said irritably. "Whatever happens now is not going to benefit Mum or Dad, is it?"

"It could pay for their care," Gyle suggested, narrowing his eyes towards Laura.

"What could?"

"Compensation."

"They'd been out for a meal remember?" Laura turned to them both. "You know Mum and Dad would have had wine with it, and don't you think there's every chance Dad would have had a whisky or maybe two after the meal?" Laura searched their faces for a response as she continued. "Work it out for yourself. It won't matter if it wasn't their fault. If Dad was the only one over the limit, that alone makes him responsible." She turned to Emma now. "Am I right?"

Emma agreed reluctantly. "Laura's right, if the police have said it was a multi fault accident then it's best we leave it there, otherwise it could be Mum and Dad facing the compensation claims."

Laura glared at her husband before walking out of the room and into the kitchen. A moment or two later he appeared at the kitchen door. "I'm sorry," he said quietly, suddenly feeling guilty about taking out his bad mood on her. "I'm an idiot, I know. I'm not good at this kind of thing; I didn't mean to upset you. I understand how hard this is for you."

Laura wiped a tear from her eye. "Really? You've a bloody funny way of showing it sometimes."

He started to smile as he walked towards her and looked into her tear-stained face, kissing each cheek. "Come on, we'll get through this." The words were warm and reassuring and he held her close to him, his head lying softly on hers. As her tears dried Laura felt a sudden surge of love as Gyle's dark mood lifted again, and she was reminded of the man she had fallen in love with.

When Emma's husband Neil arrived the next day he hired a car to make it easier for the three of them to visit the hospital. Gyle continued to work during the day but he was unusually gracious and kind to everyone when he returned, visiting the hospital with them all in the evenings. Knowing everyone was busy during the day in ITU and their minds occupied with the events there, Gyle was free to take up where he had left off with Louisa. She had accepted his excuse of having to help his parents decorate in the evenings for a few days without question, so he felt released from some of the pressure he felt had been suddenly forced on him. The situation suited him perfectly and he was in a better mood generally, enabling him to play the supporting husband role for the time being. It was Kristen's final year at university now and Scott was in the process of setting up a new veterinary practice in Blairlogie. It was an exciting time for them, the dream was coming true and Laura was really pleased. When she called to say she was coming over to visit the following day Laura was surprised. "What about the practice, Kristen, and everything you have going on there?" she asked.

"Scott said he will manage with what needs to be done at the practice Laura, and he sends his love."

"He's a good man, Kristen." Laura smiled to herself, wondering why Gyle couldn't be more like Scott, always happy with no dark side or moods and certainly no supersized ego, despite being a really good-looking guy.

"I know," Kristen laughed. "I think I'll keep him."

Laura agreed. It was a great relief for Laura knowing Kristen was coming over to see her. She had thought perhaps that her in-laws might have been a bit more hands-on but that wasn't their style. They had called to offer sympathy, but clearly they seemed to think that any practical help should come from

Laura's side of the family, without considering where that help was likely to come from. There had been little change to Marie and Fraser's condition, and the sight of them both lying side by side in the Intensive Therapy Unit was exhausting and stressful. When Kristen arrived at the hospital Laura felt the weight lifting from her shoulders. It was a physical feeling she'd often heard people describe, but she had never experienced it herself until now. She hugged Kristen and they both cried. "It's in today's local paper," she told Laura. "Everyone is really shocked and they all send their love."

"Mum and Dad have a lot of friends; do you think everyone will know now?"

"I would think so; what about you Laura, do all your friends know?"

"There's only you now Kristen."

"Jodie and Mikey? And what about Doug?

"Oh my God, I should have phoned Mikey and Jodie at least, but you know how jealous Gyle gets about my friends at Tattie Bogles?"

Kristen agreed. "Well I'm here now I'll give them a call. Surely Gyle will be okay with that now you're not working there anymore?"

Laura shrugged. "It's hard to know what he's thinking right now, but thanks Kristen." Laura smiled. "It's so good to have you here," she said, giving her a big hug.

"I know it's hell just now but you just need to hang on there," Kristen urged, patting Laura's now very large bump. "You need to think of that little baby in there."

"Do you think it'll be alright?"

"The baby?"

Laura gave a worried nod.

"Of course it will!" Kristen reassured her. "You give me your spare key and get yourself back in there with Emma and Neil. I'll go over to your place and see what needs to be done and then I'll get some dinner on for you all."

"You'll stay and eat with us?"

Kristen looked apologetically and shook her head. "Sorry honey, I'd better get back home after that and see to things there, but I'll be back in a couple of days. How long do you think Emma and Neil will stay?"

"It's hard to say, Kristen." Laura sighed. "Gyle has been really nice to them but I can see he's struggling to keep it up now, and I think Emma's caught a few 'Gyle-like' glances." They laughed.

"Right," Kristen said, nodding, "they'll be off tomorrow then?"

Laura agreed, laughing. "You know Gyle." She sighed. "Being nice is a bit of an effort for him, it doesn't come naturally and he's been nice for days now."

"He must be exhausted," Kristen teased.

"Absolutely," Laura agreed, laughing. "Oh Kristen, what about Maisie?"

"She's fine, Laura, she's with my mum and dad and Piper and Zeus just now, she's having a great time."

"Are your mum and dad okay about having her with them?"

"You might not get her back!" Kristen laughed, and Laura too. "Once we get the practice up and running I'm taking Piper and Zeus with me, so Mum will have Maisie all to her herself until you want her back." Laura looked at her sadly, fighting back tears. "Don't tell me he doesn't want her here?" Laura nodded. "Don't worry about it Laura, it might be difficult with the new baby, and if you are happy for Mum to keep her, she will think it's her birthday!"

Laura gave a smile and a little laugh. "Are you sure?"

"Absolutely and it's good to see you laugh Laura," she said as she left the hospital. "When do you expect to be back for dinner?"

"I told Gyle we'd be back for half five."

"Chin up, I'll see you some time," Kristen called as she headed off out of the hospital. Later that afternoon she called Mikey, but she was stunned when he said he had already heard the news. "My dad's just mentioned it when I was speaking to him earlier. He had apparently consoled a young rookie cop, Denise somebody, who had been in bits following a visit to break some bad news. When she mentioned the name, it suddenly clicked with my dad that I knew who she had been talking about. I was going to get Jodie to phone tonight, I didn't want to speak to HIM."

"Gyle?"

"Yes, he's not my favourite person, but you know Jodie, she can somehow reach his better nature." He laughed.

"Jodie could reach anyone's better nature. Of course she has the added advantage of being a woman, and she knows him from way back."

"I know him from way back, that's half the problem."

There was a short silence then Kristen changed the course of the conversation briefly. "I didn't know your dad was a cop?"

"It's not something I tell everybody," Mikey told her. "It receives mixed reactions, but yes, he's a detective." Kristen understood why he didn't say anything; people did have mixed reactions, especially those frequenting pubs, and when Mikey explained that should anyone be stopped for drink-driving, after leaving Tattie Bogles, he didn't want the finger pointed his way.

Changing the conversation back to Laura, Kristen explained

the situation and hoped Mikey and Jodie would call in to see Laura at the hospital, even if for a few minutes. "You'll not be able to visit the unit, but she needs a break and if you could persuade her to go with you to the café for a cup of tea, I think it would help," she told him.

"God, of course," he gasped. "I'm assuming Gyle won't be with her?"

"He's in and out at the moment, but I have a feeling that when Emma and Neil leave, he'll disappear completely into his own world again, and Laura will be left on her own to struggle through it."

"Is Laura okay?"

"She's struggling, Mikey, and she has a really sore mouth. I didn't mention it to her and she didn't offer to tell me what happened."

"You don't think it was him do you?"

"I don't know Mikey, but it wouldn't surprise me."

"What does she see in him?"

"Beats me?"

"You tell her Jodie and I will be over soon. We'll wait until HE's out of the way and we'll pop over some morning when he's at work."

Before everyone had returned home, Kristen had cleaned, washed and cooked. She left a note asking Laura to call her when she had a minute and gave her apologies at having to leave before they returned. It had been a difficult day, but for the first time in a while, when Laura came home to the smell of cooking coming from the kitchen, she was reminded of her mum and dad's home in Stirling and she instantly felt supported and loved with Emma, Neil and Kristen there to ease the pain.

5

When Kristen visited again a few days later she was upset to see Laura looking so strained. It was almost midday, she was still in her pyjamas and she looked tired and pale. The latest news from the hospital was not good. Marie had developed complications and was again in a critical condition. Emma and Neil were now back in London and their decision not to return to Scotland in the near future, unless they had to, was understandable although disappointing. Their early departure had left Laura feeling isolated and at a loss about what to do next, so she did nothing. Now the house was unusually untidy and dishes lay on top of the dishwasher, unwashed. Kristen felt mildly irritated that Gyle couldn't do more to help Laura around the house. Then after Laura explained he'd not returned home from work until the early hours, Kristen took a deep breath, stifling her annoyance. Then as Laura continued to tell her that he had overslept as a consequence, leaving for work again a few hours later in a foul mood with everyone, her irritation and growing annoyance turned to anger. "What's wrong with the man?" She yelled, then looking towards Laura's troubled expression, immediately calmed down again. It was clear the worry and stress had taken its toll on her friend and Laura was now struggling to cope with a selfish and insensitive husband on top of everything else. Kristen helped Laura to tidy up the house and encouraged her to have a shower and a change of clothes before taking her out for lunch.

"It's times like these, I miss escaping to the Ochils," she told Kristen between sips of tea.

"Well, there's no way we're hiking up there with you like that?" Kristen teased, looking her friend up and down. Laura smiled and Kristen felt relieved to see her spirit lift slightly and hoped she would leave her in a better place mentally than she'd found her that morning. Kristen returned home shortly after lunch and Laura took a nap on the sofa. She was drifting off to sleep when she started to feel sudden pains in her sides and back, waking her instantly. She sat up with a bolt thinking it was cramp, and then as the pains eased she rested again for a while, before suddenly remembering she had shopping to do. She had set herself the task of making Gyle's favourite Italian meal, parmigiana, but with added chicken, the way his mother had shown her. Tired and sore, Laura took herself out to buy the ingredients from the local store and struggled back with heavy bags. It was after four in the afternoon and Gyle promised to be back by six so she carefully prepared the meal and put it in the oven so it would be ready when he came home. Hours passed and when he didn't show by seven-thirty Laura called him. His mobile was switched off, so she tried again later, and several times after that. When he eventually staggered in the door at nine-thirty, having driven home drunk, Laura was not amused. "Where have you been?" she asked him in disbelief. "You said you'd be home by six." Then, sensing his dark mood, she quickly tried to lighten the tense atmosphere by smiling, but he was having none of it.

"What the hell has it to do with you where I've been?" he

slurred loudly, eyes bulging with rage, as he continued his torrent of abuse. "It's not as if I have anything special to rush home for now is it?" he sneered.

Laura stared at him. She was still sore from the earlier pains and tired from the day's events. Then, trying desperately to change his dark and drunken mood, she turned to him, still smiling. "I've made your favourite chicken parmigiana," she said cheerfully, bending down and carefully lifting the dish out of the oven with a tea towel. "See, it's still hot and it smells lovely." Laura felt a sense of dread welling up inside her, as she turned round to face him, realising his mood hadn't changed. On the contrary, his face was white and the anger in his eyes scared her as he lunged forwards knocking the hot dish out of her hands, splattering the contents right across the kitchen, up the walls, on the floor and over the worktops.

"That's what I think of your stinking chicken parmigiana," he yelled at her as he turned away, then turning back, "Get that bloody mess cleaned up in there!"

Laura was relieved when she realised he had taken himself to bed. Exhausted and shaken she began to clear up the mess as she wept.

The following morning she asked him why he was so mad with her. "You know what I'm like when I've had a bad day, and too much to drink!" he told her coldly, then turning the blame on her. "The trouble with you is you never learn, do you? You're so bloody stupid, no wonder you flunked uni!" It was a remark that hurt Laura, but the worst was yet to come as his voice started to rise again. "Now you want to make me out to be a bad bastard don't you? You want to make me feel bad and grovel apologies to you. Don't you?" He was staring at her, his face close to hers as she stood in silence shaking her head. If she had hoped for an apology, it wasn't going to be now. Instead he glared at her as she looked up and caught his cold stare. "And you can stop looking at me like that unless you want a smack in the mouth as well!"

Laura turned away. "Sorry," she whimpered, fighting back the tears.

"You will be," he snarled before grabbing his jacket and car keys and headed out to work, leaving Laura feeling sick all morning as the events tore through her mind time and time again. That afternoon the pains she had experienced the day before returned with a vengeance. Her due date was still a couple of weeks away but these were real pains and they were now occurring relentlessly, developing a pattern of time. Anxiously she phoned Gyle but he cut the call off. She called again and again, but he didn't answer. The pains were now intense so she phoned Mikey and asked him to come over to take her to hospital.

"You hang on honey," he told her, "I'll be with you as quick as I can." By the time he reached Lanark Road West, Laura was well into labour and he called an ambulance. "I can't risk it Laura," he said, holding her hand and trying to keep her calm. "It could happen any time now."

"Stay with me Mikey, please," she whispered as he wiped the hair away from her fearful eyes.

"I'm not leaving you," he said quietly. When the ambulance arrived, Mikey followed it to the hospital. He had tried to phone Gyle but his phone was now switched off completely.

It was midday and Gyle Jamieson was enjoying lunch with a woman he'd met in a bar the night before. He had been angered at having to return home but he knew if he'd stayed out all night

Laura would start phoning round to see where he was. He had been forced to tell this woman he had to go home to attend to the dogs and she had accepted his explanation. Now he had returned to the small hotel where she was staying and joined her for lunch. He was still annoyed with Laura for putting him under pressure and he was determined to keep his phone switched off. Later he returned to the woman's room where she helped to ease his frustration. She poured him a drink from the minibar before undressing slowly in front of him, dropping each garment on to the plush carpet. Gyle sat on a small chair near the window of the room watching her every move as he took slow sips of his drink. Then, leading him to the large soft bed, the woman stripped him naked, slowly teasing and touching him, stroking and kissing his body playfully. She took the glass from his hand, and placed it on the bedside table before pushing him gently back onto the bed. She crawled on top of him, slowly moving and writhing, and as their bodies connected she didn't stop as the motion quickened and intensified until at last he groaned loudly before relaxing, satisfied and elated. He left the hotel room an hour later, not even knowing her name. She had told him it was Caroline but he knew it wasn't, any more than he had been Keith. It had excited him and the encounter released the pressure and frustration of the night before. Walking towards his car, he quickly turned his phone back on. Eight missed calls, some from Laura and some from numbers he didn't recognise. He called Laura and was surprised to hear Mikey. It was a voice which instantly took the edge off his good mood.

"Gyle, you need to get to the Royal Infirmary, labour ward," Mikey told him informatively and unfriendly. "Laura tried to get you but in a panic she called me... and well, to cut a long story short, you are about to become a father if you are not already."

"I'm on my way," Gyle said calmly with no hint of urgency and by the time he arrived at the hospital Laura had given birth to a beautiful baby girl. Mikey was just leaving the hospital as he arrived.

"Congratulations," Mikey said. Gyle said nothing. There was no "thanks Mikey" or "are they okay?" There was nothing, and Mikey shook his head. "Thanks Mikey," he said to himself, trying hard not to feel annoyed by Gyle's ingratitude.

Shortly before Laura gave birth to her daughter, a few miles away at the Western General, Marie Duncan lost her fight for life. Delivering the news to Laura threw her into a pit of emotions. In the space of a few hours she had been angry with Gyle for ignoring her calls then panicked about giving birth alone at home; then she had been relieved when Mikey came to her rescue, and distraught that she'd given birth without her husband present. Later she had felt elated at delivering such a perfect little girl and now she was devastated at the loss of her beloved mother. As she looked into the little hospital crib and gazed at her beautiful baby lying there all bundled up in a pretty pink blanket, silent tears soon turned to sobs. Her dear mum would never see the little granddaughter she had been longing to hold; her daughter would never know her grandparents. Holding on to that thought for a moment suddenly made her feel vulnerable and very alone. It had been an emotional day and by the time Gyle arrived in the ward, she couldn't have cared whether he had visited or not. She now felt a powerful bond with her baby and an overwhelming sense of responsibility to protect her. Gyle wouldn't spoil that, not now, not ever, she

111

promised herself. As he entered the little labour ward he bent down and kissed Laura on the forehead. "Sorry honey, I got held up in a meeting. So you had the baby then? What is it?"

Laura looked at him and shook her head as she looked at the little pink bundle lying in the crib next to her. "We have a little girl, Gyle," she told him quietly. "We have a daughter."

Gyle looked at her again, without looking into the little crib beside her. "Have you been crying? What's wrong, is the baby okay?"

Laura realised he hadn't heard the terrible news. "Did no one tell you?" She was surprised. Her tears started again, turning to sobs as she eventually gasped, "My mum died."

"How do you know?" Gyle was shocked.

"Mikey called Emma to tell her I was in labour and the Western had already called her. Emma thought, under the circumstances, the doctor should tell me the bad news." She sniffed, wiping away her tears before looking into his face. "I was told the lovely news about our baby, then that Mum had died." She looked up at him. "Can you imagine what that was like? I was on my own Gyle, you should have been there."

"They didn't waste any time, did they?" he gasped, then, feeling slightly guilty knowing where he was at the time, and what he was doing, he hugged her. "I'm so sorry Laura, I wasn't expecting it."

"Neither was I!" Laura wailed. "Of course the hospital tried to call you, Emma tried to call you and Mikey tried to call you." The annoyance in her voice was evident.

Gyle looked away for a moment and then the practicalities of the situation suddenly spurred him to react. "What about the funeral? You can't do it, in here. Oh my God, that's all we need right now!"

Laura was now gazing at her little girl, lying sleeping in the clear plastic crib, as Gyle continued whining and whingeing, all of which she ignored. When he eventually stopped talking, she looked up at him. "When you are quite finished Gyle, relax," she said calmly. "Emma's dealing with everything, it's not as if we could ask you is it?" Gyle wasn't sure how to react to the remark, but, relieved someone else was shouldering the aftermath, said nothing. Laura tapped him on the shoulder. "Aren't you going to say hello to your daughter?"

"Oh my God," Gyle gasped again. "I forgot!" He looked into the little crib and smiled. "She's tiny, what's her name?"

Laura laughed. "They don't come with names," she teased. He looked up, almost startled by her remark; he had never even thought of this bump Laura had been lugging around for months now as a baby. Names had never crossed his mind. The reality of him being a father suddenly hit him and he wasn't quite sure how to handle it. "I think you should give her a name Laura, you'll be better at that kind of thing."

"I thought you might say that," Laura said softly, "so I have decided to call her Kenzie. Her name is Kenzie Marie Jamieson."

Gyle looked down at his daughter. "Hello Kenzie," he said quietly, staring at the little infant sleeping peacefully. "What do we do now?"

"Well I would like some rest, if that's okay with you," Laura told him. "It's been quite a day. It would be good if you could bring some baby clothes in later, I left a bag in the nursery."

Gyle nodded. He looked completely lost and when he made his way out of the labour ward a few minutes later Laura was relieved. Over the next few days, Laura's visitors were more excited at the arrival of little Kenzie than Gyle had been; Kristen and Scott were thrilled with the news but saddened by the death of Marie. Mikey and Jodie shared Laura's tears while being completely over the moon seeing Kenzie. It was a strange situation for them all but Mikey was especially taken with the little tot. "Look at Daddy day-care," Jodie joked as he sat in awe of her.

Marie's funeral took place exactly a week after Kenzie was born and Jodie and Mikey came over to look after her. Emma and Neil arrived from London a couple of days before but stayed in a hotel in town. Before the funeral Laura and Emma visited their dad in hospital. As Laura looked down, clutching baby Kenzie to her, she felt pained to watch his pale drawn face as she and her sister broke the tragic news. He would be there alone now, amid the machines, which bleeped and buzzed and the tubes that connected him to life. The girls were not sure whether he heard the words they spoke to him or if he understood, but they felt compelled to deliver the sad news, painful as it was, and it was so hard for them to leave him now. For weeks following the funeral, Laura felt numb. There was still a whole torrent of emotions going on inside her head and she was pleased that Gyle wasn't around much to add to her stress. Gyle noticed the change in his wife. She seemed more distant and independent than she had been, and although it was something he had almost hoped for a few months ago, the change was now beginning to worry him. He had settled down since Kenzie was born and he tried to focus more on work and providing for his family. He now saw Laura in a new light, not just this woman who came between him and freedom, but as the mother of his child and the key player in his future family. He felt a renewed sense of pride that she was someone he could trust and rely on. When Manor Place sold, it took more pressure off him financially and Laura was relieved that her husband was at least making an attempt at being a family man for a change. Despite his lack of willingness to do anything practical, he was a calmer, happier man than he'd been for some time and Laura gradually accepted that this was her family now and she was determined to make it work for Kenzie's sake. She told Kristen that if she couldn't be the best journalist in Scotland then she would have to try to be the best wife and mother instead. Kristen wasn't surprised. "I am sure you are that already Laura," she assured her friend, while telling herself that Gyle didn't deserve the love and care she gave him so freely. By the time Laura took the baby to visit her dad again he was in a nursing home. His condition wasn't good and she felt that somehow he was aware his beloved wife had died, and he was just giving up now. She hoped the arrival of little Kenzie had given him reason to hang on to the threads of life, but then realised it was a selfish thought. Fraser had no life now, lying there in a nursing home with no prospect of returning to the life and family he loved. Now Laura sat holding his hands gently. "You know I love you lots Dad, but if you need to go now, to be with Mum, then that's okay. I'll be just fine and so will Emma. Just tell Mum we love her." Laura continued to hold his hands for a few minutes, wiping away the tears and then she kissed his cheek before leaving the nursing home for the last time, as grief gripped her throat and silent tears flowed. Hours later, after Laura returned home, Fraser Duncan let go of the fragile threads of life he was clinging on to and he gently passed away to join his beloved wife Marie. Kenzie was now six months old and the image of Laura. She was a contented happy child with a ready smile for everyone. Her little blonde curls and big blue eyes captured the hearts and attention of everyone she met.

Although she was devastated when her beloved father died, Laura also felt a certain relief that he was free and she imagined her mum and dad again together in heaven or some afterlife, winding each other up as they always had. The image gave her comfort and it was one she would return to when she felt low or sad. Fraser's body was laid next to Marie's in the little cemetery near Stirling Castle and Laura took Kenzie over to lay flowers at the graveside. It was a Thursday afternoon after she returned from Stirling to find Jodie sitting on her doorstep. Laura had just left Kristen at Blairlogie where she and Scott had been busy with their new vet's practice and she was surprised to see Jodie sitting waiting for her. "Where the hell have you been?" Jodie teased.

"Why didn't you call me on my mobile?" Laura asked, still wondering what Jodie was doing there waiting.

"I've not been here long Laura, I'm just teasing you. I didn't think you'd be far away?"

Laura laughed. "I'm just back from Stirling and seeing Kristen. Are you okay?"

"No," Jodie answered quietly, shaking her head. "Me and Mikey have split up." She looked down to the step as Laura juggled with the baby, handbag and keys of the house.

"Whatever happened?" Laura asked, completely shocked, as they struggled through the door. "Mikey's a great guy."

"I know Laura, that's why I've finished with him."

"What are you crazy? That makes no sense."

"I don't love him Laura. He is a great guy and..." She paused, looking up to the ceiling then out of the window, tears welling up in her eyes. "God how I wish that I loved him, but I've tried and I just don't. It wasn't fair to keep things going."

"Oh my God, Laura, he'll be devastated." Laura looked to

her friend in disbelief, as Jodie now took Kenzie from her, leaving Laura to fetch the pram. Jodie and Mikey had become regular babysitters and Laura always thought they looked so happy.

"Well, that's just the thing," Jodie sighed. "I was going to tell him weeks ago, and I was so scared of hurting him that I put it off and put it off." Laura sat down on the arm of the sofa. "When I told him, he said he was glad I'd said something because he felt the same, and didn't want to hurt me either! Can you believe that?"

Laura nodded. "Well, yes actually, I can believe Mikey would do that, but he's always wanted to settle down, and you both seemed so happy. I'm so sorry Jodie, it's a complete shock to me."

"We are still going to be great mates." Jodie looked up, smiling. "And I'm still staying at Mikey's until I can get somewhere else sorted out. He says there's no rush."

Laura was stunned. "I don't know what to say Jodie?"

"Oh, and we'll still babysit. You know Laura, Mikey just loves Kenzie."

"I know, he'll make a great dad one day, I'm just sorry it's not with you."

"Maybe that's it Laura, I don't really want kids. Oh I love Kenzie, but I can hand her back to you. I'm just not sure I'm cut out for it as a life choice!" Laura laughed; she understood completely. Jodie the responsible mum was not an image she could hold in her mind for long, but Mikey was different.

Jodie stayed for dinner and when Gyle came home, he was happy and playful with her. When she told him about splitting up with Mikey he told her she would find somebody better. Laura smiled; it was a remark Mikey had said to her once when he was trying to discourage her from seeing Gyle. Later that night Gyle took Jodie home and when he returned he was still in a happy and upbeat mood. Laura hoped he had now overcome the earlier bad dark days for good, and she felt content that Gyle seemed to embrace family life now, rather than resent it. He had been gentle and kind since the birth of Kenzie and they had even made plans for the future, something Gyle had never been happy to do. Kristen and Scott were still building on their dream in Blairlogie and Laura was overjoyed for them. She felt as though she had just stepped into a different world. Life was nothing like she had ever imagined it would be and she wondered what other twists and turns her life would take, where she would be or what she would be doing in the years ahead.

Laura wasn't clear when the mood began to change, but she noticed that Gyle had not been his usual self after returning from work one very wet and dull evening. He had been let down by a prospective buyer to a property which had been on the market for months and had attracted little attention. He arrived home preoccupied and when Laura asked what was on his mind he ignored her. Later that evening when she asked him to clear the kitchen while she gave Kenzie her bath he just snapped. "What do you think I am, some kind of little flunkey at your disposal?" he said, his voice rising as he continued. "Do you not think I do enough for this family, without you reducing me to the ranks of domestic servant?"

Laura looked at him in astonishment. "And when I do it? Does that make me your flunkey, Gyle? Is that how you see me, some kind of housekeeper?" she fumed.

"You've got it made here, while I'm out trying to make a

living to pay for this place. You have no idea what I do for this family, you don't appreciate any of it!" He was now on his feet peering down at her sitting at the kitchen table and yelling in her face.

"Do you think I just sit here drinking tea all day?" Laura argued, turning away. "If it makes you feel better why not take a day off work and look after things here. You'll soon see what I do to make your life a bit easier," she said brightly, trying to stay calm and without provocation.

"You can be a real bitch sometimes Laura," he went on, lowering his tone now but replacing it with a softer yet more powerful tone, aimed to hurt. "Look at me Laura, look at me. I'm a great-looking guy. I look after myself and I'm smart. I could have had anybody I wanted, anybody. But no, I got stuck with you. Take a look at yourself, Laura, take a long hard look." He reached out his hand, pointing towards her, moving his finger from head to toe. "You're nothing special, you're just a talentless bum, who is bloody lucky to have a guy like me." He looked at her shaking his head with a snide smile. "You would be nothing without me, you'd have nothing without me, but are you grateful? Are you hell? You take it all for granted!"

"Is that what you really think Gyle?" Although she was deeply hurt by this latest tirade of abuse, Laura was very much in control. Absent were the tears that would once have flooded her eyes in the months before. Instead she sat up straight from the kitchen table where she had been feeding Kenzie. "I only asked you to clear the kitchen Gyle, not throw yourself to the lions for us. It's a simple enough task, but hey, don't bother, I'll do it myself if it's too difficult for you." She then looked him up and down. "I think you'd better lie down in a darkened room until you can regain some self-control. You know, it's really not an attractive look." He was startled, and as she lifted Kenzie from her highchair she turned to him again. "Oh and another thing Gyle," she said quietly and calmly, without raising her voice even slightly. "Don't you dare speak to me or raise your voice like that again in front of Kenzie, she doesn't need that from you or anybody else for that matter." She turned and walked out of the kitchen and up to the bathroom to give Kenzie her bath. She was shaken from his latest rant, and sat for a moment while she tried to calm down, congratulating herself on her strength of self-control. By the time Laura came back downstairs, the kitchen was clean and Gyle was sitting watching the television. He said nothing and Laura was determined she wouldn't thank him for clearing up the mess. They sat in silence all evening and in the morning the conversation was limited to what had to be said or answered, before he left for work.

When she spoke to Mikey later that day he told her that Gyle obviously felt a bit sorry for himself. "He probably feels a bit jealous of you and the baby Laura; you know she does take up a lot of your time."

Laura agreed. "I have to do what I have to do for Kenzie, Mikey, and yes, it does take up a lot of time, but what can I do?"

"Why not surprise him Laura, you know, do something spontaneous, something unexpected. Show him he does mean something to you both. I am sure he would love it, you know how much he likes attention!"

Laura laughed; Mikey was right, Gyle loved attention, and she agreed he had been pushed to one side lately. "Thanks Mikey, that's just what I'll do." It was good to have a friend like Mikey, Laura thought; he could give her a guy's perspective on things and this time, she was sure he'd hit the nail right on the head. Later that morning she discarded her jeans in favour of a little dress, she curled her hair a little and dressed Kenzie in a pretty dress and little cardigan. She then made her way into town and to McArdle and Baynes to take her husband out for lunch, hoping he would be there when she arrived. Instead it was Janice the administrative assistant and Heather the sales assistant who came to greet Laura and the baby. As they fussed over Kenzie, Laura asked when Gyle was likely to be in. "Oh he's gone to collect Gavin from the airport," Janice told her. "They should be back soon. Gavin's been on a recruitment drive looking for a dynamic new sales executive. Someone who will make the company bubble and fizz!" Janice raised her eyebrows as the others laughed, enjoying her take on the boss's new ambitious drive to increase sales.

"I would have thought business was booming, judging by the amount of time Gyle spends here!" Laura sighed, but caught sight of the puzzled looks and in particular from Andy, who worked with Gyle. "Have I got that wrong?" Laura asked cautiously.

"No, no!" Andy was quick to answer. "It's just work, work, work, here all the time these days, we need an extra pair of hands."

"Oh good." Laura smiled. "Gyle is just exhausted when he comes home at night."

"I bet he is!" Andy said quietly, winking towards Dawn, the lettings assistant who was standing close by.

"Maybe I'll be able to see more of my husband when the new person arrives?" It was a question nobody answered as they all continued to flock around the baby between telephone calls. Laura noticed that the office was quiet. "Is Gyle free for lunch, do you know Janice? Could you check his diary?"

Janice called up the electronic diary on her computer. "Mmm he has one appointment with a Mr and Mrs Henderson out at Murrayfield."

"I can take that one," Andy shouted across to her. Laura was pleased she seemed to have chosen a good day to call, and she was pleased to see Gyle and his boss Gavin enter the large office.

"What are you doing here?" Gyle asked, slightly startled.

"I'm here to take you out for lunch." Laura smiled.

"Lucky you Gyle," his boss teased.

"I have an appointment," Gyle protested.

"It's okay Gyle, I'll go!" Andy called, looking over to that side of the office.

"Right then, let's go," he said cheerfully to Laura as they left the office and stepped on to the busy street.

Back at McArdle and Baynes the surprise visit had provided a topic of interest among the staff. "Why did you lie for him?" Heather asked Andy. "You know we haven't been busy. God knows where Gyle gets to these days?"

"What could I say?" He lifted his hands up to his jaw. "You know what he's like, and going home exhausted?" He looked across the room at the disapproving faces.

"Poor Laura," Heather said quietly, shaking her head.

"And that appointment in Murrayfield?" Andy continued, as the others looked on eagerly waiting for the next piece of gossip. "It's not Mr and Mrs Henderson, it's a recent divorcee, Mrs Henderson."

"You're kidding?" Janice was shocked, but the others were less so. "You don't think?" she started.

"Who knows?" Andy cut in. 'But I know one thing, Gyle won't be pleased I'm going in his place!"

As they walked along Princess Street, Gyle was shocked by Laura's surprise visit, and not as happy as she hoped he might be. "What on earth possessed you to drop into the office Laura? Do you not realise I'm busy? I can't just drop everything when you call by, and now I've let Mr and Mrs Henderson down."

"I'm sorry Gyle." Laura looked at him. "I can see you've been a bit stressed out, and you know, now this little madam is here," she said, kissing Kenzie's rosy cheek, "I haven't been able to give you the time and attention you deserve." She looked up at him, smiling. "I just thought you needed a bit of us time, and a break!"

Gyle tried to stifle a smile. "Okay Laura, but don't do this again." He put his arm around her, reluctantly giving in to the impromptu lunch date and sighed as she pushed the pram along the street. "Where are we going?"

"Gianni's!"

Laura made her way home after lunch feeling she had accomplished something special and she congratulated herself on the way she had handled the latest situation. However, she still worried a little about much of what her husband had said before. She was suddenly made aware just how dependent she had become on him. Where would she go, and what would she have without him? The house was solely in his name, she thought, or it could even be in his father's name. She didn't know for sure. She could have no claim on it if it was. She had no qualifications, no job. It was partly his fault, but she would ultimately pay the price if they split. He would still have his job and a roof over his head – and his parents to help him out. Laura suddenly felt very scared, and very vulnerable. If she left now, she could move into her parents' home for a while, but even that would only ever be a temporary solution. She could offer Kenzie nothing without him and the realisation of the impact failing university had made to her life depressed her. It was something she should consider again. Kenzie was now a little older, and the possibility of finding a nursery might be a possibility if she was accepted back at university.

That night she ran the idea passed Gyle. "If I could go back to uni, and put Kenzie in nursery, I would probably only have to do a year, and then I would be able to work and contribute to the household," she cheerfully told her husband.

"How much is that going to cost?"

"I don't know? I might be able to get a student loan again."

"Oh yes," Gyle said sarcastically. "Then as soon as you start work you are going to be paying back that loan and the original one so you'll have nothing left! Meanwhile I'd be forking out a fortune in childcare!"

"But I would be qualified and it could benefit us later."

Gyle looked at her. "No, it's too much of a drain on my finances just now Laura, maybe in a year or two, but not yet, and as far as Kenzie is concerned, you had her, you look after her!" Laura was disappointed, and angered by his last remark, but she didn't rise to the bait and said nothing. She had hoped he would have gone with the idea, but she needed his support financially and accepted he had a point. Their finances were stretched a bit too far on his salary alone, so she was forced to abandon the idea. Gyle continued to run hot and cold with his emotions towards her, and she sometimes found the strain of it difficult to cope with. She wondered what kind of mood he would be in every time he came home, it was never the same two days in a row and although she tried to get to the bottom of things he never gave anything away. Laura realised he was secretive and she began to wonder what happened during his days away from her, because he rarely spoke about the ordinary things anymore, the people he'd bumped into or the chatty office conversation. There was a side to Gyle she realised she didn't really know. Mikey had told her about the shady deal he'd been involved in, yet he had still never mentioned the fact that he knew Mikey. The more Laura wondered, the more the whole thing intrigued her, and when Jodie called her to ask if she was free to meet for lunch she grabbed the chance. She would ask Jodie more about her husband, and his past.

They met a few days later at Tattie Bogles and Laura felt she had come home. Doug was in awe of the lovely little Kenzie and he gave Laura a big hug. "How's that man treating you?" he asked.

Laura raised her eyebrows. "He's hard work, to tell the truth."

"Aren't all men?"

"Not the ones I know, except him!" Laura laughed. "He used to come in here, didn't he, before we met?" She looked at Doug. "What was he like? What don't I know about him?"

"That's a funny question to ask Laura," Doug answered, not sure what to say next. "I don't know what you do know, or don't know already, and to be honest Jodie knows him better, maybe you should ask her?"

Jodie looked at him. "Thanks," she said sarcastically then, turning to Laura, "I am surprised he settled down Laura, to be honest. He's a player, did you never wonder why he never had a steady girlfriend before you?"

Laura looked surprised. "That's just the thing Jodie, he never talks about ex girlfriends, and I have no idea who his ex-girlfriends are."

"You know one of them," Jodie reminded her. "The one he was with the night you first met him, Natalie?"

"Oh yes," Laura suddenly remembered. "He finished with her because she was too materialistic and wanted more than he was willing to provide, he told me that one." Jodie laughed as Doug gave out a sigh before turning round and headed back behind the bar.

"Leave me out of this one," he said before serving his next customer.

"Gyle didn't finish with Natalie that night Laura. She was still living at Manor Place for at least two weeks after that. Rumour has it she walked in on him with another woman." Jodie looked at Laura and then across to Doug who promptly lowered his head and carried on drying glasses behind the bar. "Apparently, she'd forgotten her bank card and nipped back for it at lunch time. She was surprised to see his car outside because he said he was entertaining clients!" Jodie almost shrieked the last part of the sentence. "Can you believe the nerve of the man?"

"Why didn't you tell me all this before, Jodie, when I first met him?" Laura was surprised and saddened by the sudden revelation. "At that time you didn't want to know him, remember?" Jodie glanced up at her and towards Doug, who had taken a renewed interest in the conversation, at a safe distance. "Then you went out with him. Mikey told you to be careful and, I guess the bottom line is that nobody expected it to last, and to be honest we all thought you'd bin him after the first week."

"I still don't understand why you didn't tell me then?"

"By the time I realised you two were serious, I reckoned, err I should say we reckoned that he'd changed. As far as we knew he'd never had a steady girlfriend before, and we just thought that his philandering past was because he hadn't found the right one. After all he was free and single. I suppose you could say, we thought he'd found the right one in you, so it didn't seem fair to cause trouble between you."

Laura listened intently. "I can see where you are coming from Jodie, but in hindsight I wish I had known a bit more about him. I can't believe you were all talking about the situation and left me clean out of it!" She sighed then looked towards Doug, still at the bar, and again to Jodie. "He's not an easy person to live with and he's not easy to pin down sometimes."

"Oh," Jodie responded, quietly. "You know what Mikey thinks about him."

"Yes, I do but that goes way back to a work situation Jodie, it was nothing like this." She looked down at Kenzie who was sleeping in her pram now and she felt a sudden dread that she had made the biggest mistake of her life, getting involved with Gyle Jamieson. Later that evening Laura found it hard to speak to Gyle, without imagining the scene Natalie had faced when she walked into the flat in Manor Place. Then she remembered it had only recently sold. What if he had 'entertained' clients there? she wondered, and it suddenly became clear why he didn't want to take her to Manor Place in the beginning. It was because Natalie was still there! Her mind was buzzing with it all and she found herself drifting away from the present conversation she was trying to have with her husband. "Hello, earth to Laura," he teased. "You were miles away, have you got something on your mind?" He was in a good mood and Laura hated spoiling it. She knew how easily he could go off on one of his nasty twisted rants so she just smiled. She wanted to challenge him about Natalie but couldn't find the way to begin. "No, I was just daydreaming, wondering if the property market is picking up now?"

"It's terrible Laura, hardly a sale going through at all. It's a worry."

"That's awful Gyle, I guess it's the same everywhere just now?"

"Yup, we have to chase every sale and make every effort, that's why McArdle and Baynes are recruiting someone new to the team, to introduce new selling techniques and boost sales."

Laura smiled. His answer hadn't matched the reason Andy had given her earlier, that they were rushed off their feet and needed an extra pair of hands. No, there was something not right and Laura decided to keep that to herself for the time being. "No wonder you've had to work so hard Gyle, poor you." She stroked his face and smiled. "Run off your poor wee feet, slaving away just for us. Things are bound to get better soon. Can I get you a beer?"

"Mmm, that would be great, thanks."

The next day Laura called Mikey for advice. "How do I bring up the subject without getting Jodie into trouble for telling me? You know what he's like if I say Jodie told me, he'll be round there like a rat out of a hole."

Mikey laughed. "Good analogy."

"You know what I mean?"

"That's just it, I do!" he said, still laughing. "And if you say Natalie told you, then that wouldn't work either."

"I don't even know Natalie." Laura was getting a bit frustrated at the lack of options. The line was quiet for a while as they both thought.

"Are you still there?" Mikey called, suddenly.

"Yes, still here and wondering, feeling sick to the stomach."

"I've got it, it has got to be the only way. The anonymous telephone call!"

"Who, how, what?" Laura was taken by surprise.

"I'll call in a favour from my cousin Judith. She was let down badly by her fiancé a few years ago in a similar way, so I know she will be up for it."

"Are you sure Mikey, but how will it work?"

"Just make sure you are out and Gyle's out and I'll get her to leave a message on your landline answer phone."

"You'll need to get the timing right Mikey, because if he gets the message before me he'll just wipe it, and say nothing."

"Mmm." Mikey thought for a moment. "You're right and he'll also be alerted to the fact that someone out there is ready to tell you and it'll give him time to create his own story. We'll have to synchronise our time, Laura, and keep it real. I'll leave you to phone me, when the time's right, and I'll give Judith a call this afternoon to give her a 'heads up' on things."

Three days later Gyle was in another mood when Laura insisted he take time out to go with her to buy a baby walker for Kenzie. She was now walking round the furniture and Laura thought a little walking aid would be fun for her but it was just too bulky to take home on the bus. The arrangement had caused him to delay his plans slightly after work and he was irritated by the sudden demand on his time. Laura knew that when they arrived back home, he would simply drop Laura and Kenzie off at the front door with the pushchair and parcel then head straight off. She would pick up the message soon after.

"It's important, is it, this err... meeting you have?" Laura quizzed

"They are all important Laura, you know what the situation

is like, we just spoke about it the other night, or have you forgotten?"

The message on the answer phone was clear and straight to the point. Laura smiled when she saw the little red light indicating a message on the phone then remembered she would have to be furious when she played it back to Gyle. She eagerly lifted the phone and pressed the message button and listened as it played.

You have one message. Message was received today at seventeen ten. There was a click before the message played. *Hello, this is a message for Mrs Gyle Jamieson. Do you know that your husband is a lousy cheating bastard? He sleeps around and has affairs. I have evidence if he tries to deny it, and I will call you in a few days' time with all the details, times, places, everything. The information will shock you.*

Laura gasped; she was shocked at the message, and it wasn't what she had expected. She thought the focus would be on the Natalie incident, which was after all in the past, and something she could confront Gyle with without feeling compromised. This message set all that on fast forward implying this was happening now. She quickly called Mikey. He seemed to be waiting for her call as he answered almost immediately. "Hi, you heard it then?"

"Mikey, it's not what I thought Judith was going to say? What's happening?"

Mikey sighed. "Laura, Judith wondered why someone would call anonymously almost two years after the incident. She reckons, and I have to remind you she doesn't know Gyle or you, that if he did that then, there's every chance he's done it again."

Laura was silent.

"Honey, are you still there?"

"Uhhuh."

"Look Laura, that's not to say there's anything in it but it gives you a better platform to tackle things doesn't it? He can deny it, and I have no doubt he will, but then you can ask where the accusation came from. You can lead the conversation back to the time he met you, and it keeps it more general without pointing the finger at anyone, which is what you wanted." Laura thought for a moment then agreed. This way was good. It was right in your face, but it certainly delivered the message, and Judith was right to point out the invalid purpose of an anonymous message about something, which had happened so long ago. When Gyle returned, Laura calmly played the answer phone. He was in a fairly good mood and she watched his face pale and twitch slightly as the message hit loud and clear.

"Who the hell was that nutcase?" he yelled.

Laura shrugged. "What does she mean Gyle? What affairs, who with?"

Gyle looked at her. "The woman is deranged, how did she get this number anyway, it's ex-directory?"

Laura gulped quietly. It was something she'd forgotten. She looked at Gyle, shaking her head but studying his face carefully. "Why would someone make a call like that if there was nothing in it Gyle?"

"So you are calling me a liar and a cheat now?"

"I didn't say that," Laura said quietly and trying to keep the conversation controlled. "Could it be someone from the past who thinks you let her down? Perhaps it's an old girlfriend who has realised you're married now and she thinks it should have been her, I mean, what a catch she's missed out on!" Laura said

131

sarcastically, but it was missed and she smiled as Gyle agreed it could certainly be a possibility. Astounded by the extent of his conceit she probed further. "Did you ever cheat on your girlfriends before me Gyle?" She looked at him carefully, noting the change of expression, the awkward twitchy movement for a moment, then in an instant he was cold and calm and smiling again.

"Of course I cheated on my girlfriends, it's what guys do." He laughed. "They meet up for a lads' night out and the aim is to see who can get hooked up with the hottest tart. Sex is there, it's always there and you don't say no, not ever." He looked up at her. "Everyone does it, it doesn't mean anything. It's just a bit of fun, part of a good night out if you like. It all starts off by having a laugh with the lads, followed by a few drinks, and then a few bets on who can pull who, all ending with sex. When it's over you go back to your girlfriend, or your wife and you've had a good night out with the lads." Laura was shocked. Gyle hadn't even looked guilty or remorseful. It was all part of what he'd described as a normal and good night out, and she suddenly felt sick to her stomach, as she realised she didn't have to ask if he'd remained faithful to her. His last sentence said it all. *When it's over, you go back to your girlfriend, or your wife and you've had a good night out with the lads.* Remaining calm she smiled at him, without acknowledging the impact his words had on her. "Ah well, it's a good job those days are over for you Gyle," she said firmly, "or I'd cut your balls off and serve them to you for supper!" Laura didn't wait to see his face, and she didn't hear him when he replied quietly. "Psycho."

6

Morven Stewart's arrival at McArdle & Baynes was a momentous event. The tall leggy redhead from South Africa had an air of efficiency and confidence, which stood out among the small friendly staff. Up until now Gyle Jamieson had been the confident one, but even he sat in the shadow of Morven as she moved around the room examining everything from internal brochure displays to workstation layouts. While she continued on her survey of the premises, the staff sat watching, raising eyebrows to each other as she passed each desk, wondering who this woman was, until eventually she raised her head. "Good morning everyone, I'm Morven Stewart, joining you all on the staff of McArdle and Baynes." The staff continued to stare until Cameron, the young trainee, felt brave enough to break the silence. "Can I get you a coffee or something?"

"Yah," Morven answered, with only the slightest hint of a smile, then, walking towards the small coffee area, "That would be good, maybe you should get everyone a coffee then we can get the necessary preliminaries out of the way?"

Gyle stood watching, amazed at the confidence of this young woman. Here she was commanding the attention of everyone in the room, on her first day in a new job. He gave a wry smile as he placed his hands on his chin and up over his nose then relaxed again. She wasn't even a new boss, just another sales executive, and one who would be on a considerably lower grade than him. Yet as she glided across the room, with the air and presence of a senior executive, Gyle was impressed. Cameron looked uncomfortable and glanced towards his boss Gavin McArdle for approval. Gavin nodded; he too was amused at Morven's grand entrance and the effect she was having on the unusually quiet staff, as they turned round in their seats watching her every move. "Morven, welcome," Gavin boomed as he walked towards her with hand outstretched, then pulling some chairs nearer the staff table he ushered to them to gather for an impromptu coffee break. Noting the surprise on his employees' faces, Gavin placed a hand on Morven's shoulder. "We usually have coffee around ten-thirty, but it will be good to have an early one today so you can become acquainted with the staff." Morven smiled but said nothing. Gyle started to walk slowly towards the coffee table, slightly bemused by this stunningly attractive woman, who had not even looked his way. As he approached her he smiled, giving a slight tilt to his head, "Hi, I'm Gyle Jamieson."

"Hi Gyle Jamieson," she answered before turning to other staff members, gesturing to each for their own introductions. It wasn't the kind of reaction Gyle was used to and he was puzzled by her immediate reluctance to engage with him more directly. As he listened to this new employee, watching her body language, he realised he would struggle to sum her up. Did he like her? He wasn't sure. She was certainly attractively cool and aloof, with the same style and class his mother carried. However, for the time being, Gyle was just not sure how to relate to Morven Stewart. It was clear from the reception of the staff during coffee that it was an opinion shared by them too; and it was of great relief to everyone when Gavin took his new employee out to visit a prospective new client, giving the staff time to make their observations known.

"What did you make of her then?" Janice asked as soon as the two had disappeared out of the door.

"Bit of a madam?" Heather suggested.

"I thought she was hot!" Cameron commented, with a slight blush.

"Hot?" Dawn looked at him. "You need to get out more Cameron. The only thing hot about that one is the speed she'll chew you up and spit you out!"

They all laughed.

"She's certainly rattled a few cages here," Andy remarked. "What about you Gyle, what do you think?"

Gyle looked up from his desk. "Mmm."

"Mmm?" Came the collective response.

Gyle nodded. "I don't know what to think. Maybe we should give her a chance? From what I understand she has a great sales technique and..."

"Bet she has," sniped Janice, as Dawn laughed, agreeing in approval of the comment.

"As I was saying," Gyle continued, "she is apparently very good at her job, so perhaps if we can all try being nice to her, she might turn out to be someone we will come to admire and respect."

"I'm sure you'll be nice to her," Dawn teased, as she turned to her colleagues, giving them a wink.

Gyle shook his head. "Back to work, I think ladies." A response he made clear applied not only to Janice, Heather and Dawn but to Cameron and Andy too.

After that initial meeting, Morven Stewart kept herself to

herself, avoiding office chitchat and any attempts to befriend her. Over the next few weeks offers to join staff for lunch were politely declined and she arranged her diary, some thought deliberately, to avoid coffee time. "Suits me," Heather remarked one day, when the conversation had turned to the new employee. It was a feeling shared by most of the staff, but Gyle was becoming interested in his new colleague. It bugged him that she barely looked his way and even more that she seemed indifferent to his attempts of friendliness.

The opportunities to engage on a closer more personal level had been few as Gavin McArdle made it his priority to take care of an extended induction process with his new member of staff. It had been a quiet time for property sales, and seasonally so, but now more property was coming on to the market and Gavin was being called to attend to more urgent matters. As he was about to leave for yet another appointment Gyle stopped him. "I had a call from Mr and Mrs Finlay about an hour ago, they want us to market their house in Morningside. 'The Willows', I think they said."

Gavin looked up from his briefcase, as he crammed the last of the papers into the only remaining space available. "The Willows? I know that property, it's very nice Gyle, are you going over to have a look?"

"Yes, I thought I would take Morven with me, I don't think you've covered that area with her yet, and it would be interesting to get her take on things now she's been here for a while?"

"Good idea Gyle, and it gives me the opportunity to back off a bit. I tell you, she's a bit of a closed book, that one, see if you can soften up the edges a little at the same time." Then with the last forced click of the briefcase lock he hurriedly left the office.

The Willows was a beautiful family home set in landscaped grounds of over an acre. A little stream towards the outer boundary was home to three magnificent willow trees which stood proud, their vast thread-like branches flowing down towards the calm water, caressing the soft grassy banks at each side. Inside Gyle carefully examined the immaculate and sophisticated interior, commenting on the excellent choice of fabrics and style. "Mrs Finlay, you have a beautiful home here," he told her. "The snooker and games rooms are similar to the ones in my parents' house, and I know how great that was when I was growing up, having space for my friends to come over."

"Yes." Mrs Finlay smiled. "It was a great asset when the children were younger, at least their friends had somewhere to gather, and we knew where they were. Now they are all grown, with families of their own, and as beautiful as this place is, it's becoming too big for us. My husband and I feel it is better that we move on now, while we are still relatively fit and active and we can settle into a place which will suit us better in the coming years." She looked towards Morven, who had said nothing since the first hello on arrival, and was now just walking round the house again, in quiet contemplation.

"She's the strong silent type," Gyle quipped as he noticed his prospective client carefully watching his colleague.

"So I see," she said thoughtfully. "How much do you think we should be asking, and what do you think it will achieve?"

"Oh I don't think she's worth that much!" Gyle joked, referring to Morven, then observing Mrs Finlay's forced smile he quickly brought matters back to a more professional level. "I would recommend it go on the market at offers over one-and-a-half-million and I wouldn't expect offers to be any less than one-million-three-hundred-and-fifty. A property like this has the potential to attract offers at around one-million-seven-hundred-and-fifty, when the market is strong."

"That's a bit of a difference, can't you be a little more precise?"

"Sorry Mrs Finlay, unfortunately the market has been slow for a number of years now. At one time 'offers over' meant exactly that, and we could predict almost exactly what a property would sell for." He looked out of the window. Morven was walking in the grounds now, and for a moment he was caught up in her beauty. The sun was shining on her flame-red hair as the soft breeze occasionally caught a few strands, blowing them over her face.

"And now?" Mrs Finlay prompted, bringing Gyle's attention back into the room.

"For the past few years property has been selling at prices greatly below valuation, but there are signs the market is picking up. Unfortunately there's still a lack of confidence out there, and some really good properties still don't sell."

"Do you think this will?"

"I would be very surprised if this was on the market for too long," Gyle assured her. "If I had the money I'd buy it myself!"

"That's very reassuring Mr Jamieson, thank you. I'll speak to my husband tonight and give you a call in the morning, if that's how these things are done now?"

"That'll be great, if you decide to go ahead, we'll send our photographer over to take a few pictures and get the marketing process going. Someone from the office will take you through it all." With that remark Gyle left, calling on his colleague who was standing by the willow trees. "You didn't say much," Gyle challenged her. "In fact you were a bit rude."

"Hey, it was your call, I just came for the ride," she answered lackadaisically.

Gyle shook his head and laughed. "Time to join the real world darling." Then, looking her straight in the eye, "What do you think then? How much would you recommend they sell this place for, and how much do you think it'll fetch?"

Morven looked up at the house again, and across the beautifully manicured gardens before turning to Gyle. "Peanuts," she muttered, then before he had the chance to reply she added, "about one-and-half-million, and if they are lucky and the right person comes along at the right time, tops I would say one-six."

"And that's peanuts?"

"Hell yeh."

"What kind of properties have you been selling then?"

"Properties that cut me that kind of deal." She laughed, looking at his stunned expression. "I could buy this tomorrow, if I wanted to."

"Before you wake up?"

"One day," Morven smirked, changing the subject. "Come on, last one back to the car buys the drinks." It was the first time Morven had shown any sign of friendliness, and taken aback by her change of character, Gyle found he was suddenly lagging behind the fleeting Miss Stewart as she ran to the car parked some way off.

"Tea or coffee?" Gyle asked as he opened the car, panting and sweating slightly.

"Get real, I want wine, a very large glass of it," she looked at him, "and fast!"

"You're a cheeky mare aren't you?"

"You have to be."

Several large glasses of wine later, Morven Stewart was becoming a lot easier to talk to. Intrigued by her earlier remark,

Gyle dared to ask about her past property-selling experience. "What did you mean about cutting a deal?" he asked curiously.

"Gyle, you know in any business you have to take risks?"

"Yes."

"Sometimes you have to be brave and strong enough to take those risks, the high stake risks, if you want to get on in life and achieve your potential." She reached out and touched his cheek. "You are not there yet, sweetie."

"Where?"

"You are not brave enough, not strong enough, too conformist."

"What do you mean, not brave enough or strong enough, you hardly know me," Gyle protested.

"Oh but I do, and that's another thing, you're not intuitive enough."

"Whatever," Gyle turned away. "I think you've had too much to drink."

"See!"

"See what?"

"Not brave enough. Come here." She leaned across the table and pulled his tie so his face was almost touching her own. He quickly pulled back. "Not brave enough," she scoffed, and the two sat looking into each other's eyes for a brief moment before Gyle stood up and slowly walked over to where she sat. She was still smirking at him as she watched him move towards her. Without speaking he kneeled down and grabbed her by the hair and kissed her passionately on her neck then her lips while fondling her breast. Breaking from his grasp, Morven pushed him away. "People are watching!" she gasped. He laughed as he moved back to his seat.

"Brave enough now for you?"

"No way near enough," she teased. "I thought you were married?"

"I am, kind of."

"What? You are either married or you're not, there's no 'kind of' about it."

"It's a situation that could change soon," Gyle began...

"When she hears about the kiss?"

"No it's more complicated than that, she's got issues, mental issues since her parents died. We fight constantly, and she puts me through hell. I'm not sure how much I can take, quite frankly. I've tried everything I know but it's just not working out."

"Kids?"

"Yes, a little girl, Kenzie, she's about nine months old now. That's why I stay, you understand?"

"Yah, poor kid."

"Are you married or have kids or both?"

"No way, I fly solo, it's safer that way," Morven said dismissively.

"I thought you were the brave one?"

"Oh I'm brave, but I don't carry passengers."

"Brave enough to go back to work?"

"I said I was brave not suicidal, you got to be kidding I'm blitzed!"

Gyle stood up again. "Come on then I'll take you home." Morven was already on her feet, refusing the offer of a lift home, instead insisting she take the bus. Her attempts at keeping a distance between them were obvious. Morven Stewart was a strong independent woman, that was clear and she had Gyle exactly where she wanted him.

When Gyle arrived home that afternoon, Laura was surprised. He was much earlier than usual and although he was clearly drunk he was in an unusually happy mood. "Good day honey?" Laura wasn't sure what to make of him as she played with Kenzie on the floor of the lounge.

"Great day, but I'm starving, what's for eating?"

"Dinner's not even prepared yet," she laughed.

"A sandwich will do then, anything." Laura picked Kenzie up and made her way to the kitchen. By the time she brought the sandwich and a cup of tea through to the lounge, Gyle was fast asleep on the sofa. She covered him up with one of Kenzie's cot blankets and let him sleep it off, not daring to imagine what could have made him so happy.

In the morning, the account of his time spent with Morven Stewart was very different from reality. "She's a real weirdo, Laura, and a lazy bitch to make things worse."

Laura looked up from her breakfast. "So why were you so drunk Gyle?"

"Oh, I was so pissed off with her hanging about all morning, I popped into that little wine bar. You know the one on Hope Street? Well I bumped into Ben and one drink led to another."

"Oh." Laura raised her eyebrows and poured him another cup of coffee. She was surprised, and unconvinced his reasons for arriving home early, worse the wear for drink, had anything to do with Ben. After all, she was quite sure Ben still worked miles away and he was rarely in the city during the week. "I'll need to have a word about this next time I see him, leading you astray like that," she joked, as he choked on his coffee and almost coughed the words out.

"Don't you dare, he'll think I'm a real wimp." It was enough to satisfy Laura that her suspicions were not unfounded, and as he left for work she called out to him.

"It might be best to stay away from Morven Stewart today Gyle!"

Morven Stewart completely ignored Gyle at work that morning. She sat quietly at her desk, working online and looking through some unsold properties before making a few phone calls. Gyle tried to speak to her discreetly, but she gave him no opportunity to do so. He was now completely focussed on this woman, this strange infuriating woman, who just gave him the tiniest hint of interest before closing down the shutters again, as though he didn't exist. She had teased him with throwaway comments he didn't quite understand and the depth of her character fascinated him. Her determined isolation from people had not gone unnoticed but it drew him to her; he wanted to know her more. Gyle realised he knew nothing about this woman, except her name, that she had come from South Africa, and had no children. And yet he had almost poured out his life story to her, leaving him wondering how that happened? After all, he was usually the guarded secretive one and now the roles had reversed, without him even realising. The last month at work had been frantic for Gyle, due to the usual last-minute panic to conclude sales in time for the new school term. The pressure forced his attention away from Morven Stewart and her easy acceptance of the situation irritated him; but not as much as her reluctance to pick up where they had left off after their visit to The Willows some weeks before. Gyle was eager to get to know her better and her cool, distant air tormented him to distraction. She occupied most of his thoughts at work and at home Laura noticed his mind was very much elsewhere. Laura put this down to the manic conditions at the office but Gyle's strange mood was very different from any she'd known before. He was quiet and preoccupied and he spent a lot of time just staring out of the window into the garden. Only when the market began to slow down again at the start of the new school term did Gyle have an opportunity to have a brief word with Morven. "The Willows sold for one-six a few days ago," he told her, hoping to open up a conversation.

"Mm, it's what I thought," she said without looking up from her desk, and then turning the opposite direction towards Janice sitting beside her, she asked quietly, "Have you ever sold property abroad?"

Janice thought for a moment. "No but Gyle sold a development in the Cayman Islands a few years ago. It wasn't really us, as in McArdle and Baynes, more like through us, if you get what I mean?"

Morven looked surprised. "I see," she said almost in a whisper then carried on reading her monitor. Gyle overheard the quiet conversation, and he waited for Morven to say something but she didn't.

It was a few weeks later before Morven spoke to Gyle again. He had gone to see a property on the outskirts of town, and as he walked to his car after the appointment he saw her across the road. She was sitting on a small wall and she stood up as he walked past her. "What's happening?" she asked, now walking beside him as he approached his car.

"It's been a rental property," Gyle explained, assuming she was there to see it, and trying to keep the conversation on a purely professional level. "Tenants move out in a couple of weeks and the owners want to sell. There's no point in marketing it yet, it needs a complete refurbish."

Morven shrugged, with obvious disinterest. "It's a bit different from the properties in the Cayman Islands then?"

Gyle was startled. "Who told you about that?" he asked, pretending not to have overheard her brief conversation with Janice.

"Never mind that, tell me about the development, I'm interested." It was the first Morven had spoken to Gyle in weeks and now she was standing there beside him in the street, like a long-lost friend catching up on the news. He was taken aback by her sudden eagerness to strike up a conversation.

"Not here, lets grab a coffee. I know somewhere quiet we could go for a chat." He opened the car door.

"My car's over there." She pointed to a little Suzuki Swift across the road.

"Ah mobile at last. No wine today then," he teased.

"Not yet."

As Gyle sipped the last of his coffee he watched Morven's face light up in reaction to what he had told her about the Cayman Island development. She sat staring into her empty cup, smiling for a while then looked up. "Brilliant! Pretty damn ruthless but brilliant."

Gyle smiled, it wasn't the reaction he was expecting but then again this was Morven Stewart, and he was beginning to realise that when it came to her nothing was expected. "Do you think so?" he asked. "I made a lot of enemies at the time."

"Yes, God yes, but you came out of it reasonably well did you not?"

"Enough to pay for Manor Place and the car, just over half a million altogether," Gyle said proudly but Morven laughed.

"You were shafted!"

"Get lost." Gyle shook his head dismissively.

"What would you say if I told you that together we could make millions?"

"Have you been drinking?" he laughed. "I'd say that's got to be the craziest thing I've heard in a long time."

"You think so? You think I'm crazy?" Morven was seriousl she pushed her coffee cup to one side and sat staring at him. "Well you're right, I am crazy. I am real crazy. I take huge risks for high returns but I've never failed yet. I thought the Cayman Islands deal might have given you the slightest hint of what can be possible, but hey, if you've missed it, then okay, I won't waste any more of your time." She stood up; then, reaching down for her briefcase, moved away from the table. "Thanks for the coffee."

"Wait Morven," Gyle called to her and she turned towards him smiling gently.

"You're not brave enough Gyle, and quite frankly I don't think you have the balls!" With that remark she walked out of the café, leaving Gyle even more confused than before. She had done it again; it was infuriating, she'd made crazy half statements, and walked out on a half-finished conversation, which left him wanting more. When he spoke to her again it was by phone a few days later. Morven was already at the office and Gyle was still at home. He was now desperate to speak to Morven and something told him it was going to take some time and a lot of privacy. It was the week before Kenzie's first birthday and Gyle persuaded Laura to visit a huge toy store out of town to find something suitable for the occasion. He called his mother to go with them, knowing they'd not be back until way after lunch, as was Carla's style and this would give him the time and space he needed. It was just after nine-thirty and as Gyle waved his family off with one hand, he was calling Morven's direct line with the other. "Morven?" he spoke quietly. "Are you free to come over to my place just now? I really need to speak to you about the conversation we started the other day. Pretend you are speaking to someone else, and consider the conversation confidential. Understand?" Morven understood completely, and in a louder more officious tone, "certainly sir, what was the address there?" Morven scribbled the address on her notepad. "And that's Penicuik did you say?" Morven ripped the sheet from the pad as she stood up before replacing the receiver. A few minutes later Gyle called in sick, he wanted time to listen to what Morven had to say, and he wanted to know all of it, without her floating out of the conversation again, leaving him hanging on. Gyle prepared coffee and as Morven took a few sips her eyes surveyed the stylish home of her colleague. Photographs of Kenzie hung on the walls and one or two stray toys lay on the floor. Kicking them to one side, Gyle pulled up a chair and sat beside Morven at the kitchen table. "I want to know more about this crazy claim." He took a gulp of his coffee before settling back in his seat.

"You still don't believe me?" she said playfully.

"It's not easy, Morven."

She put her cup down on the table. "Do you really think I came halfway across the world to work in a little estate agents in Edinburgh?"

"Are you telling me you didn't?" Gyle's eyes were fixed on Morven's face, challenging her to tell him more.

"Your little development in the Cayman Islands?" she started, taking another sip of coffee. "How many properties are we talking about?"

"One-hundred-and-twenty-seven," he said boastfully.

"And you made what, about half a million, right?" He

nodded. She moved her face closer to his. "Think about this. A small development of thirty-nine properties in Mombasa."

"I'm imagining." Gyle teased, closing his eyes.

"It was targeted at the American high-end second home market," she continued quietly and slowly, making sure he was taking in every word.

Gyle opened his eyes, and took another gulp of coffee. "Mm, good strategy."

"It made me six million."

Gyle choked. "What? How much?" He almost shrieked the words through a coughing fit. Morven hit his back, and then as he gradually regained some composure he threw some negatives into the conversation. "I'll bet dealing with the Nairobi authorities was a nightmare, and then there's the Kenyan builders and suppliers. It must have been a nightmare, you'd have earned it!"

Morven was now shaking her head and looking very smug. "I had no outlay at all and no hassle."

"What about planning and architects. Don't tell me they came cheap?"

"I paid nothing for either. So, are you brave enough?" she teased.

"I'm certainly more interested," he said cautiously as he stood up and walked over to the coffee machine. Then, pouring two more cups, "Tell me more."

Morven looked at him. "No Gyle, that's as far as I go until I know you're in." If you're not I can't say any more, it's all part of the risk factor. If you're in I have a contract for you to sign. If you're not we end the conversation here and I go back to the office." She looked at him, waiting for his response.

"You expect me to sign a contract based on the flimsy piece

of information you've just given me?" He sat back down at the table, running his fingers through his thick dark hair.

"Let me see," Morven began. "I've said I can make you a multi-millionaire with no outlay from you, in a couple of years at the most. I've told you it's a high-risk project, but not financially. What more do you need to know at this stage? The real question Mr Jamieson is, are you brave enough? This is what I was saying before. Can you dance with danger? Do you have the balls for it? Are you ready Gyle, to take the chances which will change your life forever?" Morven was teasing him now, daring him. "Live a bit Gyle, while you still can."

"Why me?" he asked, flattered that she was eventually acknowledging him. She had kept him at arm's length and it had driven him mad. Now she wanted him and he didn't want to say no. Morven was exciting, dangerously so, and he wanted to spend more time with her. He wanted the excitement, and if he could make a fortune having fun, then she was right. He would be crazy to pass up on the chance.

Morven was standing behind him now, her chin almost resting on his shoulder. She kissed the side of his neck then nibbled his ear. "Because I believe in you," she whispered. "I know you can do this."

He turned round and pulled her to him and kissed her. He stood up and kissed her again before pulling off her jacket, as she responded to his passion. His hands were on her breasts and he loosened her blouse, then her bra. Soon his mouth was on her breasts, licking her nipples as his hands moved slowly inside her panties. She was unzipping his jeans, her hands exploring his throbbing manhood. He led her upstairs and pushed her gently on to the bed, removing every piece of clothing. His tongue was everywhere, caressing every inch of her

149

body then he slowly moved on top of her and inside. She responded to every move he made, to every touch and every kiss until eventually the peak of their passion ended with a loud groan from Gyle. He was sweating and panting. Morven lay seductively beside him, touching her own breasts with one hand and stroking her inner thigh with the other. "Gyle," she purred and before she could say any more he was back on top of her again in a frenzied act of passion. Morven let out a high-pitched gasp before he groaned again and they both relaxed, still entwined and breathless. They lay together for several minutes before Gyle whispered, "Let's go for it!"

"What again?" Morven teased, knowing he meant something very different.

Eventually Gyle sat up on the end of the bed. "I need another coffee!" He discarded his clothes and put on his pyjama shorts and dressing gown and made his way back downstairs to the kitchen, leaving Morven to get dressed.

When she came down she coolly handed him a contract, which he glanced over before signing. "It just says you are in contract to Burlington Park Estates, and should you break contract before the end of the project you will be liable to pay the company twenty-five thousand pounds."

Gyle looked shocked. "What?"

"You are not going to back out now are you?" Morven teased.

"It would seem I couldn't afford to, even if I did want to back out," he replied nervously. "So no, I'm not going to back out now."

"Good, you are going to have to trust me. I am taking all the risks your part is very simple but I need guarantees. I'm sure you'll understand."

"Who runs Burlington Park Estates?"

"We do!" Morven smiled while Gyle gulped hard.

"Okay," he said cautiously, "tell me more."

This time Gyle listened intently as Morven explained everything before unveiling her plan to financial paradise. The development in Mombasa was the third Morven had been involved in, boosting her finances to over fifteen million pounds. She told Gyle this latest plan would be her last and would take in an ambitious three developments in as many countries. The venture was guaranteed to leave them extremely wealthy. "I guess you're sinking your fifteen million into it then?" Gyle asked. 'Making it your high-stake risk?" Morven shook her head. "Are you mad? Did I not already say there was no financial outlay?"

"It's impossible," Gyle insisted.

"Shut up and listen." Morven moved a little closer to him again. "The project focuses on developments in Cape Verde, Dubai and the Seychelles. They are high-end boutique properties, which you will sell on behalf of Burlington Park Estates."

"And we do this at work?"

"No, and yes. Not officially, but we need to set up a phone number which will be diverted to your new company mobile, and as such you might get calls at work, but I'll leave you to juggle that."

"One of the high risks?"

"I guess so," Morven continued. "But we should be halfway finished in six months, so it's not long to wing it."

"Six months!" Gyle gasped in disbelief. "The plans won't even have been passed in six months, get real!"

Morven groaned. "Relax, the plans are completed, I have

151

them at my flat. I even have a little model site, which we can photograph. I've brought this stuff with me, but we, err... I mean you, sell the property off-plan and online." She looked up, noticing the confusion on his face. "Don't worry, I'll even give you a start on that one."

"Who deals with the overseas stuff then?" Gyle asked, his mind whirling around like a washing machine.

"No one," Morven laughed. "Look Gyle, the whole scam is so damn simple, it's ridiculous."

"Scam? You never said anything about it being a scam?" He was shocked.

"Of course it's a bloody scam, you clown, but it's a good one, trust me."

Gyle put his head in his hands and groaned. "It looks like I'm going to have to."

"If you would shut up for a minute, I'll run through it." Morven was losing patience. "There are currently three active developments in Cape Verde, Dubai and The Seychelles, owned and marketed by other companies. I have the plans and documentation for them all. We need to adapt and reprint schedules, but I'll do that at the office, when I get a chance. That's another risk. First rule, no one must know about this here, I think you'll find that in your contract."

Gyle sighed. "No doubt," he said, wondering what he had got himself into.

"We market the properties on a phased build basis which will take over three years, as far as the customer is concerned."

"I thought you said six months?"

Morven looked at him. "Shhh. Yes, that's at our end." Gyle looked confused but Morven ignored the look and continued. "The properties are sold off-plan and secured by a deposit. We take money at the beginning of each phase, and there are lengthy delays, due to international transactions and red tape." Gyle was still confused, but Morven carried on. "The contracts are all signed at the point of the first deposit, and half the money for the property is paid at the six-month stage, before the delays begin. The contracts are watertight and protect us. If they back out in the first year, they don't get their initial deposit back. We send the photographs of the development as it progresses." She looked up to see Gyle about to ask another question but before he could she said, "I have all the photographs." She looked at Gyle. "You still don't get it do you?" He shook his head. "It's a good job I'm taking care of the paperwork then, isn't it?" He was staring at her now, completely at a loss for words. "Bottom line, Gyle, is that the properties don't exist!"

"What?" He almost choked again. He took a huge gulp of coffee and sat staring out of the window, then towards Morven. "You can't be serious?"

"Well, they do exist as it happens, it's just that they don't actually belong to us."

"What if people want to visit in person?"

"We tell them we don't have agents who can take them near the development for health and safety reasons, which is why we have the photographs, taken by the builders. Don't worry we offer huge discounts to compensate the fact they can't visit and we also offer free legal assistance through the red tape, which of course I take care of under different company names."

"That's very generous of you,." Gyle laughed.

"If someone did go and visit, they would see a site in progress. It's just not ours!"

"Clever and cunning," Gyle agreed but with reservation. "How can it possibly end happily?"

"Three months, or sooner depending on how things work out, towards the end of the process, after most of the money has been cleared by the bank, the company disappears and we bale. By that time the money has been invested overseas under another company name and we walk away."

"What if someone recognises us?"

"We don't sell to people here, you ninny." Morven laughed at his naivety. "We are targeting overseas buyers from Monaco, Dubai and America. They are not going to walk into Burlington Park Estates – and obviously we don't sell the Dubai property to the people in Dubai."

"Oh my God Morven, this is huge. It's a major adrenalin rush for God's sake!" He stared at her. She was cool, calm and controlled like she had just described the layout of a new house, while he was shaking and sweating and almost hyperventilating. He took a walk into the garden to calm down. It was one of those cold but sunny days and there was no breeze. He took in a deep breath then walked back into the kitchen. "When can we start?"

"Any time, it's not as if we have to present the plans is it?" Morven teased.

"Marketing?" Gyle asked.

"Web based, but I'll give you some leads to start with." Morven moved towards him and kissed him softly on the cheek. "Drink?"

"Bloody right!" Gyle gasped and reached for a bottle of wine. "Chianti okay?" Morven nodded then watched as he poured two large glasses. Gyle took two large gulps then settled down as they finished the bottle more slowly. Morven moved over to him closely as he sipped the last few drops and she kissed him. She pulled at the belt of his dressing gown and it fell open.

Her hand brushed against him. "This is turning me on," she purred as she led him back upstairs to the bedroom for another session of intense wild sex. It had been a great morning for Morven. She had achieved what she came to do, not only there in the home of Gyle Jamieson, but also in Scotland. Gyle couldn't believe his luck at the sudden turn of events and everything this new encounter would promise. As Morven hurriedly dressed for work, Gyle quickly cleaned the house, carefully clearing away cups and wine glasses. "I'll make a start on the paperwork Gyle, you don't need to worry about that side of things. I'll just need your signature on a few documents so that your assets are protected as we set up the company," Morven said casually as she kissed him before heading out of the door. "Okay," he said, finding comfort in the word 'protected'. After Morven left he ran upstairs to tidy the bed, suddenly realising he couldn't remember how Laura had arranged the pillows so he remained in his pyjama shorts and dressing gown and he would later tell her he had come home from work sick and gone to bed for an hour or two.

Later that afternoon Laura, Kenzie and Carla arrived home, laden with shopping. Gyle was in a great mood and as Laura hauled out boxes of toys and one pretty dress after another, he was happy to play with Kenzie as Laura took the presents upstairs. Carla moved to the kitchen to put the kettle on.

"We had a great day Gyle," she said. "Laura's a great girl."

"I know," Gyle agreed, amused at his mother's unusually gracious comment.

"You'd better be good to her, do you hear?"

"What's she been saying to you?"

Carla laughed. "Nothing you need to know."

The following week Kenzie celebrated her first birthday among friends and family. Kristen brought a huge cake, which looked, like a princess's castle. At the bottom it said 'Happy First Birthday Kenzie.' Jodie and Mikey arrived together although they were no longer a couple and Kenzie loved to see them. Scott couldn't take time out from the practice, so Laura was pleased to see Kristen and her mum Yvonne arrive for the party. Gyle was especially charming and thrilled in seeing his daughter toddle across the room amid the fun and laughter. By the time everyone was gone, and Kenzie was bathed and tucked up in bed he was still in a celebratory mood. "Come and have some Prosecco with me Laura, we need to celebrate this day together, now we are free from the crowds," he joked, and they sat down together happy with the great day it had been for them both. Laura smiled quietly, as she remembered the rocky start to their relationship when she first discovered she was expecting Kenzie. She could never have dreamed things would turn out so well. Here she was sipping Prosecco to celebrate the first birthday of their little girl with her husband Gyle sitting next to her. She found great comfort in seeing Gyle so happy, unaware his mood had nothing to do with Kenzie's birthday or that they were a family. He was still on a high as the morning's events flashed in images through his mind. The prospect of becoming a property magnate and a millionaire, as he saw it, still excited him and, keeping his word to Morven, he said nothing to Laura about his latest plans.

Since his last meeting with Morven, she had prepared a number of documents, slipping them discreetly between property schedules at work for Gyle to sign. She returned to her usual distant, cool self, barely speaking to him in the office unless she had to, making it difficult for him to catch even a few words with her. Eventually she provided him with a company mobile and he felt happier being able to contact her more often. When he visited her flat in Barnton, an area out of the city centre, he felt happier still. It was a small flat, not very stylish and Gyle wondered why someone who claimed to be a multi-millionaire would rent such a basic flat and not make it more comfortable. "It's a commodity," she later explained. "When the project is over, I'm moving on. You honestly don't think I would want to spend the rest of my life in this cold damp country do you?" She laughed. "No Gyle, this is my operational base, and it suits the purpose." Gyle understood. It wasn't something he'd thought about, and it suddenly hit him. When the property scam was over, he'd be rich beyond his wildest dreams, and that would open up the world to him. He had never thought about what he might do beyond that, or where he might want to live. He could live anywhere in the world. He wouldn't ever have to work again. Realising he would soon be able to adopt any lifestyle his heart desired, he found it hard to focus on what he really wanted right now, but he was pretty sure none of it would include Laura and Kenzie.

7

The interest in the Seychelles properties based at Sunset Beach kept Gyle busy, particularly with inquiries from the American market, as Morven rightly predicted. Within the first two weeks he had sold three properties each costing slightly less than four million pounds, and the interest didn't look like it was about to slow down. He wasn't too surprised, the villas looked amazing, all constructed using natural materials and muted tones of wood, rattan and pebbles. The interiors boasted marble floors, soft breezy curtains and a stunning light-oak cascading staircase. Outside a large swimming pool overlooked the Indian Ocean and the tastefully furbished deck enjoyed panoramic views, which took in beautifully designed landscape gardens. The properties were breathtaking and Gyle was happy to help prospective buyers come to the decision to buy. As he talked over plots and colour themes, he had to remind himself that none of it was real. He would have bought a property himself if he had the money and laughed at the irony of it all. Morven was efficient with the paperwork and Gyle's only task was to sign a few documents as each deal was confirmed. The Cape Verde properties in St Vincent were selling for just less than two million pounds each. There the two-storey villas boasted top quality furnishings and exotic local stone. Each property had its own gym and spa with private terraces looking over the bay of Mindelo. They were stunning, and selling faster than Gyle could cope with, especially with the incentives Morven was throwing into the deals. Free conveyance, free legal services dealing with all the red tape and free regular reports on progress all helped to convince prospective buyers they were getting a good deal. However, the big money-earner was in Dubai. Here the spectacular beachfront properties were selling for more than six million pounds each. Gyle gasped at the price when Morven told him, and he was stunned so many people not only had that kind of money, but also that they were so casual about spending it. "We're dealing with the big boys now, it's pocket money to them," she told him excitedly. "This is where it all starts to get interesting." Gyle sighed. He was terrified rather than excited. Dealing with the probing questions from extremely wealthy businessmen and Sheiks terrified him. Convincing them not to engage with their own trusted lawyers was very risky, verging on dangerous and he struggled to maintain the level of confidence Morven had in conversation with them. He was well out of their league; the conversations now amounted to high-level business deals, and far removed from the friendly polite chat he was used to, selling Edinburgh flats and houses. Although many of the questions were casual, almost conversation starters, Gyle found them difficult and uncomfortable. Engaging in conversation with these people made him feel tense and nervous and the amounts of money involved made him feel sick. As he struggled to gain a more controlled confidence Morven continued to encourage him with her usual casual coolness. "Come on baby, we're well into this now. A few more months and we can start making plans for the future. Just keep calm, look over the schedules and convince yourself, it'll all become easier." He took her advice and looked over the schedules of the Dubai properties. Each five-bedroomed villa was the ultimate in luxury, built on three floors with panoramic sea views and each with its own private jetty; they were in a different class to anything he'd ever seen before. Every villa was built to an exceptionally high standard with a roof terrace, private garden, pool and terraces looking out across the Arabian Gulf. No expense had been spared in luxury design, fittings and furnishings. Weeks later Gyle had sold four properties but the venture had made him tense and nervous again. He totalled up the value of the properties he had sold and was staggered to see that it had come to fifty million pounds already. He called Morven frantically, wanting to quit. "Gyle, honey, you can't do that yet," she soothed, then in her usual calm voice, "Remember we only get about fifty to seventy-five percent of the sale because we bale before completion. If we baled now we'd be lucky to go away with twelve million. It's not worth all that work and risk, we've still a way to go."

Gyle was staggered. "I guess we could get by on twelve million," he argued but Morven was having none of it.

"Look Gyle, I'll cut you some slack. If you want to bail at the halfway stage we can review things then, but you are going to have to sell a lot more properties before we can do that to make it worth our while. And I suppose if we bail around then, we can put clients off contacting us for a while longer and disappear before anyone realises they've been hit." She sounded so normal, casual; there was no hint of panic or concern in her voice at all, but Gyle really wanted out. He was terrified of being caught and now dreaded every email which came into his inbox and every call he had to make. When the sound of his mobile rang, he shuddered, desperately wanting to ignore it but

160

knowing to do so would only help to raise alarm bells. He couldn't understand how Morven could remain so cool, while he felt as though he was dying from the inside out. He couldn't sleep and barely managed to concentrate at work. He found it difficult to eat and Morven's conversation no longer helped as he realised more and more what high risk really meant. Gyle desperately wanted to end the scam now and forget he had ever been a part of it, but he was trapped and forced to carry on until the end.

A couple of months and several sales later, Laura was beginning to worry even more about her husband. He had become distant and agitated and he'd spent a couple of weekends away at what he described as Property Fairs. Laura wasn't too sure he was telling the truth and, sensing his strange mood, didn't want to dig too deeply. When he came home late from work one evening, she casually asked him if he was okay. He looked at her and his words surprised and worried her. "Oh Laura, sweet simple Laura, why am I not more like you?" The words were in stark contrast to his usual putdowns and he looked pale and troubled.

She turned to him. "I don't know what's going on Gyle?" She looked to see if he was listening before carrying on, speaking slowly and firmly. "But whatever it is it's not having a good effect on you. Look at yourself Gyle you are exhausted and jumpy. It's not like you at all. Now, you can tell me what's going on, or not, but whatever it is Gyle, you'd better sort it out before it kills you." She put her hands up to his face and stroked his cheek, hoping he might share the load but he turned away.

"I can't tell you Laura, and I wish I could, but then again you wouldn't understand." He was near to tears and Laura had never seen him like this before. She had a terrible feeling of dread knowing something was far wrong, but she couldn't imagine what it could be. Plucking up the courage she moved closer to him again.

"Is there someone else?" she asked, terrified he was going to say yes. It would certainly explain his absences and quiet distance.

Instead he laughed loudly. "Do you think I would be like this if there was someone else?" His answer startled Laura and she waited for an explanation but he just shook his head laughing loudly before walking out of the room, leaving her with more questions than answers.

The Dubai properties were becoming popular with buyers from Monaco and every confirmed sale put more pressure on Gyle. Try as he might, he couldn't see how they could simply walk away without being caught. Despite Morven's cool assurances, he was counting the weeks and number of sales away, eager to draw a line under the whole sordid thing. He now regretted ever getting involved with Morven Stewart; even if it had been exciting at first, the pressure he now experienced was overwhelming. He still couldn't eat or sleep and he was exhausted and nervy. When Laura suggested he visit the doctor to give him something to help him calm down, or to help him sleep, he agreed, much to her surprise, and it made her worry even more. It was uncharacteristic for Gyle to be so submissive and when he returned from the doctor's surgery a few hours later, immediately swallowing two pills before heading for bed, Laura's concern was great. As her husband slept soundly upstairs, the reasons for his deteriorating mental state puzzled her. He'd made it clear there was no one else, so what could be the problem? Laura's mind was buzzing with possibilities, eliminating each one as they came into her head. Eventually she settled on the only reason she could imagine would cause him to crumble in the way he displayed now. It had to be debt. She felt a sudden panic herself; had he allowed their finances to reach such a terrible state they may be facing financial ruin? Was he gambling? He'd certainly been out a lot lately. Was he making plans to sell the house? The more she thought about it the more her own level of panic grew. If Gyle wouldn't share his problems with her then she would have to try to find out herself; she had studied investigative journalism after all, now it was time to put it to the test. She could hear Gyle snoring upstairs and he'd not slept for days. Laura knew this might be her only opportunity to look through his briefcase and his laptop for clues. She was looking for bank statements, overdue accounts or demands for immediate payment. As she looked through the papers none of these emerged, but among the usual property schedules, a few unusual ones caught her eye, and with them some official-headed paper bearing the name Burlington Park Estates. She stopped for a moment to listen to her husband still snoring upstairs before returning her attention to the schedules. Laura carefully removed them from the briefcase, laying them down in front of her on the coffee table. She was confused; had Gyle changed jobs and not told her? Perhaps the job wasn't going well? She looked into the briefcase again and pulled out his appointment diary. It was clear all his appointments were local, and there was certainly no Burlington Park Estates that she knew about, but it was clear he was involved with the company in some way which involved overseas property. Laura gasped as she looked through the amazing schedules of properties, which had up until now been beyond her wildest imagination and she couldn't imagine why Gyle would be involved in any of them. She picked up his diary again and noticed the name 'Morven' featured in it on more days than made sense to her. He had claimed they didn't speak and yet according to his diary he had clearly been seeing her often, but never at the office. Was Gyle having an affair with Morven Stewart? If he wasn't, did she have something to do with the overseas properties? Laura quickly returned the papers to Gyle's briefcase together with the diary, as she feared she had uncovered something at least partly responsible for Gyle's state of mind. She wasn't sure if her findings were the root cause of her husband's change of mood, or just the tip of the iceberg. She reached for his laptop, fearful of what she might find. Laura gasped again as images of luxury properties danced across the screen in a slideshow, and she gasped even harder as she read the cost of each of them, which had been absent from the schedules in his briefcase. Quickly closing the file, her eye rested on an email to Morven and she took a deep breath as she read it. 'Morven, three more sales need your attention. Please process ASAP so we can bale ahead of plan when the time's right.' Laura quickly closed the laptop and replaced it back in the briefcase. Her hands were shaking as she sat staring at it for a few minutes then towards Kenzie who was playing quietly on the floor beside her. From the little she had seen, it was obvious he was involved in the selling of these properties for some reason, but whatever that was he was keeping it to himself and she had a gut feeling it wasn't good, but it was certainly major. It did answer one question, however. Morven Stewart was clearly involved. Lifting Kenzie up off the floor, Laura carried the tot through to the kitchen and sat her in the highchair while she made a cup of tea. Later as Kenzie sipped at some juice from her trainer cup and nibbled on a biscuit, Laura sat taking sips of tea, staring into the garden. She was going to have to keep an eye on Gyle, but she wasn't sure how. She didn't usually have access to his laptop so she couldn't begin to search for answers from the web unless she went to the library and then she worried what she might find. When Mikey called an hour later, Laura's mood brightened, taking her attention away from Gyle for a while.

"It's Doug's fiftieth birthday at the end of the month." His cheery voice made her smile. "Jodie's organising a surprise for him at Tattie Bogles and she wondered whether we could do a couple of duets for him?" he said excitedly. "Do you think you could get a sitter for the night?"

Laura sighed; she loved the idea of going back to Tattie Bogles and singing with Mikey again but she doubted Gyle would agree to go and it would be even less likely he would agree to watch Kenzie. "I'd love it Mikey, but I'll have to get back to you. I'm not sure I can find a sitter, and Gyle's a bit busy right now."

Mikey wasn't going to be put off easily. "Could we get together sometime anyway to go over a few numbers, in case you can make it?" he asked optimistically.

Laura smiled. "I'd love to Mikey, maybe I could meet you in town and we could look through what we've got over lunch some time?"

"Yeh that would be great." Mikey sounded delighted. "Give me a call when it's a good time for you Laura, and it's a date!"

Laura laughed at his choice of word 'date'. "Okay Mikey, I'll give you a call soon.' The interruption had been a welcome break for Laura as she braced herself again for what her life with

Gyle was about to bring to them all. Gyle slept all afternoon and through the night.

When he woke the next morning he looked so much more relaxed and even managed a smile for the first time in weeks. He looked at the clock then to Laura. "Don't tell me I slept right through!" He was shocked. "Those pills were strong, I've probably got about fifty missed calls!"

Laura stopped in her tracks. His phone! She had forgotten to check his phone and it annoyed her. "I didn't hear it ring," she told him breezily.

"That's because I put it on silent at the doctor's and kept it in my jacket pocket."

"Are you going into the office this morning?" Laura asked as she passed him some toast and marmalade. "Oh yes, I'd better get myself in and see what came in yesterday, but first I really need a shower." His mood was bright and now Laura was desperate to check his mobile while he showered. She waited until she heard the shower and quietly tiptoed upstairs and into the bedroom. Gyle's jacket lay over the chair in the room. She carefully pulled the phone out of his pocket and checked his calls and texts. He had sixteen text messages, all from Morven, but he hadn't opened them, so she couldn't read them without him knowing. She checked his missed calls. All ten were from Morven. She stood looking at the phone then heard Gyle turn the shower off so she quickly replaced the phone in his jacket again and hurried downstairs. When he appeared at the door of the kitchen, dressed in his suit with briefcase in hand, she smiled. "Has the world been looking for you then?" she asked jokingly.

"No, no calls or messages at all. I guess no one missed me," he lied, as he bent over and kissed her cheek. "I'd better get in to the office and see what's happening."

"I guess so," Laura answered as Gyle picked up the last piece of toast and made his way out of the house. "Gyle, I forgot to say it's Doug's fiftieth at the end of the month," she called out to him as he opened the door of his car. "They've called to see if we can go and whether I could do a couple of numbers with Mikey. Are you free?"

"Is it the last weekend of the month?"

"Yes, it will be, the Saturday."

"Sorry, I can't. I've another Property Fair, something that stupid bitch Morven's introduced to sell more properties. She's a real pain in the backside and I think the whole team is expected to stay over at the hotel for evening guests this time."

"Okay Gyle, I'll get Kristen and Scott to babysit and head over myself."

He stopped in his tracks and turned, surprised. "Okay then," he mouthed as he sat in the driver's seat and turned on the ignition.

When Laura met Mikey a couple of days later it was clear she had a lot on her mind. Mikey listened carefully to what she was telling him, occasionally shaking his head and covering his eyes with his hands. "Mikey," she said after she had told him what she had found, "you can't say anything to anyone, but tell me what you are thinking?"

He looked at her, his face serious and full of concern. "I'm thinking he's in something nasty up to his neck Laura. What exactly did he mean by 'bale out early'?"

Laura shrugged her shoulders. "I haven't a clue? I thought about doing some investigating to find out."

"No Laura, I would say the least you know about this the better because, if it is dodgy he will get caught out, in the end, and you will certainly be questioned too. I tell you Laura, stay well out of it, and forget you've seen any of this unless it's to the authorities. You probably know too much already."

"You don't think it's a legitimate business then?" Laura was desperately hoping it was.

"If it is legitimate why isn't it being done through McArdle and Baynes and why the secrecy if it's all above board?"

Laura shrugged again. "Because he's also having an affair with Morven Stewart?" They both sat in silence for a few minutes.

"Where did you say this Property Fair is taking place?"

"That's just it, I didn't. I haven't a clue." Laura said nervously, close to tears.

"I could make enquiries right now if you want? I could phone McArdle and Baynes and ask them where their Property Fair is?"

Laura shook her head. "What if there isn't one, Gyle would smell a rat. As far as I have been told, these Fairs are something Morven's introduced to boost sales."

Mikey agreed, and sat deep in thought before the waitress arrived breaking his concentration.

"What can I get you?" she asked, with pen poised on her notepad waiting for the order.

"Two baked potatoes with Mexican Chicken and a sausage and chips for the little one, please," Mikey said quickly, desperate to regain his train of thought. "I've got it!" he said at last. "I'll call McArdle and Baynes and ask if they are open over the weekend. If they have an event, they are sure to mention it, wouldn't they?"

"Mm," Laura agreed, "but they could have a skeleton staff on I suppose to keep the place open?"

"I can see where you're coming from but I'm pretty sure

they'd tell me if they had an event, they'll want as many customers as possible."

Laura nodded. "Okay, now what about Doug's party?"

"You found a sitter?"

"Kristen and Scott are coming to stay."

Mikey smiled. "Perfect."

As they looked through the song list Laura felt relaxed and happy. She could be free to be herself with Mikey, knowing his mood was always the same, and she felt safe in his company. Today, Mikey was in a particularly upbeat mood as he handed Laura some music he'd scribbled on a sheet of paper.

"I've written this music Laura, it has a real Scottish lilt to it, and I wondered whether you'd like to write the lyrics?"

Laura looked at the music. "It's sadly melodic," she said quietly as she hummed to the notes written on the sheet. "I could put something together Mikey, but I can't see it being party material, but would it matter if it was stuck in the middle of the happy songs?"

Mikey thought for a moment. "Actually, I was thinking that it might be good to have something sad and meaningful and very Scottish, as a sharp contrast to all the other stuff. It will make people stop and notice. It should go down well."

Laura was still humming the tune to herself, deep in thought. "I think you have a winner with this Mikey, I hope I can do it justice. I love the chorus. I'll give it a go and you can deliver your verdict on it." Mikey looked pleased and as they thumbed through the song list they chose two catchy tunes, which were favourites with the regulars. Laura was looking forward to it now.

The following day Mikey called to say McArdle and Baynes

would be open all weekend and there was no mention of any Property Fair. Laura then wondered whether the Property Fair was connected to the overseas property but without knowing where it might be, she had to put the thought to one side. But then Gyle had told her about it, and suggested it was work, now she thought about it, it couldn't relate to the overseas properties, otherwise he wouldn't have said anything about it to her. Mikey agreed to check out Burlington Park Estates online and he found something interesting. It was clear from the website that the company was owned and run solely by Gyle Jamieson, but the address was registered to an address in Barnton. There was no connection to McArdle and Baynes and, more relevant to the information he had searched for, no Property Fair, as Laura now suspected. The news of Gyle's prominent involvement would shock Laura but she had to know. "I don't know what's going on Laura," Mikey said quietly as he called that day, "but it's something major for sure. These properties are worth millions. Where has he found the finance to set this up?"

"His dad maybe?"

Mikey shook his head. "There's no mention of Alastair Jamieson, and if he was an investor he'd have to be named. And who has the property in Barnton?"

"I have no idea Mikey, it's the first I've heard. There must be a connection to Morven Stewart somewhere in this Mikey, I just don't know what yet?"

"Well Laura, I think we both know too much now already, I don't think we should probe any further."

It had been a bad day for Morven Stewart, and later for Gyle when she delivered some worrying news. Alarm bells began to ring when one of the American clients, Mr Steinberg, called that morning from Texas. "Ya know the strangest thing, Miss, my colleague asked about your company and no one had ever heard about them in Dubai," he boomed in his loud Texan drawl.

"And your friend, err rather colleague, has bought a property in the same development as your own Mr Steinberg?" Morven asked breezily.

"Hell no, he's over there on business, Miss er, Miss."

"MacDonald," Morven lied, protecting her identity.

"He was just checking it out for me, Miss MacDonald." He almost shouted the words.

"Ah Mr Steinberg sir, that explains it," Morven began to assure him confidently. "We have an exceptionally high standard of privacy regarding our clients. You know, not all of our customers want their business transactions to be known, if you know what I'm saying? We have a duty of care to protect our client's business dealings and do so with the utmost respect. After all, that's why many of our clients prefer to deal with us as overseas agents, avoiding their own country's financial scrutiny." There was a long silence.

"I got it sugar, I'll be sure 'n telling him not to go no more snooping around in future Miss and I'll be thanking you for your time."

Morven replaced the receiver and took a deep breath. It was a bit too close for comfort and it was time to make a call to Gyle. "We've hit a blip Gyle," she told him coolly. 'There's no need to panic but we do need to start winding down. I'll push the contracts through at this end and process payments but don't start any more sales."

"What the hell's gone wrong?" Gyle almost cried in panic.

"Don't worry, just some American asking questions but it's

okay, he's gone away happy. It's just a sign, when people start asking awkward questions, it's time to cut and run before they get the chance to dig deeper."

Gyle sighed. "Oh my God Morven, I'm glad we're bailing but I need to see you. I've got another seven deals about to go through."

"Well go ahead with what you have Gyle but I can't see you until we're winding up then we can get together and sign things off with a bang!"

Gyle laughed as he agreed but the news had sent him into a panic. For the first time he began to ask himself some questions. He had been so absorbed in the process and lost in the intensity of it all he realised he'd never taken time to calmly think things through. And now it looked as though he would be timed out. There were so many questions he should have asked but didn't. There was still so much unknown. He realised he knew nothing about how the company had been set up, how it would be dissolved or how Morven organised the contracts. More importantly he hadn't a clue how he would access his share of the profits. Morven avoided him at work but sent a text to say the company mobiles should be destroyed in two weeks' time. He called her. "Morven, we need to talk, can we meet?" His tone was anxious.

"Listen honey," she whispered, "I'll get a message to you soon, but I'm phoning in sick this week to have time to finalise all the paperwork. Don't phone me or contact me this week Gyle. It's all part of the final bale out. You'll need to sign off all the paperwork so we can close the account and then I'll give you the new account details and how to access your money safely. It's nearly over honey, just take a breath and for God's sake act normal." It was a huge deal for Gyle; his stomach churned permanently, his hands shook and he constantly felt sick. He felt out of control and it wasn't a feeling he was comfortable with. He found it difficult to cope around Laura, and the trivialness of her conversation irritated him, as his mind buzzed with too many thoughts and worries. Laura noticed he was jumpy again, agitated and short tempered. He wasn't sleeping again and when Laura asked him if he was still taking his sleeping pills he snapped at her, telling her they were as much use as a teardrop in a desert.

"They worked before," Laura reminded him but he ignored her and walked into the garden. "Where are you going now?" she called out to him.

"Somewhere to get some bloody peace from you," he yelled back, leaving Laura feeling troubled and uneasy.

Gyle's mood didn't improve much over the next couple of weeks and he spent more and more time out of the house and in bars in town, returning home drunk after driving home in the early hours. Laura was too afraid to tackle him and she pretended to be sleeping when he came home but lay awake most of the night worrying. When Kristen and Scott offered to have Kenzie overnight at their house so they could go to bed when they needed to and she could go to Doug's fiftieth, Laura was relieved. Gyle's mood had been strange and although he claimed he would be away for the weekend, Laura now knew it wasn't to any Property Fair. However, she was determined to enjoy Doug's party and with Kenzie safely far away from home and with Kristen, she knew she could relax and have fun without worrying about her daughter. Laura was still sure he was having an affair with Morven Stewart and the hurt cut deep as she imagined her husband spending the weekend with her.

She was terrified her whole world was about to fall apart again, but when Gyle offered to give her a lift to Tattie Bogles his sudden change of mood surprised her. He even gave her money to spend for a good night out, and a taxi home, which she felt confirmed his guilt about spending the weekend with Morven. After Laura left for the evening Gyle's plans changed. Morven called to say the paperwork was now ready for the company to be signed off, but she couldn't stay for more than a few hours because she had other plans. Gyle had hoped to spend the weekend with her in Barnton but instead now invited her to Balerno, knowing Laura was out for the evening. He was excited as he set the scene for a romantic evening, lighting candles and playing soft music. The Prosecco was on ice. Excitement overwhelmed him. In just a few hours, he would be rich beyond his wildest dreams. Perhaps he could meet up with Morven in some exotic country when it was all over, he dreamed. Beyond that he had still made no plans. He laughed as he recalled Morven's earlier words to him, *it's so damn simple*; it had indeed been as easy as she promised, now that it was over. When Morven arrived at Lanark Road West, Gyle was already pouring the Prosecco. As they sipped from their glasses, Gyle gleefully signed one document after another, hardly glancing at the tiny wording on each page. Morven carefully placed them all in her file and then into her briefcase before pulling out the details of four overseas accounts. "You can access money from these accounts, and transfer the money into your own account, but you'll need to wait for the money to clear from Burlington Park Estates to your overseas accounts before you can organise the transfer back to your current account in about ten days' time." She smiled as she handed him a 'Statement of Funds' document.

He gasped as he read it; thirty-eight million pounds. It was there in black and white and he could hardly believe it. "This is all mine?" he gasped.

"Yeh, I told you it would be worth it."

He leaned over on the sofa and embraced Morven, kissing her and stroking her hair and as she responded the level of their passion kept them there, on the sofa. Gyle was kissing her neck while removing her bra, kissing each breast as the garment fell to the floor. She allowed him to remove her panties before their passion and desire took over and their bodies entwined relentlessly, moving in sexual rhythm to a pounding beat and a breathtaking few minutes later, they relaxed and regained control of their senses. Gyle remained on a high, fuelled partly by the amount of Prosecco he'd drunk and partly because of the evening's events. It had been a perfect day for him. They lay together on the sofa for a moment before Morven kissed him gently on the cheek. He watched as she dressed; she was calm and relaxed. "This is where we say goodbye darling," she said softly. "It's been fun, but now it's goodbye and we go and live a little."

"Where will you go?" he asked.

"Ah, I have places, but it's best you don't know." She glanced up at him. "You know when things become apparent, it's best not to leave trails." Gyle felt a sudden shiver as Morven glided out of the room, out of the house and out of his life. Of course it would all come out, and fairly soon, he suspected, otherwise Morven wouldn't be moving on so soon. The reality and the enormity of it all hit him. He'd made no forward plans, no escape plan. It was clear Morven had meticulously covered her tracks, leaving him at base camp. He was the only traceable source, and the terrible truth made him feel vulnerable, very vulnerable at least until his money cleared, and then he could cut and run, just about anywhere in the world, but not yet. Morven, on the other hand, had it all planned. She already had enough funds from her previous scams, and now she was off to God knows where leaving him to make some big decisions for himself. He now realised he couldn't hang around Edinburgh for long; it was the base of the operation, and it would be the first place to be investigated. "Damn!" he said out loud. His whole life was in Edinburgh, his family and friends, it was all he knew. He walked into the kitchen and poured himself a whisky, the feeling of excitement and elation well gone. What about Laura and Kenzie? He groaned as he slammed his glass down on the worktop. "Shit!" He suddenly remembered he had told Laura he would be at a Property Fair all weekend, the perfect cover to spend time with Morven, but now she had gone, leaving him at a loose end. Laura would be home soon enough. His mind was racing, he was going to have to make plans, and fast. Once questions started and investigations followed, he would have to be as far away from Edinburgh as possible. This is what the high stakes and the high risks had meant for him, but he puzzled to know where the risk had been for Morven. He opened his laptop; perhaps he could go on holiday, and then move on, perhaps by bus or train? His heart was pounding as he finished his glass of whisky and poured himself another and sat down to consider his options.

Doug's party at Tattie Bogles was great fun and it attracted crowds of family, friends, regulars and passersby. Jodie organised a huge cake and she brought it through as Mikey played 'Happy Birthday' on the piano with everyone singing along. Laura had been there barely a couple of hours, and already she felt relaxed and happy as she soaked in the atmosphere of Tattie Bogles, surrounded by people she loved and trusted. She also loved spending time with Mikey; he was so different from Gyle, so open, so happy, and so well adjusted, so normal! She sat deep in thought, before a call to perform their duets brought her back in the room. As promised, their first song was an old favourite among the regulars but now it was time to try out their own song. Laura sat on a stool beside the piano as Mikey started to play the introduction. He stopped. "This is a song Laura and I have put together, it's called 'Where the Eagles Fly.' I hope you all like it." The crowd applauded as he began the introduction once more and smiled towards Laura as she began to sing.

When I first saw him standing there,
He caught my heart, my soul my mind.
With gentle smile, he stood and stared.
It's true what they say, that love is blind.

When a cruel twist of fate from the ice queen above
Turned his loving hands to harsh tools of pain.
And his soft gentle lips just ran out of love,
With words once tender, ne'er spoken again.

I escape to the hills and my dreams of old
Of happy times and secrets untold
And my soul drifts away, away up high
To that place in the hills where the eagles fly

How could he have been so mean to me?
No one could ever have loved him more
I loved and I cared for him so tenderly.
But fear is all mine when he walks through the door.

I see it clearly now with closed eyes and pray
I just loved him too much, so the fault is all mine.
One day I will leave him, but it won't be today
He might just come home to say he loves me, this time.

I escape to the hills and my dreams of old
Of happy times and secrets untold
And my soul drifts away, away up high
To that place in the hills where the eagles fly

They often sang this way together, but tonight as they sang the chorus, Laura suddenly felt different. Her feelings for Mikey were deeper and warmer than she realised. It was a feeling so unbelievably and overwhelmingly powerful it startled her and as Mikey glanced towards her, smiling, as the chorus ended, they shared a moment between them. Laura realised he was feeling it too; it was such a brief moment, it was true, yet in that second the strength of the moment took her breath away. She turned away, quickly denying herself of the experience, as the crowd were on their feet in abundant applause. Later she made light of it. "The crowd really bought into that one," she joked and Mikey smiled.

"Come on, let's get a drink and some of Doug's cake before it's all gone, then we can go back and finish with 'You've got a Friend,' I guess they'll all be expecting that one."

Laura hugged him. "Thanks Mikey," she said without looking at him.

"What's that for?" he teased.

"For being you," she said quietly.

When Laura arrived home later that evening she was surprised to see an empty Prosecco bottle in the recycling box and an almost empty whisky bottle beside a glass on the kitchen worktop. In the lounge, Gyle's jacket and shoes lay in a heap on the floor. Laura made her way quietly upstairs to find him sleeping soundly and came back down to make a cup of tea. Her mind was full of questions. Why was he not at the supposed Property Fair? If his plans had been cancelled why hadn't he come over to Tattie Bogles? She took more sips of tea. "Typical Gyle," she said to herself as she walked over to the sink, discarding the remaining tea before opening the dishwasher to put the empty cup in. There she noticed two champagne flutes. "That explains the Prosecco bottle," she said out loud, but it provoked more questions than answers. Was Morven Stewart here? The thought irritated her as she moved into the lounge and switched on the television. She lay back on the sofa and flicked through the channels with the remote without settling on any particular programme. She switched it off and straightened the cushions, but as she did her hand brushed over something caught on the back of one. She turned the cushion over to find the most unusual earring she had ever seen. It was a heavy silver hoop with a giraffe's head and long neck crafted in the middle. It was beautifully made, extremely unusual and very African. "Morven bloody Stewart," she half cried as she sat with it in her hand. She wanted to go upstairs and confront her sleeping husband, but she knew it would be pointless. He was very drunk and he would either ignore her or else his anger would turn on her. She put the earring in her handbag before heading upstairs to bed. Morven would surely want this back at some point, and she would enjoy watching Gyle sweat, trying to find it. She was angry, very angry as she slipped between the sheets, turning her back on her sleeping husband and tears fell silently into her pillow. Her worst fears had been confirmed, he was having an affair with Morven Stewart. An hour later she was still awake. No matter how hard she tried, or how tired she was she couldn't sleep. Images of Gyle with Morven together in her own home made her feel sick with anger and hurt. She wanted to hurt him and her. "How could he?" she cried as she crept out of bed and made her way back downstairs. Gyle was still sleeping soundly as though he didn't have a care in the world. In the kitchen, Laura opened the fridge and pulled out a green chilli, cutting it in half. She walked back upstairs and carefully pulled back Gyle's pyjama shorts, rubbing the seeds of the green chilli to the inside of his pyjamas, making sure none of the seeds were left behind. She smiled as she made her way back downstairs again. "Try explaining that one!" she laughed as she discarded the chilli to the food waste before heading upstairs to bed again.

The following morning Gyle rose early. Laura could hear him in the bathroom with the cold tap running fast. "Job done." She smiled to herself before turning over and going back to sleep to the sound of the bathroom cabinet door opening and closing as he hunted for something to take the burn out of the fiery rash. "Too bad, you won't find anything in there," she chuckled to herself, knowing she had hidden every cream and lotion that might ease the pain. When Laura finally came downstairs, Gyle was searching through the local paper for the name of the Sunday rota chemist. He jumped as she entered the room. "Do you know where there's a chemist open on a Sunday morning?" His face was winced.

"Are you okay Gyle, I thought you were at the Property Fair?"

"No, I had to come home," he lied. "I didn't feel well and now I feel awful, I think it's an allergy or something."

"I don't know where you'll get a chemist today, and the supermarket doesn't open until about eleven.' She turned away to hide her smile. "Can I get you anything?"

"No, it's okay, I'll get a shower and head into town, to see if I can find a place open."

"You might get something at the garage?"

"Yes!" he cried and hurriedly made his way upstairs to the bathroom, and Laura laughed as she heard the shower running, knowing it would have to be a cold one!

When Gyle arrived at work the following day the place was buzzing with gossip about Morven Stewart. "I have a few words of my own I need to have with her." The annoyance in his voice was clear.

"You'll be lucky," Gavin shouted from his office. "She's quit her job, just like that, no notice, no nothing and she announces, quite the thing, I might add, that she's leaving the country this afternoon!"

"What about her pay?" Janice called out.

"She was paid cash, on a casual self-employed basis. Her terms, not mine," Gavin called. Gyle felt a sudden gush of panic as he tried calling her and failed to get an answer before he remembered the phones had been disposed of. She told him the money wouldn't be transferred for ten days yet, so why was she bailing out now? He was infuriated, the rash was still burning and the hangover, banging in his head, was no better. Had the money cleared early? He would have to go down to his bank and check things out. He made an excuse to his boss and made his way into town.

The bank teller was friendly and efficient and listened carefully as he asked her to check the balances of the Burlington Park Estates accounts. Her face searched the screen before she looked up puzzled. "It's an online account sir, you can really only manage it through the online system, but I can tell you the money transferred from this account several days ago. However, it didn't transfer to the account numbers you've given me. Would you like to check the details again?"

Gyle felt the colour drain from his face. "You're checking the right account, Burlington Park Estates?"

The teller looked back at her screen. "Yes sir, it was all cleared to an overseas account last week through online international transfer."

"And the transfer was made by a Morven Stewart?"

The teller checked her screen again and shook her head. "No sir, the account is solely in your name and it was transferred to Global Property Investments."

"Ah, I see." Gyle smiled; this was what Morven had arranged to manage his money. She could have explained that a bit better. "Could I move some of it back to my own account then please?" He smiled at the teller as she looked back at her screen.

"Mmm no sir, sorry. It's an online investment company. You made the transfer more than a week ago sir." She noticed the shock on his face.

"No, I didn't!" he gasped.

"It was an online transfer sir, and it went through all the security checks before the money was moved. Do you not remember? It was a huge financial transaction. These things are very secure." Gyle felt sick, he wanted to scream but instead he just stood staring at the woman. "Sir, if you think some deception has taken place we need to alert the authorities." Her

182

tone was probing as she watched for his reaction. He couldn't bring in the authorities, it was the last thing he needed. He tried hard to look more cheerful.

"Ah yes, of course, I remember now, that explains things, thank you. You know I deal with so many accounts these days, I have lost track. I am so sorry for your trouble." He hurriedly left the teller and the bank and headed towards Barnton and Morven Stewart. If he was quick enough he might just catch her before she fled the country. "Bitch!" he yelled as he steered his car through the busy traffic, irritated by the traffic lights, and pedestrian crossings which all seemed to be set deliberately to stop him reaching the flat in time. When he eventually arrived, he parked his car in the nearest available space and ran towards the flat. He banged loudly on the door. There was no answer. He banged again and looked through the letterbox. He could see a suitcase lying on the lounge floor. It was packed but still open, then he suddenly realised Morven didn't know he had been to the bank, so she wasn't trying to avoid him necessarily. He would have to play it cool to gain access. He shouted through the letterbox. "Morven, honey, you can't leave without saying goodbye, open the door."

Morven eventually appeared, wrapped in a towel. "I was in the shower," she said as she opened the door, and as she did he pushed it hard open, stepped inside and slammed it close behind him.

"You damn bitch!" he yelled at her. "You filthy cheating bitch!" He pushed her back and her towel fell to the floor.

"You came back for one last look?" she yelled back. "What the hell's your problem?"

"You're my problem Morven. Firstly you've left me with a rash and a burning dick!"

Morven looked surprised. "Nothing to do with me," she shrugged.

"And that's nothing compared to the news I've just had from the bank." She looked shocked for a moment then returned to her usual cool self as he continued shouting at her. "You were going to cut and run with it all!" he yelled, pushing her back and around the room.

She pushed him back. "You know the score," she laughed. "High risks, remember?" She looked at him and sneered. "You lose baby, better luck next time." Her voice was casual as she bent down to pick up her towel and wrapped it round her again. "I think you'd better go. Go back to your wife and child, and your safe little job and live your safe little life. I have places to go." She turned her back on him and began to walk away.

Gyle grabbed her by the hair and pulled her back. He slapped her face. "No way Morven, you are not leaving here without settling with me first!"

Morven rubbed her cheek. "Sorry baby no can do." She was still calm. "What are you going to do? Call the Police?" She glared at him up and down. "No, I think not."

"I might just do that," he said calmly, trying to turn the control of events round in his favour. "Why not?"

Morven laughed. "I think you'll find everything is in your own name sweetie." She smiled. "I've been in this game too long to leave a trail." She threw a file towards him. "Go on take a look." Gyle grabbed the file and frantically thumbed through the documents. It was true, all trails led to himself without any reference to Morven. She was smiling smugly at him now. "See Morven Stewart doesn't exist!" she laughed. "Oh and for the record, I was going to ditch the file".

"So where's the money then? I'll trace you through Global

Property Investments," he laughed, nodding his head. "Oh yes, that's right, I know all about them. I've got you now." He moved closer, his face was almost touching her own.

She pushed him back. "I don't think so darling," she smirked. "You know nothing and my husband is taking care of that as we speak."

Gyle was taken aback. "Husband?" he gasped.

"Sorry darling, it was nice knowing you. Now if you don't mind I have a plane to catch," she said quietly pushing him to one side.

"Let me see your tickets, you bitch, where are you going?" He grabbed her arm.

"They're not here, no trace, remember? My God you've a lot to learn, but have a good look around, satisfy your curiosity – be my guest." Gyle grabbed the suitcase, scattering clothes and shoes. Morven grabbed him by the hair, scratching his face. "Get out Gyle!" she yelled. "Just get out!"

"No way bitch!" He spat in her face as he grabbed her by the hair again. They struggled and he punched her on the chin, making her fall backwards and then trip over a discarded shoe as she tumbled to the floor. He lost control, kicking her in the ribs, face, head and back, time and time again. Finally he lifted her head up by the hair and kicked her hard to her shoulder blade. "Try lifting your case now you cow!" His heart was pounding and he was sweating and shaking. He stopped the assault and looked at her as she lay still. He pushed her over. She was out cold. He bent down to listen to her breathing; there was nothing and he couldn't find a pulse. "Oh my God," he said quietly, "I've killed her!" Panic raged through every part of him, body and soul. He stood for a few moments breathing so fast he thought he would faint. He felt sick and he was still shaking with anger as he quickly began stuffing everything he could find into the suitcase, including the file. He carefully wiped anything he might have touched, door handles, walls and tables before picking up the suitcase and heading out of the flat and back to his car, throwing the case in the boot before he spun off and headed back to work.

Thankfully the office gossip had moved on from Morven Stewart's sudden departure by the time Gyle returned to work and he was able to read a few emails while keeping himself to himself, even if his mind was whirling so fast he felt dizzy and sick. He couldn't believe he had just murdered someone, deceived people out of millions of pounds and yet here he was, sitting at his desk as though nothing had happened. The horror of it all overwhelmed him. He desperately wanted to flee, but how could he now? It was inevitable that Morven's body would be found sooner or later and that would mean all staff would be questioned at some point. He couldn't risk drawing attention to himself. He would have to try at least to act as normal as he could before choosing his moment to leave, carefully. The horror of it all sickened him and no matter how he tried, he couldn't escape the image of Morven's battered and lifeless body lying on the rug in the living room of her flat in Barnton.

"What happened to your face?" Heather asked him as everyone turned to see.

"Those blasted brambles at 'Otters Drift'. You know that little cottage I went to see? The place is very overgrown, it's a death trap."

"You'd better put some antiseptic on it Gyle," Heather told him as the others returned to their work, leaving Gyle feeling sick at the irony of the words he'd just used.

8

At home Gyle was agitated and preoccupied. Laura tried to break through the wall of silence he had created around himself, but the only time she succeeded was when he snarled at her and snapped irritably at Kenzie. Laura waited for him to mention Morven Stewart, allowing her the chance to confront him with the earring, but he said nothing and a couple of days later she ran out of patience waiting for the moment to come.

"How's that Morven Stewart getting on?" she asked casually as she cooked supper one night.

Gyle looked up, startled. "What?"

"Morven how is she?"

"Why the sudden interest in Morven Stewart?" he asked, annoyed at the interruption to his deep thoughts.

"You've not mentioned her lately, that's all. I was just wondering wha..."

"She left," Gyle said quickly, cutting off her sentence.

"She left?" Laura was surprised. "When? Where?"

"For God's sake Laura, what is this, a bloody quiz? I don't know where she is, South Africa probably. She just resigned and left. Thank God, is what I say!"

"I guess that will make your life a bit easier then?"

He sighed. "Do you think so? How long will supper be I'm going out?"

Laura shook her head. "Again Gyle? It would be good to have you around sometimes, I'm sick of feeling like a single parent."

"What?" Gyle snapped. "You've a bloody nerve Laura. Single parent? You have no idea!"

Laura watched him as he moved towards her. That look was in his eyes again, the bulging stare and the ashen white face. She felt afraid. "Calm down Gyle," she soothed, but he ignored her and grabbed her by the throat. Laura tried to scream but she couldn't and instead twisted and turned until she eventually struggled free, coughing and gasping for breath. "Leave me alone!" she yelled as Kenzie started to cry. He pushed her away and sneered as she stumbled into the table, catching a blow to her elbow. "For God's sake Gyle," she gasped.

He turned towards her again and pushed her face. "Well done Laura for making me out to be a bad bastard in front of Kenzie." He glared at her and without a word he turned and walked out of the house.

"You are a bad bastard," Laura cried quietly after him, but he had already closed the door and made off in his car.

As Laura lay in bed that night, Gyle Jamieson was standing across the road from Morven's flat. He stood for a while staring up at the window, trying to comprehend the horror of the events that had taken place there. He couldn't take it in and eventually returned to his car, parked a couple of streets away. The following morning Laura found Gyle sleeping on the sofa, still in his clothes and stinking of stale booze. She stood staring at him for a while and, for the first time ever, questioned why she was still with him. This wasn't the life she had hoped for, or what her husband had promised; and it wasn't how she wanted to live her life, shackled to this uncompromising, insensitive egotistical idiot. A life that had to be lived on his terms, wholly determined by his moods. She left him to sleep and made some coffee before calling Kristen. Hearing her friend's cheery voice helped to lift the tension and she tentatively suggested she might call over to see her. "That would be great Laura, when do you plan to come?"

"What about today? Today would be really good for me."

Kristen detected the strain in Laura's voice. "I can get some cover for a while today. It might not be all day, but I could pick you up from the station if you're coming by train?"

Laura felt relieved. She really needed to get away. She looked around for some paper to write Gyle a note but in her hurry could only find little sticky notes, so her message was left in two parts. 'Gone to Kristen's, back later' on one and 'Sorry for the inconvenience' on the other. She stuck them on top of the kitchen table. He would have to get his own coffee and breakfast for once, and he wouldn't be pleased, but Laura couldn't have cared less. As the train pulled in to Stirling Station she could see Kristen waiting on the other side of the barrier for them. She waved as Kenzie took off, jumping into Kristen's arms as the barrier opened.

"Someone's pleased to see me!" Kristen smiled.

"I'm too big to run and jump into your arms Kristen, but I'm so pleased to see you too!"

It was a lovely day and when Kristen suggested a short walk in the hills, Laura jumped at the chance. "I'd love to, but we can't go too far with Kenzie, she's a bit heavier than Maisie!" They laughed as they remembered the last time they had walked carrying the little terrier. "How is she?" Laura asked sadly, "I really miss her."

"Oh Mum has her spoilt rotten Laura, as you would imagine. She's her little lap dog."

Further up the hill, holding tightly to Kenzie's hand, Laura's mood became more sombre. "I don't know what's going on Kristen, but I'm sure Gyle's been having an affair with a colleague, and I'm sure he's mixed up in something to do with overseas property sales, which for some reason he is keeping a tightly guarded secret." Kristen listened intently as Laura told her all about Gyle, his moods and his mental state. 'Living with him is hell sometimes Kristen, he's just a bully," she said quietly as tears fell down her cheeks.

"Leave him Laura. Leave him and stay with us for a while," Kristen urged. "You and Kenzie will be fine here until you can sort something out." She searched Laura's pale and drawn face. "You are just hurting yourself by staying, and quite frankly he's just not worth it!"

Laura knew Kristen was right, and she struggled to fight back the tears in front of Kenzie. "I need answers Kristen first, and you need to speak to Scott before you go inviting us to stay," she teased. "If Scott's happy, then yes, it's something I might seriously consider, but it could only be for a short while." Laura hugged her friend.

Kristen lifted Kenzie up to sit on her hip. "You need to be a good girl for Mummy," she said to her and she smiled as she cuddled in tight.

When they arrived back at Waverley Station later that day Gyle was out. Laura tried calling his mobile but he didn't answer, as usual, and it really irritated her that he couldn't be there to pick them up from the station, like any other husband would for their wife and family. She was now left waiting for the bus and she wondered whether she would be home before him. Everything was just one big guessing game with Gyle. After she had fed and settled Kenzie down, it was quite late and Gyle had still not appeared. She started to prepare a meal as her phone rang. "Gyle?" she answered without looking to see who it was.

"Err no, sorry, it's Mikey."

"Mikey!" Laura's face lit up.

"I've got some business in Balerno tomorrow, and I thought I might call in for a coffee if you are going to be around?"

"That would be great Mikey, I'll be here. I was over at Kristen's today and we talked our tongues sore!" she laughed.

"I'll bet you did. Well I'll let it recover before I come over some time. Not sure when exactly Laura, so if you need to go out, it's ok."

"No, no, I'll be here, Mikey, I'm looking forward to catching up, there are things I need to talk to you about."

Mikey's call helped to continue the happy day, but now she was alone again and there was still no call from Gyle. She ate alone and when he still hadn't come home, and continued to ignore her calls, she went to bed. The next morning Laura woke early to find Gyle sleeping soundly beside her, and Kenzie was still asleep in her nursery. She went downstairs to start breakfast and turned on the little television in the kitchen. As she poured herself a coffee the local news caught her attention. 'A woman has been found in a flat in Barnton. The badly beaten woman was barely alive when a workman found her last night, but she is recovering from her injuries at the Western General Hospital. The workman made the grim discovery when he arrived to carry out repairs for the landlord, but the identity of the woman remains a mystery. The flat had been let to students who moved on some weeks ago. The only line of enquiry the police have is an earring, which was found on a bedside cabinet.' A photograph of the earring flashed across the screen, and Laura almost dropped her cup as the image of the earring she had found clinging to the cushion on her sofa appeared on television. She quickly opened her handbag and pulled out the earring. It was the same. Laura put her hand up to her mouth. "Oh my God," she gasped. "It's Morven Stewart!" Laura was still standing open-mouthed when Gyle came downstairs. He looked terrible, huge dark bags hung under his eyes and his skin was pale and drawn. "Any coffee?" he asked tardily as he sat down.

Laura walked over to the coffee maker and poured him a cup. "A woman's been found in a flat in Barnton," she said casually as she handed the cup to him.

"How did she die?" he said, trying not to look too bothered.

"Oh she's not dead." Laura smiled, watching the startled look on his face. "But, strangely enough, they don't know who she is? It's a complete mystery." Gyle was staring at her in silence and shock. "The only clue they have is an earring they found on her bedside cabinet, apparently. They think they'll be able to identify her through that."

"Oh?" Gyle was still and staring, his coffee cup untouched.

"You know the police are really clever these days, and the forensics are amazing, they'll soon sort it out. The earring was so unusual, silver, with a giraffe. It's not sold in Europe apparently, they seem pretty sure it's African."

Gyle snapped at her. "Turn it off," he yelled. "Bloody damn rubbish first thing in the morning, and you rabbiting on."

Laura moved towards the television and turned it off. "I could help them with their enquiries Gyle, and I have a feeling you could too, don't you?"

"What do you mean?" he asked abruptly, taking a large gulp

of coffee. Laura opened the palm of her hand. "The earring was just like this!" she said quietly, now dangling it in front of his face as he turned a peculiar shade of grey. "It's Morven Stewart, isn't it Gyle?"

He jumped up, almost knocking his cup over. "Where the hell did you get that from?" His face was etched with terror as the reality began to hit home. It was indeed Morven's earring.

"I found it stuck to the cushion on the sofa the night you were supposed to be at a Property Fair, which I can only assume with some confidence never existed? You've been having an affair with Morven Stewart Gyle, haven't you?"

He looked at her and shrugged. "So what if I have, it's over now so get over it."

The glib remark made Laura really angry. "It certainly is but that's not all you've been up to is it? Oh no, you're involved in some kind of overseas property dealings aren't you?" She stared at him. His face was twisted with anger, his eyes were all but popping out of his head and the veins on the side of his face bulged as his cheek muscles twitched. Laura instantly wished she hadn't made that last remark and she was now very afraid of her husband, as she realised he was losing control.

"What the hell are you talking about you stupid woman?" he yelled at her, moving his face closer to hers.

She moved back. "It was you Gyle, wasn't it?" she said softly but moving further back still. "What did she do Gyle, dump you? Or maybe she just got a better deal with Burlington Park Estates?" she said, hoping he would calm down and explain his side of things but Gyle's temper raged now.

"How do you know about that?" he yelled again, lunging towards her and grabbing her by the hair.

"Let go of me Gyle," she shrieked at him. "It's only a matter of time before Morven recovers and tells the police it was you!"

Gyle let go of her hair and, pushing her back. laughed loudly, "You haven't a bloody clue after all, have you?" He shook his head still laughing, but it was a strange high-pitched laugh, which Laura found scary. He shook his head. "I'll tell you what, seeing as you are so bloody interested, I'll tell you all about it." She sat down, relieved he appeared to be suddenly calmer, and she listened as he explained every detail, including the assault on Morven. "So you see, it all went wrong in the end. Everything goes wrong in the end." He stood up and walked to the sink, pouring a glass of water before reaching for his pills.

"No Gyle, you can't," she screamed and ran towards him, reaching out to take the pills from his hand. "If you go to the police now, it will be a lot easier on yourself."

He caught her by the hair and pulled her back, as he had with Morven, and he laughed. "Poor sad little Laura," he sneered, "these pills aren't for me, they are for you!" He reached out and grabbed her, the look of horror on her face amused him; then, holding her tight, he stuffed the pills into her mouth then stroked her throat, causing her to gulp and then almost poured the water down her throat, making her choke at times. "Now, I'm going to sit down here with you for a while Laura, and have a little chat but then I really need to go."

"Where will you go Gyle?" Laura whispered through her tears, desperately hoping he might have a change of heart. She fearfully didn't mention Kenzie, and prayed she wouldn't wake. Gyle's mind had blown out of all reason, and she was terrified he might hurt her too. "Why are you doing this to me Gyle? All I have ever tried to do was be a good wife to you, to take care of you and love you. What have I done to deserve this?" she pleaded. "They'll find you Gyle, and you'll just make things worse."

"Sorry Laura, you just know too much and anyway they won't catch me. I'm heading down to the docks to catch a boat to wherever it's going," he lied with a high-pitched voice.

Laura was sure the events had destroyed his mental state completely. "With all the money you've made from the properties?" Laura whispered as she struggled to stay awake.

"The money?" Gyle's blood ran cold as he suddenly remembered. There was no money. For some crazy reason everything had become blurred, he couldn't think logically any more. He had still been convinced he would access the money somehow, but now Morven was still around and he suddenly realised the dream was over. All he had to show for his anxiety and trouble was a paper trail of deception, an attempted murder, and the pending murder of his wife. At least with Laura gone, he would have time to hide, there would be no one to tell any tales until the property buyers caught on. He still had time, he tried to convince himself, but he was panicking. He knew he had to go, but he wasn't sure where. He looked across at Laura who now lay asleep on the sofa. He would have to go to work as normal and make it look as though Laura had taken her own life. He'd not thought this through and groaned as he realised there was no note to explain and make things clearer. He hurriedly scribbled a note from himself to Laura saying their marriage was over and he was going away for a few days to clear his head. That would give a good enough reason for suicide and it would give him some legitimate breathing space. Then he found the sticky note still lying in the kitchen. "Excellent!" he cheered. It wasn't much, and a bit strange he supposed, but it was all he had, and it was in Laura's handwriting. 'Sorry for the inconvenience.' He left the notes beside her body before hurriedly changing then he fled out of the house, leaving Laura asleep on the sofa and the forgotten Kenzie asleep in her cot upstairs. As he drove out of Balerno, he remembered he still had the suitcase of Morven's things in the boot of his car. He would have to ditch that out of Edinburgh, and he remembered seeing a layby on a quiet road near Dunbar, some weeks before. He could dump it there, and burn the contents, but first he would go to work as normal, and everything else had to appear as normal as possible.

The morning's gossip at McArdle and Baynes focussed on the mysterious young woman who had been found in Barnton. Gyle tried to ignore it but he couldn't and he began to feel calmer as the conversation led to suggestions that she was probably an Eastern European migrant who had perhaps been trafficked and had tried to escape. It was a thought shared by most of the staff until Janice remembered another detail. "What about the earring? I don't think a poor Eastern European like that would have an expensive African earring do you?" Gyle froze on the spot. The bloody earring, he'd left it at home. Laura had held it in her hand, where was it now? He would have to race back to Balerno to retrieve it and the thought of having to face Laura's lifeless body made him feel sick. Then another thought came into his mind, Kenzie! He started to shake. He had forgotten about his daughter. She would be awake now. He wanted to scream as he slammed his hand into his desk.

"Are you alright Gyle?" Janice asked. "You look a bit strange."

"I've left my damn wallet at home," he sighed, 'I'm going to have to go back for it, oh and I'll go and see that property in Ratho while I'm out, so I'll see you soon." His colleagues nodded as he shot out of the door.

"He's been acting awful strange lately," Andy said out loud. The remark was acknowledged with a nod from everyone. As he raced back home, Gyle's heart felt as though it would thump right out of his chest. Sweat poured from his brow and his hands were clammy and shaking. Turning the corner into Lanark Road West, he was met by an ambulance with its lights flashing parked in the driveway of their home. Panic gripped him as he jumped out of the car and ran in the open front door. Heads turned as he stepped inside. "Gyle!" Mikey called from the kitchen as he noticed him enter the lounge where paramedics still continued to work on Laura. Mikey was holding Kenzie in his arms, keeping her away from the horror in the lounge, and she had laid her little head on his shoulder. A sudden feeling of guilt ran through Gyle as he saw Laura's limp body being loaded on to the stretcher. "Oh my God, what's happened?" he said, convincingly shocked.

Mikey touched his arm. "I came over for coffee and found her lying there."

Gyle looked at Mikey's face; it was soaked with tears and genuine concern. Gyle had been too wrapped up in the enormity and horror of recent events to feel anything. He was completely numb. He put his hands up to his face and felt sick at what he had become.

"She's still with us Gyle, she might make it."

Gyle felt horrified. She couldn't be okay, surely not? He was in an impossible situation now, how could he leave with this going on? And what about Morven Stewart? The horror of the fact that they would likely be sharing the intensive therapy unit terrified him. Up until now, Morven Stewart's identity was still unknown. It may be possible they would never discover who she was, if she died. Gyle stood gazing, far away in thought before a familiar voice interrupted. "I'll have Kenzie today, if you want to go to the hospital Gyle." Mikey was standing in front of him with Kenzie. The little girl made no attempt to reach out to her dad, but then she hardly knew him. Gyle suddenly wondered what would become of her if Laura died, and he felt terrible. "Mikey could you phone my office please and tell them what's happened?"

Mikey nodded. "I'll bring Kenzie back home later, about seven okay?"

Gyle nodded as Mikey made his way out of the house and Gyle followed the ambulance to the hospital. He called his parents to let them know but a message on their answer phone said they were out of the country. "Bloody great," he wailed. "I have to get a blasted telephone message to find out they are away somewhere again. Typical!" He threw the mobile across the room in temper.

At the hospital the news was uncertain. "The next forty-eight hours will be crucial," the doctor told Gyle. "Do you know how many pills she took?"

Gyle shook his head.

"Mr Jamieson, the pills were prescribed to you, surely you remember how many you had already taken?" The doctor was annoyed and Gyle looked startled.

"Oh yes, I had taken two."

"Thank you." The doctor left the waiting room to return to his patient.

By the time Gyle returned home, there was no further news and arrangements had already been made for Kenzie. Mikey called Kristen and she agreed to look after Kenzie with the help of her parents. "Kristen is coming over for her tomorrow," Mikey told him. "I guess you'll manage on your own tonight?"

Gyle looked oddly at him, and it made Mikey think again. "How about I stay on tonight and look after Kenzie? You have too much on your mind, and maybe you shouldn't be on your own?"

Gyle half smiled, grateful for the gesture, and he was eager to accept.

Later that night Mikey asked how things had been between the couple. "We were splitting up Mikey, you know she never got over losing her parents, and her sister lives so far away and she rarely calls. I reckon it all got too much for her."

Mikey shook his head, finding it hard to believe. "I can't believe she left Kenzie alone in the house?" he said.

"I know Mikey, it just shows her state of mind, she was all over the place. She's not always the happy wee soul you see Mikey, she had a deep dark side, one that's obviously taken over this time." Gyle hoped Mikey had accepted his explanation and before he had the chance to say or ask any more he added, "Look Mikey, you've been a diamond, thank you. If it hadn't been for you I don't know what I would have done, but I need to get to bed. There's a spare room next to Kenzie's if you want to crash out there?" Mikey thanked him and said goodnight.

In bed that night, Mikey's mind churned. None of what Gyle had said to him made sense. Laura didn't have a dark side; he knew her too well and she had been happy the day before when he spoke to her on the phone. She would never have left Kenzie alone. The following day when Kristen arrived for Kenzie they chatted. Gyle said a few brief and garbled words to her as he left, thrusting the note Laura had supposedly left into her hand. Kristen noticed he was agitated as Laura had described and she didn't feel easy about what had happened. After Gyle left for work it left Mikey and Kristen to talk freely.

199

"What do you make of the note?" he asked.

"Odd," Kristen replied. "We both know what's been going on, right?" Mikey nodded as she continued. "She had a whole lot of stuff going on there, and considering Laura's a writer, the note just doesn't add up. She would have had a lot more to say than that."

Mikey agreed. "Gyle told me they were splitting up, he left her a note. Maybe that's tipped her over the edge?"

Kristen shook her head. "No Mikey, she was thinking about leaving him."

Mikey looked surprised. "She was?"

"And did she mention the overseas properties?" Mikey nodded.

"And that earring she found, just confirmed his affair."

Mikey looked surprised. "Whoa, backtrack on that one."

"Did she not tell you? I guess she would have, she just told me when she came over yesterday."

"What was it?"

"She found an earring, caught on the cushion of the sofa. It was an unusual one, silver, with a giraffe, I think she said."

Mikey's face fell. "It belongs to a mystery woman, who was badly beaten up in Barnton," he told her. "They found one earring and they were looking for the other one. Did you not see it on the local news?"

Kristen shook her head. "We don't get Edinburgh local news. Oh my God Mikey, what do we do?"

"We make sure Laura's safe before anything else Kristen. As far as Gyle is aware, only Laura knows everything. If Gyle is responsible for the assault on that mystery woman and also for Laura, then she is seriously in danger now. I just hope it's not too late. I need to have a chat with my dad!" Kristen made a cup of coffee and Mikey turned on the television. The local breakfast news was just finishing, and they caught the end of an update saying the mystery woman had disappeared from the hospital early that morning without speaking a word to anyone. They never did find out who she was but a hospital spokesman said they were concerned for her welfare. Mikey turned to Kristen. "Would you believe that? I wonder if Gyle knows?" Kristen nodded. "I'm sure he will, sooner or later. Where can that earring be, do you want to help me look for it?"

"I'd better get back home with Kenzie, Mikey, Scott will be waiting, but call me, and thanks". She looked at the note again, and tears welled up in her eyes. "I can't believe she would do something like this Mikey, I just can't."

Mikey hugged her. "We'll need to pray for her now Kristen. Pray to God she makes it," he whispered, hardly able to speak as his voice wavered with emotion. Then he watched Kristen's car disappear out of the road end with little Kenzie strapped tightly in her car seat, as he wiped the tears from his eyes.

Gyle Jamieson listened to the news on the car radio on his way to work and laughed loudly. "She's gone!" He cheered, repeating the words several times. The news was like a breath of fresh air for him but it hadn't come as too much of a surprise. If he thought about it logically Morven wouldn't want to attract attention and she needed to avoid questions or any interaction with the police, so it was all good news for him. That would be something less for him to worry about now. He just had to deal with Laura, find the missing earring and dispose of it.

The sun shone brightly on the Paradise Blue yacht sailing towards the harbour of Lefkada in the Ionian Sea. Jan Van

Hoek was on the deck watching the shoreline become closer as he approached. He looked anxiously towards the decked marina for his wife Louise and smiled when he spotted her long red hair blowing gently in the breeze as her golden highlights glistened in the bright sun. She waved to her husband as the yacht neared and as it docked Jan leapt off the boat, running towards his wife, pulling her tightly to him. "Darling your poor face." He kissed her bruised and swollen face gently and tenderly. "What did that brute do to you?" he asked as he winced, looking at her bandaged shoulder and tightly bound wrist.

"It's okay darling," she purred. "It's all over now. I did what I had to do; it's all part of the risks. You know that."

Her husband smiled. "Enough now Louise, do you hear me. It's far too dangerous, there are too many risks, and you know he could have killed you."

She agreed. "He almost did, but more importantly now, did you move the money?"

"Oh yes, it's all moved, fragmented, companies opened and dissolved, money moved and moved again. We're all good honey and they'll have a job tracking us down."

She sighed. "It was all worth it then."

"Who were you this time?" Jan asked

"Morven Stewart!"

"That's very Scottish, and you've left no trace?"

"None at all!"

"What about your accommodation, no trace there?"

"I bunged a bunch of students some cash they couldn't refuse to move out early, and it suited for the time I needed it."

"Good girl, Louise, you are a genius." He kissed her again. "That's it then babe, a life in paradise awaits us, beginning on the Paradise Blue. Let's go for it!!" They stood on the deck of the yacht as it left Lefkada and disappeared towards the horizons of the crystal clear waters of the Ionian Sea.

Back in Edinburgh, Mikey found the missing earring under the sofa. It had fallen during Gyle's assault on Laura and now it sat on the console of Mikey's car as he made his way to see his father at Lothian and Borders Police. Inspector Martin Macrae listened carefully as his son told him everything he knew about Gyle Jamieson and Morven Stewart. When he finished Inspector Macrae took a deep breath, sat back in his chair and sighed. He put his hand up to his forehead and shook his head. "The problem I have with this, Mikey, is that everything you've told me is basically little more than gossip, as far as the police will be concerned. Not that I'm doubting you son, but it's all hearsay." Mikey groaned. He understood what his father was saying. It did sound that way, now he was relaying all the details. "The important thing son is there's no evidence."

"What about the earring?"

"Where did you say you found it?"

"At Laura's," Mikey said, passing the earring across the table to his dad.

"I'll hang on to it for now Mikey but it doesn't prove anything, does it? If Gyle Jamieson was having an affair with the woman, then she could have lost it at any time during their relationship." Mikey looked at his father, frustrated at the tardy process, which all seemed perfectly explainable and legitimate the way it was now presented. "You say this Laura tried to take her own life?" Mikey nodded. "It could be then that she has concocted all of this in her head, and been able to convince you it was something more than it really is. It's not unusual for paranoia to take over when the mind is unbalanced. She probably believes it all herself. That's how the police and the medics might view it."

"Damn!" Mikey uttered. "The thing is Dad, I know Laura, and she is as sane as you and I. There's no way she's made any of this up."

"The other snag, if you could call it that, is the fact that the woman you say is Morven Stewart has disappeared without a trace, without speaking to anyone. And more crucially to an investigation, she has gone without making a complaint or a statement. The fact that you've found her earring is irrelevant now. You say the woman was Morven Stewart, but she could have been anyone, we have no trace of a Morven Stewart anywhere!"

Mikey groaned. "I can see where you are coming from Dad, but it's not helping. What about McArdle and Baynes, she worked for them? And what about the properties and this Burlington Park Estates?"

Inspector Macrae shook his head, as he checked his desk computer. "I have no line of enquiry to check on this woman. There's just no case, no complaint. As far as this Burlington Park Estates is concerned, there have been no complaints against the company to Lothian and Borders Police, nor from any overseas source. And, here's a funny thing," he said as he clicked away at his keyboard. "There's no website for them."

"What? What about company records then?"

His dad nodded. "Yes, there's always that, but without a complaint we have no line of enquiry to follow, so we can't investigate. Maybe this was all in Laura's head too?"

"NO!" Mikey jumped up. "There must be something we can do, what about Laura?"

"Unless she comes round, it will undoubtedly go down as suicide son, sorry. She had a lot going on, people have killed themselves for less."

"Not Laura," Mikey said quietly and firmly, shaking his head.

"Look son, I know it's hard for you to accept, but it's not unusual for close friends and family not to believe their loved ones have been capable of suicide but it happens, tragically it happens all too often." Mikey's father felt helpless, and sorry he couldn't do more for his son.

"Listen Dad, please, if only to humour me now." Mikey tried another tactic. "Just supposing Gyle Jamieson has engineered a major overseas property scam, which for some reason has not become apparent yet, and Laura found out about it?"

Martin Macrae felt obliged to listen. "Go on," he encouraged.

"Let's just say he was having an affair with Morven Stewart, who was in on the property scam – and Laura found out about that too? Or perhaps it all went pear-shaped and Morven cheated on him and tried to dump him? Perhaps she even threatened to tell his wife?"

"I'm not sure where you're going with this Mikey, but go on I'm still listening."

"Okay, hold on to those thoughts for now. Gyle quarrels with Morven Stewart and he loses the plot big time and beats her up, leaving her for dead, then when he gets home Laura confronts him and threatens to call the police. Gyle loses it completely and forces pills down her throat. She never takes pills by the way, so that's strange in itself."

"I hear what you are saying Mikey, and yes, it's all perfectly possible, but you have to realise that at this stage it's all circumstantial, and there's absolutely nothing we can do. Remember there have been no complaints!"

"Okay Dad, but just, for the purpose of this conversation you can say what I am saying is true, then wouldn't you agree that while Laura is still alive, Gyle will be panicking? She's holding her own but he might just try to finish the job!"

"She's in intensive therapy Mikey, there are people around her 24/7. He wouldn't have the opportunity."

"And the first day they move her to a ward, God willing she pulls through? He will be desperate to stop her talking!"

His father smiled. "Okay Mikey, I hear what you are saying, and I guess there is something I can do, but I'm not promising the Superintendent won't bin it. You've just made an official complaint, as flimsy as it is, so I'll log our conversation, and you never know something might emerge."

"Thanks Dad." Mikey's emotions were everywhere.

"This Laura, she means a lot to you doesn't she?" Mikey nodded. "Well you get yourself over to the hospital and see how she's doing."

"They won't let me in, I'm not a relative."

"Oh I'm sure you'll find a way Mikey, if you try hard enough. Remember though, it's vital you keep this to yourself not only for your own safety but for any investigation there could be."

Mikey smiled, suddenly feeling encouraged there could be a way through it all and set off for work again.

Later that day he spoke to Kristen and told her the frustrating news. "It seems at the moment Kristen that as far as the hospital are concerned they are certain Laura tried to take her own life. Do you think it all got too much for her and she did sink into a deep depression for a vital few minutes and downed those pills in desperation?"

"I spoke to Gyle, Mikey, that's exactly what he is saying, and he has a bloody good alibi: he was at work. There is one thing Mikey, he is desperate that nobody goes in to see her. Why do you think that is?"

"So she doesn't get the chance to tell anyone what happened?" Mikey suggested. "I'm worried for her Kristen."

"Me too. She must have been desperate to leave Kenzie alone. Oh my God Mikey, it's beginning to look like she did do it but why would she do this?" Kristen began to cry and Mikey felt helpless.

"How is Kenzie?" he asked, trying to take Kristen's mind away from Laura for a few minutes.

"Oh she's great Mikey. Mum has her a lot, and she's having a great time. I have her from dinnertime, through the night. We're working it out just fine, and you can come over to visit whenever you want." Kristen was still crying as she replaced the receiver and Mikey felt a sadness he had never known before. As the conversation ended, Kristen felt helpless as images of Laura flashed through her mind and she was unable to think about much else. Gyle's insistence that Laura should have no visitors angered her, making her worry even more. Concerned that his partner was heading for a breakdown, Scott suggested he cover the surgery calls and encouraged Kristen to take a few hours out. "Your mum's looking after Kenzie, so why not take Zeus and Piper for a walk up those hills."

"Laura's hills?" she teased. It was true it had been a while since she had been that far into the hills, or to their special place. The practice and home seemed to have taken up a lot of her time lately and the dogs had made do with shorter, more frequent walks along to the park. A few moments later Kristen and the dogs set off from the access road at Blairlogie Meadow.

The dogs were bounding away and returning excitedly, and Kristen was sure they knew where they were going. Kristen felt a calmness sweep over her as she watched them chase each other, catching a fly nip to a shoulder or hind leg before running off. It made her think about all the times she would make this same walk with Laura. Scott had been right to suggest it. She suddenly felt very close to Laura, here on these hills. Eventually when she reached their special place, Kristen sat down on the soft wild grass and looked across towards the castle. It was a strange day; here at the summit soft cloud clung all around while a short way down the sun lit up the hillside, making the landscape glisten as it connected with the damp rugged growth. Looking towards Stirling Castle and further towards the Pentland Hills and Edinburgh it was clear and bright. Zeus sat panting beside Kristen, then he slowly lay down and rolled over on his side as Piper continued to explore and sniff everything around them. Kristen watched them both. They loved coming to this place Laura had brought them so many years before. She smiled as she remembered Laura at this very spot, and how happy they had been then. This was always her special place, a place she so kindly and generously shared with Kristen. Now here she was alone, while Laura lay fighting for her life over there, towards Edinburgh and within the scope of the hills she loved. None of it made any sense to Kristen. What had she missed? What had gone so terribly wrong? Why now? Kristen knew Gyle was a handful and a hurtful man in so many ways and his only true love was himself. She knew of his many affairs, his thoughtless and cruel remarks and she had urged Laura to leave on so many occasions but she had always phoned later to say they had resolved their problems and things were better. It was all she wanted then, to be a good wife and mother and she lived for the good days they shared together. After her parents' accident Gyle had been selfish and cold while Laura faced the worst time of her life. Kristen remembered it well, Laura had been left to face the worst time of her life, with little or no support from her husband and she had been so desperately unhappy back then. Months later, following her parents' deaths, she had been completely devastated, so overwhelmed with grief it had even made Kristen's father John shed a tear or two. After surviving all of that, what could possibly be worse, and enough to make her take her own life? She certainly didn't believe Gyle's story that it was because they were splitting up; Laura had been considering that herself. It was a question she couldn't answer, nor believe she was asking herself. She stood up looking at the full view in front of her then turned a full circle, looking far into the hills behind. She looked up as two eagles hovered for a short time as if to say "we know, we're watching," before heading back into the hills behind. Piper and Zeus were both up on their feet now, heads cocked to one side as they watched Kristen spin round, looking all around and up towards the eagles. Then she stopped and spoke softly and pleadingly. "Help me, please. Help me to understand this, you who know Laura better than anyone, please tell me why?" She stood for a few moments as the cloud gave way to warm bright sunshine and as it did, the answer came to her; it had been so obvious. Kristen gasped as she drew her hands up to her face. "Oh my God," she yelled. "Thank you, Thank you," she shouted to the eagles as their silhouettes disappeared into the distance and to the hills all around her. She looked down again to see the dogs looking up, wondering what the command meant. "She didn't do it!" she told them, and then looking out across the sprawling city in the distance she yelled again. "She didn't do it!"

Scott was just returning from a call as she arrived home and Kristen was jumping with excitement. "I know Scott, I know," she gushed at him as he was opening the door to their home.

"You know Kristen? You know what?" Scott was surprised.

"She didn't do it Scott."

"Who didn't do what?"

Kristen took a long breath. "She didn't try to kill herself. I asked the Ochil Hills. The eagles were there too. I asked them for the answers and they were given." Kristen took hold of his hand as she studied his startled expression.

"Have you been drinking Kristen?"

"No, of course not."

"You've not had a fall then?"

"No Scott listen..."

"No Kristen, you listen. I know how upset you've been but I've just been speaking to Gyle." Kristen groaned as Scott continued. "It all seems pretty straightforward Kristen. The poor girl never got over her parents' accident and it was pretty tough for her watching her dad waste away in a nursing home, robbed of his senses. When they both died it sent her over the edge. Apparently she's been a bitch to Gyle and they've fought. Kristen, the poor girl's just had enough and taken a handful of pills." He looked up at her as Kristen stood shaking her head as Scott continued. "At worst, maybe Gyle has been a bit economical with the truth about the fight they had, I'll bet it was a humdinger, but doctors haven't raised any concerns, they are quite clear."

Kristen listened impatiently, unconvinced and in exasperation cut in. "Scott, you don't understand," she pleaded. "Laura doesn't take pills, not ever."

"She obviously did this time."

"No Scott listen. When Laura fell and broke her arm at school she was in agony but she never took the painkillers. Even when she's very ill, no pills."

Scott felt sorry for Kristen having to face her friend's terrible tragedies. "Honey, I know this is hard for you, but you know she did this time, that's why she is lying in hospital. They had to pump the damn things out of her stomach, at least what was left of them. So I'm sorry for stating the obvious but she did take them. People do crazy things when their mind is unbalanced."

"No Scott," Kristen was having none of it. "Something's not right. Do you honestly think she would leave Kenzie in the house alone? Did you know she knew stuff about Gyle that could lead him to jail?"

"What stuff?"

"I can't say yet, but I will tell you, I just found out myself when she came over the other day. So, Scott, I hear what you are saying but you are wrong, and I need to go and see her."

"You can't, you know what Gyle said about visitors?"

"I'm going Scott and stuff Gyle bloody Jamieson, he's responsible for this, I'm sure of it!"

"For the love of God, Kristen," Scott wailed. "What are you saying?

"Listen, really listen Scott. Laura didn't do this. I sat at the top of those hills at our special place and I asked for answers and they were given. I know you find that hard to believe but it's true. She didn't try to kill herself."

Scott stared at her. "It was an accident then?" Kristen shook her head.

"Ah I see it now Kristen. We go to the police and tell them Laura didn't try to take her own life officer. How do you know this sir? Oh the mountains told me!" He looked at her, shaking his head in disbelief. "I don't think so!"

"They are hills," Kristen corrected him. "And I hadn't intended going to the police to tell them that, but I just know for sure now. Laura wouldn't have tried to kill herself and she wouldn't have taken pills."

"Well how did the pills get into her stomach then?"

"They were forced there by Gyle Jamieson!"

Scott groaned. "I don't believe this Kristen, what are you saying? I know Gyle can be a bit of a bastard, but murder?"

Kristen nodded. "I'm serious Scott, and I need to get into that hospital to get some answers whether he likes it or not!"

"Laura's unconscious," he reminded her. "And you need to examine your own thoughts and Mikey's. Don't you think you've both allowed yourself to be convinced that it wasn't an attempted suicide, because you can't accept that explanation? Now, you've been up to the hills, to Laura's special place, and you are suddenly convinced beyond all reason. Don't you find that strange, and perhaps a wee bit emotional? And now you think the answers will come from Laura?" Scott tried hard to convince Kristen her thoughts were improbable and emotionally driven.

"Not from Laura, I don't know who from, but I'll find out. The doctors have been fed a line from that man, a line of total rubbish and I need to set the record straight."

"Without any evidence at all?"

"I'll get the evidence, somewhere, somehow, it has to be there." Kristen looked pleadingly towards him now, reaching out to hold his hands. She was determined, that he couldn't deny, and as he looked at his partner standing there before him, desperate to find the answers, he knew he had to go along with whatever she wanted to do, if only to find some closure. He didn't want to risk being the one to stop her from trying. He pulled her to him and held her for a moment. ""Well you are not going alone Kristen. If there is a remotest chance there is something in this then you had better not go on your own. If you can leave it until tomorrow and make sure your mum can still have Kenzie, I'll ask Richard from Doune to cover the practice, he's usually off on a Thursday."

Kristen hugged Scott. "Thank you," she whispered.

9

Kristen and Scott arrived at the hospital the following morning just in time to see the back of Gyle's Mercedes disappear out of the car park a short distance ahead of them. "Excellent," Kristen cheered, delighted with their good timing. As they entered the IT unit a young man at the reception desk met them. "We're here to see Laura Jamieson," Kristen told him, smiling.

"Are you a relative?" he asked.

"More or less," she said. "I'm a very close life-long friend and I'm looking after her daughter. I really need to see Laura, please," she said, tears welling up in her eyes.

The young man pulled a face. "We really only admit relatives to the unit," he said apologetically.

"Look, if anyone asks, just say I'm her sister Emma, from London."

The young man looked at her with surprise.

"Emma's in Geneva on business and she won't be visiting this week." She looked up at him. "Please, it's important."

He looked at her pitiful face. "Go on then, but just five minutes." He then led them through to scrub up and put plastic gowns over their clothes before making their way to the huge unit. In the centre of the room a group of monitors sat with images of all the patients, operated and watched by three practitioner nurses. Over to the right, they could see Laura, wired up to more monitors as they tracked her every movement, or lack of it, watched carefully by a nurse sitting by her side. She stood up as Kristen and Scott approached. "Hi," she said, smiling.

"How is she doing?" Kristen asked, not offering to tell them who they were.

"She's doing fine this morning," the nurse said encouragingly. She had a bit of a shaky start but she's turned a corner. Err, her husband has just left, you just missed him."

"We saw him leave, just as we were arriving, typical eh?" Scott joked.

"I'll let you have some time with her, I'll just be over at the central monitor, watching her. Try talking to her, it sometimes helps to hear a familiar voice."

Kristen thanked the nurse and took a seat beside Laura's bed. "Laura," she whispered. "It's Kristen." Laura's hand twitched slightly.

"I think she knows we're here Scott."

"Keep talking to her," Scott urged.

"My mum and I are looking after Kenzie, she's fine Laura, and she's safe." There was another stronger twitch of her hand and a slight movement of her head. Kristen looked towards the central monitors to see the nurse glance across.

"Was that a response?" she asked.

"I think so, nurse. I just told her I was looking after her little girl."

The nurse came over. "That's excellent, that's just the kind of thing she needs to hear." She looked at Laura and held her hand as she now lay still. "Keep talking to her, I think we're getting somewhere."

"She didn't try to take her own life you know," Kristen told the nurse but she just smiled, dismissing the claim. Mikey was right, as far as the medics were concerned it was a clear-cut case of attempted suicide, and until such times, as someone can prove otherwise, they would have to go along with that. Now she turned her focus to her friend. "Laura, if you can hear me squeeze my hand." There was nothing. Kristen looked up at Scott. "Maybe we imagined it?"

"I don't think so, Kristen," he said, studying Laura's face. "Try again."

"Laura, if you can hear me, just try and squeeze. Come on honey, little Kenzie needs her mummy." There was nothing, then a slightest little twitch of her hand again. "Was that a response to what I said Scott, or was it an involuntary twitch?"

Scott shook his head. "I don't know Kristen, just keep talking to her."

"I've been up to your hills Laura, I saw the eagles this time. They know you are here. Honey I know it's hard but I need you to let me know you can hear me, even if you can't talk yet. So if you can just give me one more squeeze, I can go back to Kenzie and to the Ochils, and the eagles, and tell them you're going to be just fine. Oh, and someone else who is desperate to know, Mikey." Another faint movement of Laura's hand now touched Kristen's and she knew then that she was coming back to them. "Laura, listen to me carefully. Don't squeeze Gyle's hand when he comes in honey. Okay?" One slightly weaker twitch now, but a response all the same was felt by Kristen's finger. "I think she's tiring now Scott. I think we should go, but we need to come back. I'll try to find out what I can about Gyle's movements from the lad in reception on our way out." She bent down and kissed Laura's forehead. "Love you Laura, hang in there, we'll be back soon." Laura's right eyebrow moved very slightly, making Kristen and Scott smile.

"Anything more?" the nurse asked as she moved away from the monitors and back to Laura's side.

"Not really," Kristen told her, hoping to avoid a forced attempt to bring her round.

"It takes time." The nurse's comments were encouraging. "See you soon."

The young lad at the reception desk was very helpful. "Laura's husband comes in every morning for a little while before work and that's it really. He phone's a lot during the day, mainly to see if she's coming round. Some people find it difficult visiting unresponsive patients, I'm sure he'll be here more when her condition improves."

"I'm sure he will," Kristen agreed, sarcastically. "Can I come back tomorrow?"

The lad nodded. "I don't see why not, so long as it's just a short time."

"Look, maybe it's best you don't tell Gyle we were here, he's a bit precious of her, he told us not to visit and to give her rest. I'd be grateful if you could keep this between us?"

The receptionist looked surprised. "Of course. You know, it's conversation that will bring her out of this, we've done all we can medically, he's got that wrong."

"You've no idea," Kristen said smiling as they left for the morning. Later she called Mikey with the good news, telling him about her experience on the hills.

"I came to the same conclusion, Kristen, it's the only thing that makes sense."

"Well I've had the confirmation now," she told him, delighted and relieved Mikey was on the same wavelength as her.

"We need to get through to her before Gyle does," he said worriedly. "I've been thinking about nothing else for days now. We need to persuade Laura to pretend she has no memory. It's the only way we are going to save her, until we can do something about him. I'm sure he's just hanging around now to make sure she doesn't talk before he shoots off somewhere. It's just all about timing."

Kristen agreed. "I think you've hit the nail on the head Mikey, why don't you go in sometime?"

"Do you think I'd get away with it?"

Kristen thought for a minute. "I have that young receptionist lad on side, I think Mikey. I'll tell them Laura's brother has arrived from abroad and ask if you can visit for a short while before you go back again."

"Where have I been and why?"

"Afghanistan, in the army?"

"Gee thanks."

"Well, how could they refuse a hero solider?"

Mikey laughed. "Excellent."

"Scott and I will go over tomorrow, and I'll speak to him then."

"Great stuff!"

By the time Mikey visited with Kristen, Laura was much more responsive. Mikey carefully and slowly asked Laura if she had tried to take her own life. She shook her head. "We didn't think so. It was Gyle wasn't it?"

Laura's face twisted and a tear fell from one eye.

"Stop, Mikey," Kristen whispered, "you are upsetting her." She looked over to see the nurse looking across. "I'm so sorry honey but we are all with you, you need to pretend you have lost your memory. It will take too long to explain, can you trust us?" Laura smiled as her eyes opened and closed again. "Okay Laura, you can't remember us or Gyle or even yourself. We need you to do this to keep you safe." Laura squeezed Mikey's hand tight and Kristen smiled at him, and then Laura.

The nurse came over. "Is everything alright?" she asked curiously, having watched the conversation.

"Yes, we're getting some responses, but I'm not sure she knows who we are?"

"Oh, surely she'd remember her brother and sister?"

Kristen shrugged her shoulders. "I'm not sure she does." They looked at each other, trying to stifle a smile. Within a few more days, Laura was out of danger and prepared to move to a medical ward out of intensive therapy. She knew now why she had to keep up the pretence of memory loss, but it was a situation keeping her in hospital and she desperately wanted to go home to see Kenzie. "Laura, we think Gyle might run off somewhere, now he thinks you have lost your memory, it gives him time to carry on the facade that you were splitting up and now you are okay, he can go without suspicion," Mikey told her.

"What if he decides to stay? You said yourself there has been no case brought against him, so why would he want to flee? He seems to have got away with the Morven Stewart incident."

Mikey agreed. "Time's running out for him Laura, with the property. There is no way it won't all come out soon, and he will go down for a long time for that one. Then there's what he did to you? He's living on borrowed time."

"Unfortunately, Mikey, there's no proof of what he did to me."

Mikey sighed. "You sound like my dad!"

Laura smiled, laughing slightly. "I think I should just go home."

"You can't. What if he tries to kill you again? It's not unusual for people who have tried to take their own life once and failed to try again. He'd have a perfect excuse."

"Mikey's right," Kristen told her. "You are only safe while you have no memory, but do you really want to go back and live with him? And could you be sure you'd be safe?"

Laura shook her head. "No."

"Then come and live with me and Scott, until it all ends."

"How can I do that and pretend I have no memory?"

"I'll phone him and tell him I spoke to one of the consultants before he went off on holiday. I'll tell him he believes you may never regain your memory, and that time living where you spent your childhood could help establish some foundations to build new memories on. One of us will take you home and you can collect your things before coming over to our house. Job done. It will give him time to decide what he's going to do, while keeping you safe."

Laura held Kristen's hand, and looked up at Mikey. "I love you guys. Thank you," she said quietly.

A week later, Laura moved in with Kristen and Scott, relieved to be away from Gyle and out of hospital, and delighted to have Kenzie back with her again. Mikey was keeping a close eye on Gyle's movements, and everything seemed to be unbelievably normal. "You know I think he's got away with it all!" he told Laura one day when he phoned to see how they were.

"How does that happen?" Laura was amazed. "It's just not right is it? You wouldn't believe the luck of that man!"

As Laura's health continued to improve at Kristen and Scott's a month later, Gyle's luck was beginning to run out. Lothian and Borders Police received an enquiry regarding an argument, which had developed over a property in Dubai. Two purchasers in Monaco appeared to hold similar documents relating to the same property. It had been a chance meeting during a corporate event. Two men sat chatting in a bar about business, life and travel and the conversation moved to property and then Dubai. The men couldn't believe they were both in the process of purchasing property in the same small waterfront development. They marvelled at the layout and furnishings, right down to the colour scheme and the views. A little further into the conversation it began to look a little too much of a coincidence to be true, and it then became apparent that they had not only both bought property in the same development but they had, it appeared, bought the same property! Shocked by the revelation, their investigations led them to an address in Edinburgh and Gyle Jamieson's name appeared on each of the documents both men held. The police began to investigate.

The sun shone brightly in Blairlogie, and Laura was making plans to go shopping in Stirling when her phone rang. "Laura, how are you, it's Gyle." His voice was formal, and insincere.

"Gyle!" Laura was surprised at the call. It had been some time since he called and he had yet to visit.

"I'm sorry I haven't been over to see you honey, I just thought I'd give you some space. Has it helped, living back on your home turf? Can you remember anything yet?"

Laura was cautious. "I'm sorry Gyle, I know this must be hurtful, but I just can't remember much at all, I have flashbacks sometimes, and..."

"Oh?"

Gyle's sudden interruption amused her, and she continued. "It's all about school, but it's muddled up like a dream. The doctor seems to think it's a good sign, but there's a way to go yet."

"Mmm, I guess so. Oh well, I'll let you enjoy your day, Laura, take care won't you and if you ever begin to remember me, honey, do know I am here and I love you."

"Okay," Laura whispered, shaking her head. "Unbelievable!" she yelled to herself, as she replaced the receiver. It was obvious he had just phoned, to make sure he was still safe, and had enough time to make plans when the time was right without attracting suspicion. He had heard nothing more about overseas developments or Burlington Park Estates and hoped any enquiries from worried former clients had drawn a blank. It looked as though Morven had covered his tracks as well as his own. At least she had done that, even if she had taken all the money. If questions were ever to be asked now he'd had enough time to make plans and he could be free, just like Morven. Laura's memory loss had given him the time to draw breath and think calmly again. Perhaps he would bump into Morven on some faraway island and have a laugh about the whole thing? He was drifting away in his own dreams of running a beach bar somewhere. He would change his name to something well known locally, and he would learn to speak the language. It would be easy, he imagined, as thoughts carried him away again, to some far-off land. His thoughts remained far away for the next few days until a knock at the door one early evening was set to burst his bubble. Two police officers stood on the doorstep making tentative enquiries about overseas property. It sent Gyle into a panic and he denied just about everything. "No, I have never had a business in Barnton, officer," he told them, convincingly. "Yes, I am an estate agent but I work for McArdle and Baynes." "No, I don't deal with overseas properties, neither do McArdle and Baynes." The police officers were probing but not intrusive, as Gyle struggled to think of ways to avert their attention from him. "You don't think someone has stolen my identity do you?" he offered, hoping to change to focus of their investigation. "It's early stages, sir," the officer answered tardily as he jotted a few words down in his notepad. "The details we have at present are vague. If you could check your bank accounts are as you might expect them to be, that might be a good place to start sir. If you notice something you can't quite explain, then it might be best if you are in touch with us. If there's any more from our side, we'll be in touch again. Thank you for your time."

"Thank you officer." Gyle smiled as he showed the two men out of the house.

"Shit!" he yelled. "Bloody shit." The visit had sent him panicking again. He knew it was only a matter of time before others would be making enquiries, and one would lead to another. Now was a good time to run, before Laura's memory returned to add fuel to the flames. Over the next couple of days Gyle stopped dreaming and started to make firm plans to move abroad. He borrowed a few thousand pounds from his father, using Laura's circumstances as an excuse and made an airline reservation to Greece. He would spend a day or two in Greece, then catch a ferry to other Greek islands, keeping on the move to begin with. It would be easy to pay cash on ferries, and he could then disappear for good from one of them. His dark hair and swarthy complexion would help him to blend in with the crowds; he wouldn't stand out and nobody would remember him. As he sat in the kitchen of his home in Lanark Road West, his thoughts now turned to Laura and Kenzie. A sudden but short regret rushed through his mind as he considered what could have been. He had been so stupid, now he was facing a life on the run. What would happen to the house? He sighed. Laura should have the keys to the house, he at least owed her that much. In another five days, he would be gone. What a fool he had been, to throw his life away for what? He would be nothing more than a penniless beach bum, if he were unlucky, but it was better than a life behind bars. He groaned loudly then turned to make some coffee and as the machine gurgled and hissed, and the aroma filtered through the rooms, he decided to phone Laura the following morning. It would be best to phone when Kristen and Scott were at work, he thought, and he would tell Laura he was going to America on business then slip the keys of the house in her bag when she wasn't looking. Hopefully she would forget he was going away. He realised time was now running out and he bitterly regretted, and not for the first time, ever being involved with Morven Stewart. Gyle's call to Laura the next day surprised her. It was mid-morning at a time when he would normally be at work, or valuing a property. It was unusual for him to phone at all, and Laura was puzzled by his sudden interest in her welfare. "Laura, hi. I thought I might come over to see you and Kenzie tomorrow morning for a little while. Would that be okay with you?"

Laura hesitated. "I guess so Gyle, what time were you thinking?"

"Morning, if that suits?"

Laura agreed, but alarm bells rang. It was unusual for him to suddenly want to visit on a day when he would normally be caught up with work. Kristen and Scott were out on call so she phoned Mikey with the news.

"What do you think?" she asked him.

"I think the police are on to him Laura. I asked my dad the

224

other day what was happening and he said he couldn't say, but I could tell the issue was still in his mind."

"What will be his next move then? Why does he suddenly want to come and see me and Kenzie?"

"I don't know Laura, but while you can't remember there's no one to confirm any details, so I would be careful what you say. What time is he coming over?"

"He said morning, and I've just remembered that Kristen and Scott are going to be busy with some hill sheep tomorrow so I'm going to be here myself."

Mikey thought for a while. "Do you think Yvonne might take Kenzie for you?"

"Why are you saying that Mikey, you're scaring me now."

"You have to admit it's a bit strange for Gyle to come all this way, in the morning, out of the blue?"

"It can't be much Mikey, he must feel he is in the clear, there's no need to pursue things. Maybe he is going to try to get me to go back with him, now Morven's out of his life? He's cheeky enough."

"If the police are on to him? He must know they will want to speak to you Laura, and that could be just the trigger to bring back your memory, as far as he is concerned, don't you think?"

"I see where you are coming from. I think I can handle him okay Mikey. I'll get Yvonne to take Kenzie for a while, he was never that interested in her anyway and I'll let you know how things go."

That night Laura sat watching television with Scott and Kristen when the local police called. "Laura Jamieson?" the tall sergeant asked. "Do you mind if we come in and ask you a few questions? Is your husband with you at the moment?" Laura looked up at the police officer and in an instant she knew it was the beginning of the end. Questions led to more questions and soon a radio call led to someone from Lothian and Borders arriving to ask even more questions. "Why didn't you report this to the police Laura?" one asked, and she explained what Mikey had told her. "And you say you have no evidence of any of what you have told us?"

"That's just it officer," she started. "That has been the problem all along. I don't have anything, I've just guessed my way through it based on snippets of information, which I'm led to believe would amount to little more than gossip. I found the earring and confronted him with it, the police have that, and I found papers in his briefcase and laptop, but I had to put them back. I was suspicious, nothing more, and if I am being honest I was more upset about his affair with Morven Stewart."

The Lothian and Borders detectives looked at each other then back to her. "Tell us about Morven Stewart?"

"Well, that's the funny thing, I don't know anything about her except that she worked with Gyle at McArdle and Baynes on a self-employed basis. She was only there a few months and left. Gyle was having an affair with her and I am sure he is responsible for the assault on her."

"Assault?"

"There was nothing you could do about that either, she didn't make a complaint and she left hospital without anyone knowing who she was."

"And where does she fit into all of this?"

"I think she was involved with Gyle in the property dealings."

"And that's what led you to attempt your own life Mrs Jamieson?"

Laura laughed. "I didn't attempt to take my own life officer, my husband tried to kill me." The officers looked at each other in amazement. "He thinks I have lost my memory, and I'm pretty sure that is why I am still alive," Laura said softly. "Kristen and Scott and Mikey have helped to protect me."

"Mikey?"

"My friend Mikey Macrae, Inspector Martin Macrae's son."

"Ah, yes, I'm with you now."

"Mrs Jamieson, we needed to speak to you before we apprehend your husband. The net is closing in on him and if he contacts you again, it's vital to our investigation that you say nothing about this visit. Is that clear?"

Laura nodded. "He's coming here tomorrow morning." The police officers made notes before making their apologies for the intrusion and left.

"What now?" Laura asked Kristen and Scott. "What do I do now?"

"Take great care Laura, try and find out as much as you can from him tomorrow but do it casually through chat and then phone the police."

Morning arrived and Kristen and Scott headed off to the hill farm on Myreton to carry out their work with the sheep there. Yvonne arrived to take Kenzie to the park and Laura paced up and down waiting anxiously for Gyle. When he arrived he looked nervous and awkward.

"How are things?" Laura asked cautiously.

"To tell you the truth Laura, things are not good without you to look after me. I was hoping you would be coming home by now to be a family again."

"I'm sorry. I am better than I was, I think. I feel less stressed; I'm much calmer now. I think being here has helped."

"Do you think you will ever come back to me Laura?"

Laura shook her head. "I am so sorry, Gyle. I don't know you, you are still a stranger to me in so many ways, so I can't say?" She smiled at him but he looked unconvinced by her answer. His sudden affection surprised her, but she soon realised none of it was real. He hadn't asked how Kenzie was or where she was. No, his visit had a purpose, and she wondered what it might be.

"Any chance of a coffee Laura?" He asked as he took a seat in the kitchen. She nodded and poured him a cup from the filter machine. She handed it to him, white with one sugar. "I remember some of the good times we had, Laura, you studying and playing your guitar." His mood had suddenly changed. "You were good, Laura." She smiled. "Do you remember that night at Tattie Bogles, when Kristen and Scott came to see you play with that guy? What was his name?"

Laura shrugged. He was testing her.

"Mikey, I think. Yes that was it. It was Mikey, a real little tosser."

Laura looked at him, wondering where the conversation was leading, as he carefully studied her reactions.

"I visited your parent's grave on my way Laura, such a shame. I told them all about you, relieved they'd died so you wouldn't have to look after them!"

Laura struggled to fight back the tears, he'd hit a nerve, she couldn't hide her pained reaction and the tears just flowed. "You bastard Gyle."

"I thought as much!" he yelled. "You've not lost your memory, it's funny you remembered my coffee, the way I like it! You are just biding your time, aren't you? You bitch!" He lunged for her and she threw the milk in his face; it was the nearest thing she had to hand. As he grabbed a towel to wipe

228

the milk from his eyes, Laura screamed and ran. The dogs were barking loudly, locked in the utility area, and she hoped they would alert someone near as she fled towards Blairlogie Meadow. Laura came across the path she and Kristen used often; it was thick with growth and not overly visible. If she could keep herself reasonably hidden she could make her way to the top of the Ochils. She doubted Gyle would find her, or be able to keep up with her. She had her mobile in her pocket and she texted Mikey as she hid. 'Gyle crazy, please help.' Then she made her way up through the hills, keeping to the areas of the heaviest growth. She stopped occasionally and listened. She could hear him some way off heading up another path as he shouted, "Laura! I'm coming for you Laura, you won't get away!" She was terrified as she headed higher up the hills with Gyle some way behind but pursuing still. She weaved her way through the thick gorse, taking time to take cover. She couldn't see him, but he had an advantage. He was looking up and in her direction. She had no idea whether he knew where she was, but she wasn't stopping for long. She prayed her mobile phone wouldn't ring, giving her location away, and then it gave her an idea. She would phone Gyle's phone and listen to see if she could hear it, but first she would put her own phone on 'silent mode'. She called and could hear it ring. He wasn't too near and she was sure he was tiring. He would soon tire before her; he wasn't fit and Laura knew these hills, she knew where to hide and where the best paths lay. Gyle was ploughing through the most difficult terrain and it was slowing him down, but she was still in a panic. If he caught up with her he would easily overpower her, and throw her off the hill, without too much effort. What a way to end her life, at the foot of the hills she loved. She made her way as quickly as she could, widening the distance between them. She caught glimpses of him now and then, as he struggled upwards. Then she came to a clearing and looked down towards the road. She thought she could see Mikey's car, but she wasn't sure, and then in the distance blue lights, flashing as the cars sped towards the hills. If she could just keep up the pace she would be fine, but she was tiring too and the police would have no chance reaching Gyle before he reached her; they were too far up. Laura's heart pounded as the hill terrain became sparse. There were fewer places to hide and she was sure Gyle would hear her heart beating it felt so powerful. She hid behind a rock and sat still, listening to Gyle climb. He was wearing a suit and shoes, the most unsuitable attire for a hill climb, and Laura watched as he slipped and tumbled occasionally before gaining ground again, desperation and determination driving him on. She had almost given in to the thought that he would inevitably catch up with her, perhaps at the summit. She took a deep breath, and carried on ahead. She stopped and looked back, she could still hear Piper and Zeus barking down below from Kristen's cottage but then there was more barking, louder and closer and in a sudden moment, out of the blue, the barking became even louder as dogs came bounding up the hill. Then there was a loud painful yell as the dogs jumped at Gyle, dragging him to the ground, followed by police officers. Laura sat and cried. She put her head in her hands and just sat, trying to catch her breath, relieved. When she took her hands away again she could see Mikey running up the hill towards her.

"Mikey!" she cried and ran to meet him, almost jumping into his arms.

"Oh my God, Laura, I thought I'd lost you!" he cried breathlessly as he held her tightly to him and they clung to each other for a few minutes. "It's over Laura, it's all over now," He whispered, kissing her cheek and he held her tightly to him again.

"Did you get my text?" she asked, pulling away slightly and he laughed.

"Yes, I did, but not before I got the heads up from my dad."

"Your dad?"

"Yes, Kristen and Scott heard the dogs barking and they could see you from Myreton Hill. They watched as you ran towards Blairlogie Meadow and they knew something was wrong so they phoned the police. One call connected the incident to all units and Dad called me, but I was already on my way through. I didn't want you to be there with Gyle alone!"

"Oh Mikey! What would I do without you?"

"I hope you never will Laura, I love you!"

Laura looked at him and hugged him. "When did you realise that?" she laughed.

"I've always loved you, right from the moment I first met you."

"I'm a married woman!" she scoffed.

"Ah well, we'll have to do something about that then won't we?"

They hugged again and kissed. Then looked down the hillside and up to the summit. "These are my hills Mikey," she said softly. "They've saved me, again, this time it's with your help, and Kristen and Scott." She touched his cheek. "I love you too Mikey." They looked down to see Kristen and Scott running up the hill as the police and their dogs moved back down with Gyle Jamieson, securely in handcuffs. Laura, Mikey, Kristen and Scott continued up to the summit as they watched the police cars speed their way along the Hillfoots Road and off into the distance. "Thank you," Laura said to everyone, through silent tears then, turning to the hills, "Thank you!"

A year later, Gyle Jamieson was in Saughton Prison, serving thirty-five years for deception. They never did find Morven Stewart, or rather Louise Van Hoek, or any evidence she ever existed. It can only be assumed she is living her life in paradise, with husband Jan, just as she had planned, leaving Gyle to take the blame for the property scam. Laura filed for divorce and it was uncontested. She didn't push for an attempted murder charge against him, claiming the house in Balerno as part of the settlement, in return. Kristen and Scott are now married and expecting their first child. Jodie Lewis landed a good job in television as part of an investigative research team for a documentary-style programme. Mikey and Laura plan to marry soon in Logie Kirk and Kenzie is excited to be a bridesmaid. They live in Stirling now and regularly visit the Ochil Hills, their own special place.